Days of Love and Crime

BRADLEY DAVENPORT

for Tiffany Pierce

Days of Love and Crime

Also by Bradley Davenport

Brown Ridge: Shootin' Noise
Monster Fantastic
Mansfield

Disclaimer

This is a work of fiction.
Resemblances to any peoples is purely coincidental

BRADLEY DAVENPORT

GROOVY TIME

1

Gunnster, Oklahoma

Peter Sanders and Kelly Finny were sitting in Peter's red Ford Pinto at Rama-Zampa, a drive-in cinema. The place was beside a small body of water called Water Front. A lot of people would picnic at the little piece of water, then they'd catch the movie that night. Peter and Kelly had done just that, they had a little picnic earlier. Peter talked her into going to a movie called *Star Wars*. Kelly didn't want to go to the movie. But she loved her boyfriend and knew he wanted to see the movie, that he'd been anticipating it for some time. Peter thought by telling Kelly they were going to a drive-in, that they wouldn't have to leave the comfort of their car, that it would entice her to see the film. The movie was released that day. Peter wanted to see it as soon as he could. He didn't want to hear what happened before he got a chance to see it.

It was nice out—not too cold, not too hot. From the sounds coming from the other cars, cheers and applause, it seemed everyone was enjoying the movie. Peter looked at his girl and couldn't read whether she liked it or not. He hoped she liked it. He'd bought the tickets and didn't want it to be all for nothing.

"This is good, isn't it?" Peter said.

She moved up in her seat. "It's okay, I guess. It was a little slow at the beginning. It got a little better. I like the main guy, he's boss."

"See, it's not all bad," he smiled. "You have to look at the good in things, babe. It's like no other movie you've seen before. It's fascinating. That could be us one day, having a space adventure."

"At least it got me out of the house."

"Well, that's what I'm here for, the best distraction a girl could ask for."

She smiled. "You really are my knight in armor."

"Glad I could be of service. Hey, babe, it doesn't get much better than this. You know how many girls would die to be in your shoes right now?"

"Yeah, I can probably write the whole list for you."

"I'm a popular guy, what can I say?"

"I know."

"I managed to get you, didn't I? No one else matters."

"You mean that?"

"Of course."

"Thanks."

He said, "That mean I'll get lucky tonight?"

She laughed.

"When are your parents getting back?" he asked. "It's really nice they didn't make you go with them."

"Friday."

"Oh, man."

"They were gonna stay the weekend, but Dad has to get ready for court next week. It's a murder case."

"I dunno about you, I couldn't do it. The thought of someone's life in my hands, that would be too much. I don't know how he does it. Stress must be a killer."

"Before they left he starting in about law school again," she propped her right elbow along the frame of the passenger's window. "Same story, different day. He does his best to annoy me."

"When's he gonna get it through his thick head you don't wanna do that?"

"Got me."

"You guys just need to sit down, and tell him straight-out you don't want it."

"I need to. He knows. I just get nervous when I have to talk to him about stuff like that. He says how he just wants the best for me. He tells me how he doesn't wanna see me broke without a good job. That's okay and all, but he isn't me, make sense?"

"I get that. He needs to understand, though, that you need to make your own life. You're the one who has to live it, not him."

"Would you tell him that?"

"If it comes to it," Peter told her. "I'm not afraid of your old man."

"Better not say that too soon."

"Yeah, well, guess you don't know me that well. I'll tell it right to his face. He won't know what to say. I mean, what could he really do to me? It's not like he'll kill me or anything. We're both men."

She leaned her head back. "I tell ya, I'd love to see that, babe."

"Hey, what can I say?"

She laughed. "Oh, man, you're something else."

"I know, right? Well, come on, what's he gonna do?"

"He always jokes he has a gun he hasn't killed anything with yet."

"That true?"

"Oh, he's fine. He wouldn't really do anything. He's all talk."

"Doesn't scare me any."

"I know, I know," she said. "I just feel like since he's my dad I have to listen to what he says."

Peter said, "You don't have to do anything you don't want to. You need to take control."

"Yeah."

"It'll be okay, you'll see."

"I don't know about that."

"Just trust me. It won't be that bad. It's not like anything is going to happen to you or anything."

"Maybe you need to come with me?"

Peter laughed. "I don't think so."

Kelly's father, Ed, worked for R&W Law. He'd been a lawyer for them for almost nine years. He wanted her to be a lawyer. He told her there was good money in it, and that it was important to have a career to support your family. He'd opine at great length on how great the justice system was, how great it was to live in a country that breeds fairness. He told her that in his brand of law sometimes people needed to go to prison, and that sometimes you ran into very bad people out there. Ed, he wanted to run for public office one day. He was a good man. Her mother, Maggie, worked part-time as a teacher's aide. She was working toward getting her English degree at the local college. Kelly thought it was funny that when she started college in the fall of 1977 she and her mother would be going to the same school.

"I'm gonna get more soda," Peter told her. "You want anything else?"

"I can take another drink."

"Okay. Any candy or anything?"

"Just the soda."

"Okay."

"I don't need to eat anything else."

"You sure? I'm buying. I guess we should've gotten a couple burgers before we came out. I wasn't really thinking at the time. Too stoned."

She laughed. "I'll be fine."

He opened the car door. "I'll be right back."

"I'll be here," she gave a little wave to him.

"Better not leave."

"Don't worry, babe."

"Oh, you're a funny one."

"You know it."

"That's why I love you."

"You better."

"Don't have to worry about that."

"Let's keep it that way."

They kissed.

They loved how the other felt.

He got out of the car and headed to the refreshment stand. When he got to the stand there was a line. As he stood waiting he talked with a few people. They talked about things they liked about the movie. He got some drinks and candy. After some more talk, he headed back to his car. He knew that the movie would be the subject of conversation in the days to come. The boys at the warehouse were gonna have a field day with this one, he thought. He, along with them, was into comics and sci-fi. He couldn't wait to talk to them about it.

He worked at Landis for two years making ladders and tools. He liked the job. It could've paid more, but what job couldn't? It paid the bills, and kept him in grass, and that was all that mattered to him. It kept him from being homeless. One night on his way home from work, after a twelve-hour shift, he stopped at Krans, a little grocery store about an hour from where he lived in Gunnster, to get stuff to make sandwiches. When he got to the checkout he saw the dumpy girl he wanted to spend the rest of his life with. Even though she was a large woman she was exactly what he wanted. After some talk, he found out her name was Kelly. She gave him her number and the rest was history. On their first date, they went to Bumpers & Boomers, a place that offered roller skating and an arcade. The place also served pizza and other things. Both of them had a great time. Kelly's parents, they loved Peter. They were thankful someone came along who liked their daughter, someone who didn't just look at her as a joke. Peter had planned to ask her hand in marriage.

As he was walking back to his car he glanced at the

other cars. It was a wonderful night, he thought. Everyone seemed to be enjoying themselves. A white 1972 Pontiac GTO sitting in the very back of the clearing caught Peter's eye. He entertained the thought of walking over and telling the person he liked the ride. He decided against it. He didn't know if the driver would want to fight him. He wasn't sure why they'd wanna fight, but he wanted to make damn sure he didn't give anyone a reason. The car was parked under a dimly lit light pole.

There was someone sitting in the Pontiac. The person was dressed all in black with a mask. The driver took a .45 caliber handgun from the front seat and got out of the driver's door. The person walked over to where the other cars were.

Peter looked at Kelly, and pointed at the screen, just as the young hero and the princess were escaping the bad guys by swinging over a landing to the other side.

"Oh, honey, that's pretty awesome!" Peter slapped his knee.

Kelly gave a dismissive wave toward the screen. "Maybe."

At that exact moment, a .45 caliber handgun came through the driver's window of Peter's car and fired a few times. The two inside slumped over with bullet wounds. The shooter reloaded, moved to other cars, and continued firing until the gun was empty.

2

Forrest Crumb, a short blonde guy with a dark mustache, sat on a park bench looking at a newspaper and drinking his morning coffee from a styrofoam cup. The women who walked by looked so fresh and beautiful. He watched as some kids ran up and down the street. At that time of day there weren't many people in the park, just a few doing their morning walks and jogs.

As Forrest continued reading someone walked to the other side of the paper. Forrest looked up, nodded at the man and told him to take a seat.

Forrest said, "Glad you could find the time."

"How's it going, man? Why did you wanna meet here?" the guy looked around. "It's a little too early. My brain has a time it shuts off. This is around that time."

"I'm a people watcher."

"I was just thinking—"

"What?"

"Isn't it a little high profile?"

Forrest looked over at some girls walking. "You wear a mask, it'll be fine. Come noon, there'll be a lot more people here. Kids and adults will clutter this whole area. And no one knows you around here."

"How can you be sure?" the man sat on the bench. "You wear a mask, too. I can say the same about you. Let's face it, we're in the same line of work. You aren't better than anyone else."

Forrest slid the paper to the guy. "You're getting a lot of press. Things might be getting a little too hot out there for you, you think?"

"I read."

"You better be careful."

The guy cleared his throat. "Don't have to worry. I know what I'm doing. Been doing this awhile, and I don't need any advice from you. Thanks for showing an interest in my well-being."

"I could give a shit about you. They lock you up, I'll help them melt the key. I'm concerned with you flipping on me. You get caught out here doing something stupid, wanna reduce your time so you turn on me, spill the beans about shit I do, tell them everything about me? I, as I'm sure you can appreciate, can't have that. Nope. Things can't go like that for me. Not while I'm alive."

"I wouldn't do that."

"Says you."

"Callin' me a liar?"

"I'm just sayin' self-preservation gets the better of us all. The fear of a life behind bars isn't that accommodating to people in our line of work. It's okay, happens to the best of us."

"Work? That's a good way to put it."

"Servitude?" Forrest offered. "We all have a purpose. You have to plow through whatever is twisting your mind and get to business."

"What's your purpose?" the man asked.

"My purpose? I guess you could say I was put here to disrupt the order of this, spin a little chaos into this fucked world. A little anarchy never hurt anyone. I figure it like this: I'm gonna die one day, no doubt about that, why not cause some madness until then? Do whatever I can to break this fine thing they've built? Serves them right, all of those rich politicians living in their expensive houses, living their fake lives. Fuck 'em. Something has to give."

"Good idea. Keep 'em guessing. Let them stumble around the labyrinth for awhile... See if they can navigate through that haunted maze you have. See if they can figure out just what the hell is going on. Gotta keep it above level, all of it. You have to do what the story calls for. There's something there, you just need to get to this gnawing truth."

"You're funny over here, you know that?"

Forrest said, "You're one to talk."

The man lightly pounded his fist into the paper. "It frightens me, to be honest. I don't know what it is. Everything is just a big clutter. It's all fuzzy, and I can't see through the haze. It hurts, my head hurts sometimes. I don't know what to do."

"If it's real, you might just need to nip it, take care of it forever."

"That's easier said than done."

"Why?" Forrest said. "Look at it like this, if you get caught you can plead insanity. Hey, it's not your fault. It just might save your life."

"It was all Dobbs."

"Oh, I see."

"Yeah."

"That right there, That's a problem. What are you gonna do about it?"

"Not sure. What can I do? Do I twist myself off the planet? Run and hide? Get myself arrested? He'll find me no matter what I do. There's no out-running him."

"I'm sure you can."

"You don't know him like I do. He'll call on more demons from Hell to hunt me down and end everything. Best not piss him off."

"Wouldn't want anything like that to happen."

"It wouldn't be smart. Next thing you know they'll be coming after you. If I kill him he'll just move to another host."

Forrest ran his finger on the side of his cup, and looked out into the park. "Shit... I don't believe in that stuff. I'm not saying you're lying, I just don't believe that."

"Better start."

"Never have."

"Well, you'll regret that soon enough."

"How do you figure? Just because you believe in something doesn't mean I have to."

The man sighed. "Don't let the blanket cover your eyes. You have to see the light, see what's around the corner. You don't want anything bad to happen, do you? It's a whole thing. This is on a level you can't even comprehend."

"Don't feed me that shit," Forrest said.

"Have it your way."

"That's the way it's always been."

"I'm just trying to help those who need it."

Forrest laughed. "Well, I'll take a pass on that one. I don't need help. There's not a soul on this Earth I need anything from."

"You're a tough one."

The guy Forrest was talking with, Mort Bosworth, was a murderer. He was tall and lanky with wild hair. At that time, he had killed twenty people. Mort always told Forrest about how his cat, Dobbs, told him to kill. He said that Dobbs was from Hell and he selected Mort to kill. Mort killed his first person in 1972: a friend since childhood. The two had gotten into an argument over a girl. The friend had her. Mort wanted her. Mort went to his friend's house, and the conversation turned aggressive when the topic of the girl came up. Words went back-and-forth for some time, and then Mort picked up a vase on a table and threw it at his friend, knocking the guy to the ground. The vase didn't break. Mort proceeded to pick it up and slam it down on the man two more times, then, he went into the kitchen for a knife. The cops who arrived on the scene would later tell reporters the man was stabbed ten times. in the murders that followed, Mort always wore a mask to hide his identity.

Forrest, on the other hand, killed for the hell of it. He liked chaos. He would say everyone has to leave their mark on this world. He knew his time was limited, so he had to destroy as many people as he could. He killed at random. Forrest didn't need to have a beef to end someone. Forrest, at the time, had killed eight people. Neither he nor Mort had any plans of stopping. Their paths crossed at Hive, a nightclub that had just opened. Mort was one of the bouncers. The guy who started the club, Bob Nance, was also a childhood friend of Mort's. As the tale went, Mort and Forrest had a few drinks at the club before they went to a few other bars. They became good friends. They told one another about their evil deeds. Mort told Forrest all about Dobbs, how he was a creature from Hell that was sent to give Mort orders. At first, Forrest didn't believe the story. He told Mort that he might want to think about telling the cops a different story when they finally caught him.

Forrest said, "It's not your cat they'll be after. Those boys, they're getting pretty smart nowadays. I suggest you leave before the heat gets to be too much."

"And go where?"

"Wherever you'd like. Get a nice place on the beach. Find a nice girl and shack up. There are a lot of beautiful ladies in the world."

Mort shook his head. "Nah, I can't do that. Maybe you should move, think about that? Why did you call me, anyway? To talk about this shit? Tell me I need to skip town?"

"Just to touch base. Make sure you aren't edging toward anything to be concerned with."

"I can take care of myself. If I get caught, then that's

how that went, that's how it's gonna be. You only live once."

"If that's the way you see it."

Mort scratched his head. "I could go for some food. You want some eggs and bacon from down the street?"

"I know how these things can plague a mind—"

"They make a pretty good milkshake. You have to taste it for yourself, I don't do it justice."

"That right?"

"Yeah, it's nice and rich... worth every penny, sir! It's important to treat yourself."

"That's what I'm told."

Mort said, "Yeah, yeah, yeah, when all the cities, states, and countries crumble to the ground, I'll be standing there laughing while I drink my shake."

"I see. You have it all figured out, right?"

"You know, did I ever tell you that's where I met that Linda girl?"

"I don't remember."

"The paper went on about how a popular cheerleader was senselessly killed a few months ago."

"Yeah."

"She was a nice waitress, always had a smile on her face. First time I ever walked in there she was working. She looked so pretty. I was sold."

"You do her in?"

"Dobbs, he came to my house and told me to put her down."

"And what did you do to her?"

Mort looked ahead. "Something happened. She's far from here, that's for sure. Somewhere out in the universe. Never told me where she was going. Maybe, maybe one day she'll come back."

"You don't know what happened to her?"

"Might be landscaping the sky in some other reality."

"What does that even mean?" Forrest asked.

"What does it mean? All in one. Who knows? Maybe if you ask the blue dogs by my house they may tell something. You can try to ask Dobbs. Not sure he'll tell you."

"Oh, I see."

Mort chuckled. "Last time I saw her she was in a hole."

"You do know what happened to her?"

"I was told she got out."

"Who told you that?"

"He did."

"How did he know?"

"Told me where she was resting. Not sure how he knew."

"Resting, that's what you call it?"

"Face down in the dirt."

"That sounds more like it."

"I try to make things seem prettier."

"Oh, is that it?"

"Better than what it is."

"Yeah."

Despite being friends the two never discussed what they did. The two men decided to go down the street to Don's Hot Place for some eggs. The diner was nearly empty. As the two drank coffee and had some eggs Forrest told Mort he had an idea.

"Give it to me, partner," Mort said. "I'm all ears. Always interested in new ideas. After awhile, you have to spice things up. You can't always do the same thing, you know? A man walks a couple miles in one direction, a car pulls along, says, 'Get in, fucker!' What is one gonna do? That guy tells you if you don't get in he'll fucking kill you. Don't know about you, but I don't wanna die."

Forrest said, "Good to hear. Thanks for seeing me this

morning. I know it messed with your routine. Cartoons are enjoyable."

"Yes, sir! I love those things. Thought it'd be righteous to make 'em."

"Think you could do that? I dunno, you have to have some skills. You can't just go charging in there and make one of those out of thin air."

Mort shrugged. "Yeah, well, whatever you say. Just get to it, get to get, get to it! What's this big elaborate idea of yours? Give it to me straight, bubba."

"How would you feel about getting a partner?" Forrest asked.

"A partner? Whaddya mean? Like a wife?"

"No."

"Girlfriend?"

"You and I can be a criminal team."

"Are we a football team?"

Forrest laughed. "Not exactly. We don't have enough people for that. No, I was thinking of a chaotic master-piece. Double mayhem. They won't know what to do. We'll be everyone's nightmare. Think of it, man, we'll make history. Everyone will be talking about us for years. They'll write books about us. We'll destroy the world."

"Here's the thing, for people to write about us or any-thing, we'll have to be caught first. I don't know about you, I don't have any plans on ever being caught. Hell, I know as soon as they find me I'm dead."

"They can write about us without knowing anything about us."

"I'd have to check with Dobbs. He gave me strict or-ders to do it by myself. I don't think he'd allow it."

"Maybe I could talk to him for you?"

"He only talks to me."

Forrest said, "Sure I couldn't convince you?"

"I'm good."

"Ah, come on, man, we can double our numbers. It'll all work out, you'll see."

"No offense, but I'm gonna pass."

"Have it your way."

The two finished their meal as they talked about other things. After he finished Mort stood, thanked his friend for the talk and walked out of the place.

When Forrest was done he drove around town for a little while. He was about to head back to his house when he saw a girl walking down the road. The girl, short with brown curly hair, wore a pair of cut-offs. Forrest pulled along side of her.

"Hey, there!"

She turned her head. "Hey."

"How you doin'?"

"I'm good."

"Nice day for a walk."

"It is."

"Need a lift?"

"Nah, I'm fine," she shook her head. "I don't mind walking."

"You sure?" he asked.

"Yes, sir, I'm good."

"Where you going?"

"My friend's place down the street."

"That's nice."

"We're going swimming," she told him.

"They have a pool?"

"Yes, she does."

"Pools are nice."

"Especially on warm days."

"You're right about that," he said. "Say, your name isn't Willow, is it?"

"No, why?"

He laughed. "Because the name of the road," he pointed at the sign with the name of the street: it read Willow Red.

"No, no, my name's Janet."

"Oh, okay. Just thought I'd check."

"Yeah, that's what it is."

"Nice name, dear."

"Thanks."

As she kept walking he crept beside her.

"I don't wanna be rude or anything, but I have to tell you, you're looking really good today."

She smiled at him. "Thanks."

"It's my pleasure. I'm just a guy who knows true beauty when I see it."

"Well, thank you, I think."

"You think?"

"You aren't one of those perverts, are you?"

"What do you think?"

"I'm not sure."

"I can tell you that I'm not," he told her.

She nodded. "Okay."

"You don't have anything to worry about."

It became clear the girl wasn't going to get into his car. He let her go on her way as he hung back. She turned and started walking up a driveway. He sped up, passing the house and hung a left. She thought he was a creep. When her friend let her in she told the friend about the guy. When Forrest came back around no one was in sight. He crept his car up the drive of the house.

When police arrived at 200 Willow Red it was reported Janet Webb, 24, and Casey Thorn, 25, both were shot several times. The calls came in from neighbors who said they heard gunshots. Sadly, no one saw who did it.

3

Bencroft, Arkansas

Harlan Reeves stepped out of Rites prison into a fine Monday afternoon. He looked into the sky and felt free. Harlan was a slender man with a sharp jaw. He had a shaggy beard and brown hair to his shoulders. The sun hung bright and high. An airplane glided above. He retrieved the black sunglasses from the brown envelope his personal possessions were in. A black 1966 Dodge Challenger waited outside for him. Harlan grinned and gave a low snort as he walked toward the car. Denny Long sat behind the wheel. While he waited on his friend he lit a cigarette from a pack that rested on the dash. It was June and summer was in full force: hot and humid. Beads of sweat started to bubble on Harlan's forehead. Denny cranked the passenger and driver's window down. Denny had long brown hair with a bushy beard. Harlan and Denny had known one another for almost ten years.

Harlan ducked his head in the passenger's window. "Hey, buddy! What do ya think of this weather today, huh? Fuckin' Arkansas, am I right?"

"Glad to see you on this side, brother," Denny nodded.

"Same to you."

"Gettin' in or stayin'? Doesn't make a difference to me."

"Oh, you old fool," Harlan hit the hood of the car with his hand. "Still a card, I see. Nah, I don't wanna spend one more lousy minute in this damn place. Want me to see if they wanna fix you a place in there?"

"Better watch it with that. And don't hit the roof."

"Or what?"

"Don't make me hit you," Denny said. "Come on, it's hotter than Hell out here."

"What's wrong, can't stand the heat?" Harlan laughed.

"Enough of that."

"If you say so."

"Just get in."

Harlan got in.

They sped out of the parking lot and down the road.

Denny said, "Think I should speed? Those pigs will run out here all crazy, wanting to get someone. Just imagine the chase. They'd throw me in a cage. You'd have to hitch home."

"Then, I suggest you don't do that."

"You think?"

"I do."

"Well, maybe another day."

"That'd be best."

Denny looked at Harlan. "You'd bail me out, right?"

"Sure."

"Right on! Can't afford having Mal find out. She'd kick my butt."

"Could you blame her?"

Denny said, "She'd be okay."

"Just add it to the list, right?"

"It's always something."

"I know what you mean."

"What can you do?"

Harlan sat back in his seat. "You have no idea how great it is to be out of that dirty place."

"I can imagine."

"It's greater than anything you can think of."

"That so?"

"Yeah."

"Hope I'm never in as long as you were."

"It's a rough thing, man. One of the things that kept me going was knowing the world was waiting for me. But there were nights where you wonder if it's worth it or not."

Denny pressed the gas harder. "Well, you're home, buddy. You have a lot to be thankful for. We just missed having you around."

"Thanks," Harlan said. "I met a lot of people. But in there it's strange, even though you meet this person in their darkest hour you never really know them, what makes them tick."

"I can understand that, sure. You have to almost become another person. You sure need to learn how to deal with things without dropping your guard—you drop that, my friend, you might as well give up the whole fucking thing. Might be better just to go out a start digging your own grave."

"Exactly."

"It takes strength."

Harlan was sent away for three years after getting pinched for a robbery. Denny was supposed to be there but got a tempting offer from the girl he was dating at the time. He never told Harlan. As far as he knew Denny fell asleep. The next day he learned Harlan got locked up. Denny felt a little guilty about it for the first two months. He figured if the subject came up he would deal with it. He knew Harlan wouldn't like it one bit. He might even kill him. But he told himself that that's the way things go sometimes. When you enter a life of crime sometimes bad things happen to you. He was fine with that.

"Where to?" Denny asked. "We can stop at a corner and get you a girl? It's been awhile since you've got to do that. It's a crime if you ask me."

Harlan looked out the window. "I'm thirsty."

"You got it."

They drove to Izzy's liquor and got a few six-packs and continued down the road.

Harlan said, "Got any weed?"

"Not on me," Denny said. "Need to get some before too long. I have some, but it's not gonna last."

Harlan looked out the window again. "We should start growing our own stuff."

"I thought about it a few times. I dunno, I start to grow, then I'll start to sell. I don't wanna go through with it. Knowing my history, that wouldn't be the best idea."

"Yeah, you don't wanna be a part of that place I just left from. You'd do anything to stay out of there."

Denny said, "We're gonna party tonight. Hope you don't have anything to do tomorrow 'cause you're not gonna make it."

"No worries," Harlan said. "I just need to report to my probation officer tomorrow. But I can do that at any time. I don't have anything going on. Hell, I disappeared from this place."

"Right on, man."

"I'm excited about this new journey."

"You should be."

"I'm free to get as drunk as I want."

"That's the spirit."

"Just glad I can."

Denny said, "Did you get any booze in there at all?"

"Every now and then."

"That's wild."

"Sure is."

"I'm sure there's a lot you need to catch up on."

"I'm gonna get so twisted I'll be feeling it for the next week."

"That's groovy."

"Hey, man, I need to do this for my soul."

"Sounds good."

Harlan cracked one of the beers and drank it as they continued talking. Harlan asked how things had been since he'd been away. Denny started to tell him how he got fired from the gas station he worked at for being late too many times. He said how he wasn't worried, that he could find something else faster than he could blink. But nothing ever really changed in Bencroft, Arkansas. Things moved pretty slow. If anything of significance ever did happen Harlan would've already heard about it from someone on the inside.

Harlan said, "You need quick cash, you can always get it the easy way."

"I might."

"Just don't get busted."

"I don't plan on it."

"I'll tell ya, you don't wanna end up in that damn place we just left. Hell, man, I wouldn't want anyone to go through that bullshit. I did everything I could do to survive."

Denny shook his head. "I can understand that, sure. You gotta do what you have to. Don't think anyone would fault you for that. If it was me, I'd skip the country."

"Mexico?"

"I'd go to Canada."

"Never been there. Seems nice."

Denny snorted. "You remember Ricky Stanley?"

"The guy we got that truck of weed from that time?"

"Yeah."

"What about him?"

"He moved up there about a year ago."

"Why'd he do that?"

"Said he needed to get away from all of this around here. Anyway, he came down for a visit a few months ago and said it was pretty nice. Told me I needed to come up there. I thought about it for awhile. Have stuff around here to take care of."

"I know what you mean."

"But I'd go."

"Not me," Harlan finished his beer. "I love it here. Couldn't live anywhere else. I barely made it this year. I can't do anything like that anymore. Gretchen, she wouldn't be able to take it. She'd leave. I don't know what I'd do if that happened."

"I hear ya. Women, they make us who we are. Sure, we don't want to admit it, but there it is... Take it however you want. Believe me, it's a damn struggle at times."

"Yeah."

"You navigate yourself the best you can. Hope for the best, that's all you can do."

Harlan said, "My baby, she's been my rock. Don't know where I'd be without her."

"You don't have to worry about that now, right?"

"One never knows."

"Yeah."

"For now everything is good. You have to ask yourself when is it all gonna come crashing down again, you know?"

"It's best to not think about that."

"You're right."

When he was inside, Harlan's girlfriend, Gretchen, visited him on a normal basis. For the most part, she was supportive. But that type of thing can only last for so long. After awhile one gets exhausted by seeing their loved one locked up. He knew it was hard on her. He suspected her of taking up with another guy. It wasn't like he could blame her. He was away and everyone has needs. The days he spent in his cell, he came to terms with everything. It was a harsh reality to think she had sex with other guys, and that she let others inside her. Whenever he thought about it he got in an angry mood, and you didn't want to be around him when he was in one of his big fits. He could be a mean guy when he wanted to. There were a few people he hoped it wasn't. He didn't think he'd ever kill them, just hurt them very badly. He didn't want to go back to the dark place he just got out of. If it came down to it he'd just hire someone to do the murder.

"Thanks for doing this," Harlan told Denny.

"Think nothing of it. You'd do the same for me."

"Yeah. Still, I don't wanna seem ungrateful or any-thing."

"Needed to get out of the house. Mal has been bustin' my balls."

Harlan chuckled. "Oh, man, what's she spazin' about these days?"

"Anything and everything."

"It's always something with that one."

"She's always been like that."

"Can't be that bad," Harlan said. "At least you have a good woman, even though she bitches all the time. I know guys who'd give their nutt for a gal."

"Half the time I just tune her out," Denny said.

"You don't wanna test her."

Denny said, "We have good days. Don't get me wrong, it's not all bad. I think she's just going to need more time before she trusts me completely again. Shit drives me in-sane."

"I can understand that," Harlan looked ahead. "How do you think Gretchen's doing?"

"Okay, I guess. Mallory would know more than me.

To me, she seems fine. We all went out to dinner the other night. She was in a good mood."

"She talk about me at all?"

"Just that she couldn't wait for you to come home."

"Good to know, good to know. You know of any guy messin' around with her?"

Denny looked at him. "Not that I've seen. Believe me, if she was you'd know before now. Someone would've come up there to tell ya."

"You sure?"

"Of course."

"It's something that's crossed my mind a few times."

"I wouldn't worry. She could've blown town. She stuck around."

"If she did, I couldn't really blame her. I think if it was the other way I would've bailed. But she stuck it out, put up with my shit."

"That's a lot of shit," Denny laughed.

Harlan looked out the window. "Anything new since we talked last?"

"Nah, nothing at all. Just the same old stuff."

"That bad, huh?"

"Could be worse."

"Could be where I was."

"There's that."

"Hey, if nothing else you have better food on the outside. Think it's a fuckin' crime they have people eat that trash."

"Know that's right."

"Every now and then they feed us pretty good," Harlan cracked another beer. "It's funny what you take for granted.."

"Yeah."

"Lack of pussy, that was my real problem."

"I couldn't imagine that."

Harlan gave a laugh. "Think my lady and I, we're gonna make up for a lot of time lost."

"Good for you. That's one of the best things about this mud pit."

"Yeah, man, there's always a girl somewhere. Some night when your girl's gone just roam around a bit. We need a sign advertising all the fine pussy around here."

"You haven't stepped foot in Bencroft in awhile and you still know that's how it goes."

"Sometimes change just fucks things up."

The two talked the rest of the way home. As they passed the stores and restaurants on Main Street Harlan was starting to feel more at home. As a few cars zoomed passed he glanced out the window. They turned off Main onto Mulano. A few twists and turns and they headed down Epstein. As they approached his house Harlan saw a few cars in the drive. They all belonged to those he knew.

Harlan said, "What's that?" he pointed to his driveway.

"What?" Denny said.

"She having a party?"

"May have cooked something up."

"Looks like something I can get into."

"See, I knew you'd like it."

"Think we should've stopped for supplies?"

"We have enough," Denny said. "If we need whatever we can always step out later."

Harlan thought it'd be fun to cut loose and get drunk. It had been awhile since he got to party. As soon as he started to greet people his girlfriend came out the front door. He looked over at the person he was talking to. She ran into his arms. Gretchen was a very tan girl with long brown hair. She was wearing a light blue dress with flowers all over it. She was happy to see him. She'd been waiting for so long. She went on visits most weekends. She never really knew when he was going to be set free.

"Oh, baby, baby!" Gretchen told him. "I'm glad you're back."

"Good to be here," Harlan brushed her hair. "How's it going, mama?"

He loved her crystal blue eyes and smell.

"I couldn't wait," she said.

"Me either."

"Glad to hear it."

They kissed.

"I love you a lot," he said.

"You better," she smiled.

"Oh, look at you! Don't know what I'd do without you."

"I would've found you at some point."

After he got everybody's attention he gave a speech. He thanked everyone for coming and sharing the special time with Gretchen and himself. He went on to talk about how important family and friends were. Some of the people in attendance he hadn't seen in over eight years. He told everyone they looked good, and said if anyone got too drunk or stoned they could crash on the couch or the floor. He didn't want anyone to get hurt.

Harlan was walking around, talking to people about this and that. The beer was nice and cold. The weed was good. Things were only going to get better from that point on.

He walked over to Denny.

"Having a good time?" Denny asked.

Harlan grabbed a cold beer from the cooler. "It's nice, man. Thanks. Hell, I feel fucking great. We'll be having more of these, brother."

"You're right about that."

"I don't know where I'd be without you guys," Harlan

said.

Denny said, "Don't think about that now, man. You're home now. Time to relax. Look forward. You can do anything you want."

"That's the way to look at it."

Hollers and cheers came from everyone.

A few people from up the street came down to join. For the next couple of hours everyone ate and drank.

4

Mort opened his eyes, blinked, looked at the ceiling fan, and remembered he had to be at work. He crawled out of bed and went to the restroom to get a shower. He looked at the time: it was 2pm. He had to be at the club by 4pm. He didn't want to be late. He was already on his last string, and his boss told him that if he was late again he'd be out of a job. Mort couldn't afford to be without a job. He didn't want to go through all the bull with having to find a new place to work. He went to his fridge, and got some stuff to make a sandwich. It crossed his mind to just call his boss and tell him he was sick. He figured there was something he could do, something to read, something to watch on television. In the end, he decided to suck it up and go to the club. Before he walked out the front door he got a little bag of cocaine—it was gonna come in handy later. Most of the time he was there until 7am. He had to be alert. He walked out to his car and got in. It was a bright day out. As he sped away he flipped on the radio and cranked the volume. He loved rock n' roll. He sang along to The Rolling Stones.

When he got to the parking lot of Hive he sat in his car for about ten minutes. He imagined what would happen if he drove his car straight through the front door. He thought maybe he should take out someone right there in the parking lot. He always dealt with small bouts of rage. The thing was, he needed to find ways to channel his dark thoughts. He told himself he'd blame it on the cat. He'd tell them Dobbs made him do it. They'd just think he was crazy. It was all the cat's fault! If he was in an asylum at least he wouldn't be dead, but then, he'd be remanded to that place. He'd still have his freedom taken from him. He decided against it. You couldn't arrest a cat. The thought of a cat being locked away in a cell made him smile for a minute. He told himself he'd come and visit it whenever he got a chance. No matter what happened he'd take the fall, he guessed.

The thought of living a long life wasn't a thing he was really interested in. He just wanted to have as much fun as he could before he died. After he took a little snort of coke he got out of the car and walked inside. It was still awhile until they opened for business, and the place looked totally different. Music was coming from the DJ booth over by the dance floor. A few people who worked there were walking around, talking to each other about whatever. Their laughter was sharp, eyes wide, fashion was loud, and energy was wild. Two guys told him they were going outside to smoke some grass, and if he'd like to join. Mort turned down the offer. The guys laughed, and said it was his loss and more for them.

Hive was among one of the four nightclubs in Gunnster—it was the hottest spot to be. People would say how much they enjoyed Hive compared to the other places. People liked the drink prices. They like the fact they could visit with friends, get wild, and not feel their wallets were being raped. The atmosphere was great. Most people were always smiling and in a good mood. They were easy-going. There were a few bad eggs, but that's expected with everything. When things would get out-of-hand that's where Mort came in. It was his job to ensure everyone who walked through the door had a safe experience. Most nights when he was there he was the only bouncer, with the exception of weekends. He was good at what he did. Most of the time he liked the work. His job was one of the ways he found his victims. There were a few times he'd make sure to remember their information, and then after they left the club he'd start the hunt the next day. When he noticed someone looked underage he'd let them in anyway. He didn't care. No one really cared. Everyone just wanted to have fun and enjoy everything, experience whatever they could.

Mort walked over to the bar in the front. The guy on the other side, Gordon Debock, was cleaning and drying glasses and mugs. Gordon was an African-American with long dreadlocks that hung to his shoulders. He had a medium build with a thick beard. He was humming to himself.

"Debock, how's it going?" Mort said.

Gordon looked up. "Hey, hey, buddy! There he is!. Hey, brother. You know, doin' what I do, takin' care of it."

"I know how that goes."

"Someone has to do it," the man shrugged. "Way I see it, man, everyone needs to make some green. Have to get it somewhere."

Mort chuckled. "Yeah, yeah, I know."

"You catch it," Gordon laughed. "You gotta know how the game works!"

"Right about that."

"Don't have all the answers, but I get by."

"Hey, who does? Just day-by-day, you know? You have no clue when it'll all end. Why spend it all in this place?"

"This is better than most. Beats workin' at a slaughter-house."

"It does. I never worked at one, myself, but I could only imagine."

"I can tell you it's not very fun."

"Yeah."

"Worked at one for five or six months. Up there going to Greenshore, you know?"

"Yeah, yeah, okay. You don't say?"

"Surprised I was there that long."

"I couldn't do it."

"The whole time I couldn't eat meat. You know how hard that was? I like a good burger and steak."

"Meat's good, there's no denying that."

"Yeah, I had to leave. Plus, the smell, it was unreal."

"Oh, boy, that would get to ya," Mort said. "You get fired?"

"Didn't show one day. Boss called. We got into an argument. I said a few things I probably shouldn't have. He told me not to show up again. It was for the best, really. That wasn't my style."

"Don't see how anyone can get behind that."

Gordon placed two clean glasses on the bar. "But no matter where it comes from, the money sure feels good in your wallet."

"You can say that again."

"It's all means to an end," he tapped his index finger against the side of his head. "Big plans in the works."

"What would that be?"

Gordon laughed. "Gonna open my own joint."

"Really?"

"I'm looking at a few different places. Hadn't found the right one yet. I have some big plans. I can see it all now. Big picture. It's the best play right now."

"No shit?" Mort said. "When the fuck was this? First time I've heard about it."

"Didn't want it to blow up in my face."

"Sounds good. When you get things going I'll come with ya."

"You sure about that?"

"Sure."

"Gotta tell you, it's gonna take awhile."

"Just keep me posted."

"Will do."

"I can do whatever you need. I'm a team player."

"Yeah, I know. I have to figure a few things out first. There's a lot that goes into it."

"When you get ready, I'll be there."

"Thanks."

"Might wanna come in as a partner."

"That'd be fine with me."

Mort took a seat on a stool. "I tell you, this place always amazes me."

"How's that?"

"This whole place, it's pretty damn hip. The amount of tail that walks in here, is absolutely fascinating. Hell, I don't have to tell you. If you want a girl, just take your pick. We have all types."

"Yeah, it's pretty nice."

"Yes, indeed."

"Gotta love all the nice candy."

Mort shook his head. "They can go someplace else. They come here because we have the hottest and loudest music, the biggest dance floor, the largest selection of booze, and all the excitement you could ask for. Something for everyone!" he looked over at the music booth. "My man, Sticks, with the music, gettin' the crowd goin', movin' to the beat. It's at a moment like that you take a warm woman, get your boogie on."

"Sounds about right."

Mort glanced over at the guy playing the music.

Gordon said, "He ordered a new system."

"Who, Sticks?"

"Yeah. He's getting a new sound system put in here."

"What's wrong with the one we have?"

Gordon shrugged. "I don't know anything about that shit. I just know when something sounds good. Have to ask him. He said they were gonna install it tomorrow or the next day."

"I'll have to ask about it."

"All that tech stuff, it's beyond me. People say it's gonna be the future, I don't know about that. Things are gonna get too big one of these days. It's all gonna end. I don't wanna be around when that day comes."

"Hopefully not too soon. I still have a lot to do."

"Naturally. Think everyone thinks that. But, you know, we can't go forever."

"Change, it may not be what anyone asked for—"

"I know, I know."

Mort asked where their boss, Sinclair Armstrong, was. Gordon nodded to an office in the back. "He's been back there for awhile. Not sure what he's doing. Think he has a girl back there."

"Really? Well, good for him. We should all be as lucky."

The man laughed. "If she's still back there you should ask about a sister in her family. Talk the two of them into a wild romp."

"There you go! That's what you gotta do. Might as well give it a shot, fuck."

"Shit... I couldn't... Man, Sin, he'd throw my black ass on the street, kick me to the dogs. I couldn't afford that. Have too many tricks who like to spend my money."

"Sounds like a mess."

"It can be. See, thing is, you have to know how to navigate through the craziness. It took awhile but I think I have it down. Thing is, they always wanna change the game. You have to anticipate anything."

Mort said, "If you ever need someone to take one or two off your hands, I'm your man. Just point them to this guy," he pointed to himself.

"Thanks for taking an interest, but I think I have it under control."

"I'm here if you need it."

"Thanks."

"Yeah."

Their boss, Sinclair, didn't really care if they had a drink or two before work. The guy was an addict himself, so he was quick to look the other way. As Sinclair would tell all of the guys. "You gotta do what you gotta to get through the night, push yourself, push, push yourself to get through the crazy night." Sinclair took the place after the original owner, Bob, committed suicide.

They had a few laughs as they shared some stories. Gordon told Mort about one of his girls, Rosa, and how she stole some cash and his car. He said that she got mad because she found he'd been sleeping with her best friend. A few days later she slept with one of his good friends.

"Damn," Mort said. "I'd lose it if someone did that to me. Don't know what I'd do."

Gordon shrugged. "At first I didn't really know. I mean, lots of things crossed my mind. I knew if I threatened her she'd call the cops. Something like that, I couldn't have it. I just walked away from the whole scene."

"Probably for the best," Mort said. "Cops get involved, that's a whole new problem. Next time we see your ass, you're in a fuckin' cell facing ten years."

"I don't need that."

"Hear that."

Gordon continued cleaning glasses. "Best to stay away from all that negativity. I'm trying to improve myself."

"That's good."

"It's about reaching the next level of understanding. I've been taking this class for two weeks now. A friend of mine, she said I should check it out. Sorta like a twelve-step program. Each week it's a new level. Instead of being angry, lashing out on the world, you take a breath, walk away. Best thing, hang a bag and punch it. Write your feelings down, that's another thing. I dunno, I might take a crack at writing something."

"Better than resorting to some criminal ways of getting peace."

"No peace can ever come from violence. You should come with me next time we meet."

"I might take you up on that. Yeah, man, I can see that. They have nice looking tail at these meetings?"

Gordon laughed. "You'd be surprised. Sexy girls are the most fucked-up. Some of the stories I could tell you. Of course, you see these people on the street, everyday lives, you wouldn't even know they were crazy as shit. I guess if you got to know them, sure, you'd see how un-hinged they are."

"You have to wonder about that, about what people are like behind closed doors, about the masks they wear and things they do. I'm sure you'd be amazed by what you find out."

"Probably right."

"The more and more I walk this Earth, the more I see it. It's out there like they can't understand who they are so they transform into what they think people want to see them as."

The man behind the bar shook his head. "Think you're on to something. I can see it. Yeah, yeah, you can't trust someone like that, though. Not a good way to advertise yourself."

"Exactly."

Mort said, "You said Sin was in the office?"

"You gonna see him about a raise?"

"Just need to run a few things by him."

"Good luck."

Gordon said he had to get back to his duties. Mort went over and talked to Sticks for a bit.

Mort walked to the back where his boss' office was. He gave a sharp knock and a voice on the other side told him to come in. He opened the door to a dark-haired, thin, man sitting behind a desk.

"Hey, Mort," the man said. "Glad you could make it. How's everything going?"

"It's all good. What can I say? Still don't have the answer to life."

"Don't think anyone is gonna solve that one."

"Of course."

"You always have people trying."

"They have too much time on their hands."

"This circus we call life, right?"

"Tell me about it," Mort chuckled.

Sinclair slid a little mirror with cocaine on it across the desk. "That's where a lot of us find ourselves these days. It's in the air."

"Yeah," Mort said.

"There's nothing we can do about it."

"Same story, nothing changes."

Sinclair told him to take a seat.

"Thanks," Mort said. "Hope I wasn't bothering you?"

"No worries," Sinclair said. "I just came out here a bit before you came in."

Mort snorted two lines of the coke.

Sinclair said, "Yes, yes, yes, my connection came through today. Started to wonder if I was gonna have to go to another guy."

"That right?"

"He said that he got drunk the other night, it just slipped his mind. Not sure if I believe that. Guy has a history of forgetting things like that."

There was a door on the back wall of Sinclair's office that led to an apartment. Sinclair stayed there a lot so he could keep his eyes on the place, and for the nights when he got too drunk to drive. He was always bringing girls to the room.

Mort said, "So, you ready for another night of excitement?"

"I'm bursting over here," Sinclair grinned. "You spend one night in a joint you see what all of them look like. The same, the same. Nothing new around here. But people come for the fun, you know? I'm looking to find me a little number tonight. Might as well, right?"

"Sure."

"You should get one, too. Take a little trip to paradise, have her show you her kitty cat."

"Working the front door lets you see who comes and goes. Not really a fan of the ones that already have boyfriends."

"In the event you get a girl you can use the place in back," Sinclair nodded to the apartment behind him.

"Thanks."

"All I ask is that you change the sheets."

"I'm guessing you have extra?"

"In the closet back there."

Mort gave a smile. "You're always looking out for us. You have to respect that."

"Hey, hey, it's all good with me," he laughed. "Get something goin', and you have it there. Get to groovin' on each other. Oh, man, what do ya know, you get the prize of the night! Sneak over, tell Sticks to play something extra special. It'll be smooth sailing from there."

"That's what the plan is."

"Just play your cards right. Better watch your wallet, though. Don't wanna end up broke because of one of these little girls here."

"Shit, I don't have much to lose."

"I hear that, buddy. I've always been plagued with money problems. If there weren't any issues I'd think there was a problem. But that's something for another day. It always hangs there, looms over everything I do."

"I get that."

"Some of it is due to the ex-wife."

"I don't have one of those yet."

"Don't. They cost too much money. It would've been cheaper for me to hire someone to kill her."

Both men laughed.

Mort said, "While I have you here, I want to ask if you can throw some more hours my way?"

"I'll have to check things out," Sinclair sat back in his seat. "Can't really promise anything. Things are getting a little tight. Business isn't an easy thing all the time, you know?"

"Pretty tight? What am I supposed to do with that?"

Sinclair shrugged. "That's the best I can do. Sorry. Maybe in a few weeks it'll look better. Fuck, man, what did I just get done telling you? I have money problems of my own. Bills. You have any idea how much it costs to keep this fuckin' place open? And it all could be for nothing. We could all be out of a job within a month. We need all these guys to continue to come in. I get it. I dunno, ask me again in a few more weeks."

"That doesn't do me any good now."

"I know, I know. I know what you're thinking, that I'm holding out on you or something?"

"Not at all."

"Listen, if you need to go someplace else for some extra cash I understand. We can work some kind of a schedule out."

"Yeah."

Sinclair said, "I wanna keep you on."

Both of them did more of the cocaine.

They talked awhile longer. Mort kept asking his boss about extra hours, but Sinclair wouldn't give in. He kept telling Mort that no matter how much he wanted to give him what he wanted he didn't have it to give. After some more back-and-forth Mort tossed his hands in the air, telling him he gives up. Mort got up and left. He went back up front to talk with a few of the others. Mort voiced his disappointment to his co-workers. They told him he had no choice but to turn the other cheek. Mort joked that he should just kill the boss. Everyone laughed.

They turned on the neon signs, started the music, and opened the doors to whatever desire people of the night wanted. Most nights there was a line outside the club. But they started something new that night, and they were all excited to see how it would go. Instead of having customers waiting in line for them to open, they should just go ahead and open earlier.

All sorts of characters were chatting, dancing, drinking, having a good time. bellbottoms and flashy colors were all over. People were on the dance floor cutting the night up. The DJ was hot and fresh, pumping out all of the groovy dance music. They would switch between disco and other types of music.

Mort walked around as the place erupted. His job was to make sure nothing got out-of-hand. He had been involved in thirteen fights while working at Hive. There were all sorts of crazy characters who enjoyed the nightlife. Every now and then a few rotten apples would wander in off the street. He learned very quickly how to get a tough exterior when it came to those types.

No one he worked with knew anything about his murderous ways. Most everyone he worked with liked him. There were a few who thought he was a little strange. They really couldn't point to just one thing, just that he acted a little strange at times. There were a few times he showed up to work all sweaty and tired. There were times he didn't show at all. When questioned he'd just shrug it off, saying he didn't feel good. It all was a little too eerie for some. Others, they'd say Mort was a delight to be around. They would say he was good to have a drink and smoke with. They said he was a great person to have a conversation with, yet, he never let anyone too close.

As he was walking the floor, checking everyone out he spotted a sweet little redhead at a table with some other girls and guys. He liked the way she looked. He walked over to the table. He asked the girl for her number. He didn't realize she was there with one of the guys at the table. After some commotion, Mort hit the guy, making him fall to the floor. The other guys at the table jumped up to assist. After the fight, they were thrown out the door.

Everyone continued enjoying the night.

Later on, after they were closed everyone had a few drinks. As soon as Sinclair told them he was going home everyone else started trickling away.

After everyone left Mort came back and let himself back into the club with his key. He went to his boss' office. He found some coke and cash. While in the office he stumbled upon some paperwork that had Sinclair's home address on it. He figured it'd be a good time for an early morning visit to his boss' house.

He drove out to the house. He sat across from the house listening to the radio, debating if he should go inside. The gun was ready to go, and he had no problem using it. At one point he got out of the car. He stood in the breeze for awhile, but then got back in and drove away.

He'd do it another day, he thought.

5

As the days passed Gretchen told Harlan if he wanted to keep living with her he had to get a job. The first few days he didn't find anything. Everywhere he went when they found out he had been on the inside, they turned him away. He thought they had something against ex-cons. His thought was that if he served his time, and paid his debt, everyone should forget about the sins of the past. Not everyone agreed with his philosophy. He didn't understand it. He felt like someone was out to get him. His girl made him promise he wouldn't go back to a life of crime. She couldn't take it if he got caught and did time again. He reluctantly agreed. Gretchen told him about an ad she read in the paper about the local college, and how they were looking for janitors. He applied and got an interview.

The day of the interview Harlan was really nervous. His girl kept telling him to calm down, that everything would be okay. She told him if they turned him away it wasn't the end of the world. He had his doubts. Within the first ten minutes of the interview, they said he had the job. Harlan went home and they celebrated. They got drunk and had sex in every room of the house. The both of them felt so good. It looked like things were shaping up. Around the same time, Gretchen got a new job at a burger place, World of Beef.

Harlan said, "Babe, things are looking better for us every day. That's something to write home about."

"You're right," she said.

On his first day of work, Harlan got his assignment from, Fred Williams, the head groundskeeper. He was tasked to oversee building eight. Building eight was where the English and History classes were held.

"You sure you're up for the job?" Fred asked.

Harlan nodded. "Sounds pretty simple to me."

Fred chuckled. "You don't need to be a doctor to do this. You just have to do a good job."

"No problem there."

"That's good," Fred told him.

They were sitting in Fred's office.

"I'm a hard worker," Harlan said.

"Glad that's the case. Around here, we have a high turn-over rate."

"How come?"

Fred opened the top drawer of his desk and took a pack of cigarettes out. He took one and offered the pack to Harlan.

Fred lit up. "See, the problem with a lot of people who worked for me was substance abuse. It's none of my business what someone does outside of work. When you're here you're expected to stay clean and sober. I mean, hell, I'm not one to shy away from the occasional drink. Grass, I had it once and didn't like it. The guy who lives next to me, I went to his brother's place and had some. It wasn't for me. Plus, I didn't wanna be one of those burn-outs. I have too much going on."

"Sir, you don't have to worry about a thing," Harlan said. "I'm straight as an arrow. Only time I take drugs is when I'm sick."

"If you are caught with anything like that it'll be im-mediate termination."

"As it should be. And just so you know, my criminal past isn't even an issue anymore. I've turned things around."

"Just like that?"

"Yes, sir."

"I hope so for your sake. If you get into any trouble

we'll have to part ways," Fred ashed in an ashtray on the desk.

"No problem."

"Good. Glad we understand one another. You have any questions for me?"

Harlan nodded. "Can't say as I do, no."

"Now, the work itself, it's not hard at all. You just need to show up every day and do a good job."

"No problem."

"You stick with it and there are good things in it for you."

"Like what?"

Fred handed a couple of papers to Harlan. "Here are all the benefits, information on health insurance and 4O1K."

"Oh, thanks."

"Hope it works out for you."

"That'd be good."

Fred sighed. "The thing is, like all facets of life, you have to really want it. Don't just do it for others. Do it for yourself."

"Yeah, yeah, I know."

"You gonna let me down?"

"I'm not."

"You sure? I mean, fuck, we'll call this whole thing off right now. My girlfriend has a retarded brother who needs a job. Think I should give it to him?"

"I can do it."

"That's what I like to hear."

"I have a lot riding on this, sir. I made a promise I want to keep."

"Promises are easy to say but hard to keep. Not always, but I'm sure you know what I mean."

Harlan took out his own cigarettes and lit one.

The two talked awhile longer as they smoked cigarettes and drank soda. Fred had the girl at the front desk get some. Both men commented that they'd rather be drinking a beer,

"Any hour is good for beer," Harlan said.

Fred laughed. "Off the record, I'd have to agree with that."

The men laughed.

"But like I said before...," Fred stated.

"Of course."

6

Houx College was named after John M. Houx, a 12th-grade English teacher who was killed when he was hit head-on by a speeding motorist as he was on his morning run. The driver was arrested and charged with manslaughter. The whole town came together to mourn the fallen teacher. They decided to name the college they'd just built after him.

Harlan arrived at 7am sharp and went to the Administration building. He wanted to make a good impression. He was going to save up and buy Gretchen a ring. He loved her very much. He wanted to show her he'd never go back to his old ways.

Harlan started his life of crime at the age of eighteen when he stole some beer and weed from his neighbor. Shortly after that, he started dealing a little weed and breaking into cars. About six months later he broke into his first house. He and his friends got out of there with some cash and jewelry. They divided up the money between the three of them. The other guys didn't have girlfriends, so they let Harlan have the jewelry for the girl he was dating at the time. The house break-ins lasted for a few more months until he got arrested. The police had been keeping tabs on him all along. Some of his friends sold him out. He spent a few months in jail. Two days after he got out he found himself behind bars again for the same thing. While inside he got a few additional months for fighting. When he got out, at first, it seemed as though he had cleaned up his act. But then he found himself needing fast cash, so he went back to what he always did. After a little while he and Denny started doing small jobs together, breaking into houses and cars. Everything was going well until one night:

The plan was simple, he and Denny were supposed to break into an average small house, nothing special—that was the night Denny never showed. After waiting on him for a bit Harlan decided to go in alone. He didn't know the neighbor was in the homeowner's backyard. Tom Hicks, he was returning some work tools. When Harlan was inside the house Tom saw him from the outside and raced in. The two men started fighting. After knocking Harlan out Tom called the authorities.

Down at the station, after a few hours of being questioned, Harlan never gave them any information. It didn't take police long to figure out the break-in wasn't an isolated incident. They had more than two dozen reports of break-ins in the area.

After some time, he confessed to five other robberies. No matter how hard they pressed he wouldn't give up the fact he had help. They told him he'd take the fall alone. He seemed to be okay with that. He wasn't a snitch. When he called Gretchen and told her what happened she hung up on him. He knew he fucked himself. The day he stood in front of the judge, he honestly thought he'd just get probation. He got three years. With good behavior, he was out in two.

It was hard on him when he first went to prison. He didn't fit into any group. He knew how to handle himself if someone ever threatened him, and it came in handy within the first two weeks. This guy, Ray Dalton, confronted him in the lunch room. Ray wanted to protect him. Ray was a big bald guy with tattoos all over. Harlan told him it was okay, that he could protect himself. Ray, not liking this, told Harlan he better let him or else.

"Or else?" Harlan said.

"You'll be sorry," Ray stared at him.

Harlan gave a dismissive hand. "Shit, man, whatever!"

"What? What did you say?"

"You heard me, you have trouble hearing, stupid shit?"

"I'll fuck you where you stand, man!"

"Sure your boyfriend won't get mad?"

"I'm tellin' you now, motherfucker, you're gonna get it. If you don't wanna end up with a bloody face you'll shut your mouth."

"Fuck you," Harlan said.

"I'm warning you."

"Think I'm scared?"

"You should be."

"What, your bitch mom teach you how to fight?"

"That's right, keep it up, tough guy."

"After I finish here I was gonna go to your mom's house. Said she wanted some real dick."

"That right?"

"She was just saying something about you not being a good lover."

"You should stop why'll you're ahead."

"Like the head your wife gave me last night?"

"Sure."

"She told me I needed to pay a visit to your sister tonight."

"Seeing as how you're in here, I don't think you will make that date."

"You wanna call her, tell her. While you're on the phone tell her you won't be there either."

Ray walked toward Harlan and gave him a hard push. Harlan came back with a right jab to the jaw, then a fast left. After a knee to the groin Ray went down. Harlan kicked him a few times before some guards ran over and broke things up.

"You want any more?" Harlan shouted. "You know where to find me, cocksucker."

After some counseling, Harlan promised he wouldn't

get into any more fights. He was told if he was involved in any more fights it would just add time to his sentence. A lot of time was spent in his cell where he thought of ways he'd gone wrong. He thought about Gretchen and how much he loved her, that her love gave him the spark to keep going. It was nice to know someone was waiting for him to get out. During his time on the inside, he made a lot of friends. A lot of people liked him. He was assigned to work in the kitchen, which he really liked. He had a knack for cooking. If nothing else it helped pass the time. Finally, that glorious day came, the day he was released.

7

Harlan liked all the students he met while at work. There were a lot of girls he thought were really foxy. The work itself, it wasn't his first choice by any means but it was some money. And it made his girl happy, and he wanted to prove to her he was the man she hoped he'd be. It was a struggle for him, having to answer to anyone besides himself. He had to take a big gulp and swallow his pride.

One day, as he was walking to his car in the parking lot, he saw a small group of guys and girls around a van. He gave them a wave as he passed. One of the guys asked how he was doing. It was a Friday and he was glad to welcome the weekend. He was going to spend the whole weekend with his baby.

"Can't complain," Harlan said.

The guy, who had big black goofy hair came over. "Good day, huh?"

"What do you mean?" Harlan said. "I guess. Just finishing it all up."

"Where you going?"

"Home," Harlan opened the driver's door to his car. "Been a long day."

"Home? Why you wanna go there?"

"See my baby."

The guy snorted. "Got a big date?"

"I just miss her."

"That right?"

"Yeah."

"That's sweet," the man said. "Nothing quite like that girl at home, huh? The weekend in front of you. Just the two of you. The moments we live for, you know? That one little bit of paradise that makes it alright. Just having that, it can make the world a better place."

"You know how it goes."

"I do."

"It makes the world go around," Harlan said.

"Women, women, women, you gotta love them."

"Yeah."

"Where would we be without them?"

"Wish I knew."

"That's the question of the ages, my friend. Men have been trying to figure that one out forever," the guy told him.

"Got that right."

"I dunno, something about that sweet muff."

"It's something like nothing else, I tell ya."

The guy laughed. "It's one thing that makes life worth livin'"

"Yeah."

"Sometimes when you're having a bad day, just look at one of those fine, beautiful creatures, and everything else becomes a shadow."

"How poetic," Harlan said.

The guy nodded. "It's a gift."

"You should write for the movies," Harlan laughed.

"That would be boss."

"Wouldn't it, though?"

"You know it."

"Yes, yes, yes!"

"That's a good one."

"I do what I can."

The guy introduced himself as Rod. He asked Harlan if he wanted to come party with him and his friends.

Harlan said, "I can't. Have to get home."

"Oh, come on, man!"

"Seriously."

"Just a little bit."

"I dunno."

Rod turned back to his friends, and pointed to a blonde girl. "See that girl?"

"Yeah."

The girl he pointed to was dressed in a white skirt and yellow blouse. He asked if Harlan wanted to get with her.

Harlan looked and shrugged. "Who wouldn't?"

"Alright."

"But I need to go back to my girl. She'd get pissed if I didn't come home."

"I don't know what woman wouldn't. The trick is not to get caught. Do anything but that. Man, you get caught, they'll kick you in the dick. They'd never let you forget that shit. The minute you thought they did, they'll throw it back in your face. Believe me."

"I wouldn't want that."

"No, sir."

"They would end us."

Harlan said, "Can't have that happening to me. It'll ruin my plans."

"Can't have that."

It didn't take much convincing for Harlan to join their party.

"That's what I'm talkin' about, man. It's all about having fun, that's why we were put on this planet. You have to get anything you can."

"I get that."

"Get some booze, other stuff, that's where it's at. All you do, find a little honey and that's that, my friend. Just ask if she has a sister for me. If she doesn't have a sister I'd take her friend."

Harlan looked over at the others by the van. "Guys have enough grass? I can always swing by my place, pick some more up."

"We're good," Rod said. "I have a bunch."

"Really?"

"I have good connections."

"That's what it's all about, you know? Stay connected all over the fuckin' world."

"They always come in handy."

"It's always good to keep people on the hook."

"You know what it's all about."

Harlan walked with Rod over to the van where the others were.

"How are you?" Harlan asked the blonde wearing the yellow blouse.

He thought she was so beautiful.

"Well, hello," the blonde said. "I'm Tiffany."

"Tiffany?"

"Tiffany LeeAnn Bosworth."

"Nice name," Harlan said.

She smiled.

"It's refreshing meeting someone who's willing to tell you all three names."

She laughed. "I'm as straight as they come. What you see is what you get. That's just me. Act the same around everyone."

"That's the best way. Wish more people were like that."

"We're hard to find."

"But you're out there, that's the important thing. Fight the good fight for us all."

She grinned. "I try."

"That's all you can do."

"Positive vibes, you know?"

"Exactly."

"It's just the way I am."

"Not a bad way to be."

"Wish everyone felt the same."

"Know what you mean," he told her.

"And you are?" she asked.

"Harlan, Harlan Reeves."

"Nice meeting you."

"I have to say, it's not every day you meet someone with such beauty."

She smiled. "Oh, stop it."

"It's true."

"I dunno about all of that, but thanks."

"Trust me."

"I don't hear that often."

"People need to tell you that all the time."

"Should tell them that."

"I will."

She laughed. "The last guy who told me that cheated."

"That's a shame."

"But he made his choice."

"That's a way to look at it."

"Not the best one, I have to say."

"That's what they tell me."

"A lot of truth behind it."

"Yeah."

"Things will get better."

"Indeed."

"They have to."

"I guess."

Her long blonde hair was a burst of sunshine. Her blue eyes were bright and calm. Her smile could warm the darkest place. He could trace the outline of her breasts through the yellow blouse. The thought of her nipples brushing against the fabric sparked interest in him. He wanted to see and feel those breasts. Her long legs ran forever. Her pale face draped a blanket of joy over him. He wanted to get to know her, everything about her, good and bad. As he looked at her he wondered what she was thinking.

They talked a little more while the others were talking over something else. Harlan asked Tiffany if she'd introduce her friends. Their names were Blake, Chuck, Connie, and Janelle. Connie said she was Rod's girlfriend. They all looked bright and fresh. As they talked around the van Blake rolled a joint and passed it around. Blake was a short guy, built like a mountain. He had long brown hair and a bushy beard. He was wearing a blue shirt that had little rips on the front. Harlan didn't think he looked like the type that would attend a college class or anything.

"Glad you could join us," Blake told Harlan. "Any friend of Rod's is cool with me."

"Thanks," Harlan said. "We actually just met. I do janitorial stuff here."

"I know," Blake said. "Seen you around. So, you like it? Like cleaning after all the shitheads up here?"

"It's okay, I guess. It's a straight way to pay the bills."

"Verses illegal ways?" Blake asked.

"Done my fair share of that shit. Before I came here I was locked up for a couple years."

"Oh, man."

Harlan said, "It's not a pretty place in there. Do your best to stay out of there."

Blake said, "Hadn't been yet."

Harlan told all of them about him being in prison. He went on to say how he made a promise never to go back to that place.

Blake handed the joint to Harlan. "Get ready for the ride, dude. We're expanding on a different plane. Strap in, it may get a little bumpy!"

Harlan took a big hit, then exhaled. "Yes, sir, that's where it's at. Some good stuff you have here," he held the joint out. "I need to get some of this shit. Getting blasted on this, that's what dreams are made of."

"Take it if you like."

"Oh, yeah? Think I might need to meet your connection."

"I can make that happen."

"Groovy."

Blake chuckled. "It takes you to many places. Some you didn't know existed. Have a few different kinds. It's like this, they all get you high. Some are just more mellow than others."

"Just point me in the direction."

"Right on, man! That's what we like to hear 'round here, brother."

Chuck took the funny cigarette, inhaled and exhaled. "That's the good thing about it, you know, you can always grow more if you want. Sure he won't have a problem parting with more if the cash is right."

"Not an issue there," Harlan told him.

"Good, good, good," Chuck said.

Chuck was another guy with long hair. He was thin and tan. He was sporting a pair of dark brown bellbottoms with a light green t-shirt.

Blake said, "Sex, drugs, rock n' roll, that's what it's all about, brother! It's the best, you know?"

"I need to get some for the show next week," Chuck said.

"You in a band?" Harlan asked.

"Oh, not me," Chuck laughed. "I don't have any talent like that. No, no, no, it's this music festival thing."

"Nothing beats live music," Harlan told him.

"Supposed to be a pretty groovy time. I can't wait."

"How many bands are gonna be there?"

Chuck said, "A few. I know Lazy Men and Screams are gonna be there. Some others, I forget."

Harlan shook his head. "I like Lazy Men. I have all three of their albums."

"Me, too."

"Saw them in Texas last year. They put on a really good show. It could've been me, though. I was fucked-up at the time."

"Right on."

"It's always amazes me, folks like that, they inspire greatness. They're just normal dudes like us."

"They're good."

Blake said, "All that fuckin' music is great. Blaze up, man!"

Chuck said, "Another day, another way. You gotta take what you can. Come on, come on, come on all of you! Hey, Rod, you have your guitars? We can rock! Turn this party up a few notches."

"Better not dump beer on them again," Rob told him.

"Man, I wouldn't do that."

"Better not."

"I told you, I was still tripping at the time."

"That's what they all say."

"If you had the shit you would've been tripping, too."

Rod said, "Most likely."

"Hey, man, you know it's good when it's good."

"You're right about that one."

"Of course."

They talked about music and getting stoned for a little bit. Harlan started to think these were good people to get to know. He asked why they never approached him before. They told him they needed to make sure he was a cool dude, that he wouldn't narc on them. Rod told him he saw him getting high on campus a few times. Rod talked it over with his girlfriend, and they decided to invite Harlan into the fold.

The girls, Janelle and Connie, like Tiffany, were

blonde. All three had the same body shape. You could've sworn they just walked off of a modeling shoot. They laughed and joked as they got high. All three girls were outstanding.

Harlan found a phone and called Gretchen. He told her that Denny and a few of his friends were going out drinking and that she shouldn't wait up for him. He knew if he told her what was really going on she'd get pissed. She said it was okay, but she didn't like it. She wanted to spend time with him. When he got off the phone he asked whose vehicle they were taking. Rod laughed, telling him he could leave his car in the parking lot and they'd come back for it later.

"Should we get any beer?" he asked.

Rod said, "There's a lot at the house, but we could always use more."

"Righteous!" Harlan said.

"Come on, you'll love it," Tiffany said.

"I'm sure I will. I'm pretty cool with everything. I've never been too picky."

"That's good."

Blake howled. "Everyone wants to know my friends, be my friends, hang with my friends, fuck with my friends! How's it gonna be?"

8

They went back to Rod's house, about twenty minutes from the store. There were a few cars parked in the yard. They walked through the front door and people were sitting on the couch. More people hanging around in the kitchen. Rod introduced Harlan to everyone. All types of characters were hanging around, all chatting and cackling about everything. One of the guys, John Ballard, was confined to a wheelchair. He explained that he was in a car accident one night while drunk. He was sentenced to a life in the chair. He had a tray on his lap with a big bag of grass. he was a round-faced fellow with red cheeks and black hair. A green floppy hat rested on his head. He told everyone if they wanted to smoke he'd roll them one.

"There's more than plenty to go around," John said. "If this isn't enough for you I have a whole galaxy here," he reached down, and grabbed a black bag that was sitting beside his chair. "All kinds of mind-fucks here, boys and girls," he dumped the bag onto the tray. There were several little plastic bags full of pills. "I have all you could need here. Take your pick. They say these are mind-altering, pushing the boundaries of reality, going to another existence. You can be whatever you want on this stuff. If I don't have it, it's something that hasn't been invented yet. Oh, my, all the good times, yes, sir. Come on, come on, I have what you need right here. The guy who first introduced me to these, he told me I could go far, that there are different vibrations out there, that I need to walk around in my own mind for awhile. I tell ya, I take one of these pills and the next thing I know I'm walking on the moon. Isn't that a trip, me walking, right?"

"That's something, alright," Harlan said.

"You can do anything with this,"

"Groovy."

"You'll be feeling really good."

Harlan took a pill.

John said, "You must think a guy in a wheelchair doesn't have much to offer, am I right? That like, when you look at me you think I'm half-dead or something?"

Harlan didn't say anything.

"I'm here to tell you, buddy, I have a lot to give. Make no mistake about it, my friend. I'm not just some pill pusher. There's more to me than you know. What do you know? I can do what most can't. People, they always try to tell me I can't do anything."

Harlan gave him a strange look. "I didn't think any-thing. I don't even know you, man. What's the deal? Just havin' a good time and you start in on all this personal stuff. It's okay. Calm yourself. Why bitch, man? It's just a party. You know, cut loose, have some fun? Mellow-out. We're here to get high and drunk."

"You know," John continued, "before I got into this damn chair I was respected. Now, people look at me with pity. I don't need anyone's pity, motherfucker. They just come to me for their damn drugs now. I'm just one of many doctors around here. I'm nothing fuckin' spe-cial. I'm a dime-a-dozen. People come up to me, talkin' all this jive all the time. I don't care what they say. We're friendly toward one another, but it ends there. Nothing goes deeper."

Harlan gave him another look. "Hey, I think your mind's twisted. Think you better lay off that shit. You need to get some sleep. Wake up tomorrow with a clear mind. It's not my fault you're in the chair."

"I can see through you, though. You're just like the others, sure. I see you running reports in your mind, like a court stenographer."

"You don't know anything about me. What are you talking about? I think you need to think about a few things. Look, nothing is perfect. I think you've had enough. I'm a nice guy but you're pissing me off."

Rod said, "John, you need to calm-the-fuck-down. I won't have you talkin' to my fuckin' guests like that. I thought we talked about this the other time. It's my place, dude. I'm your friend, but this has to stop."

Chuck said, "Tell ya what, John, I'll pick you up tomorrow, and we can hang out. We can go someplace and get higher than hell. We can do anything you want. I'm not working or anything. It's good. Sound like a plan?"

John's face grew solemn, giving a dismissive wave. "Sorry, sorry, oh boy, I'm sorry. Didn't mean to go off like that. Sometimes I forget, I forget that people aren't against me even though I'm against this chair. See, the night of my crash my baby died. I loved her. She told me not to drive. I didn't listen. I told her I was fine to drive. I mean, yeah, I had six beers but I was okay. Wished she would've forced the issue. If she had she'd be alive today. Anyway, I flipped the car and we ended up in a deep ditch. She died on the scene. For a long time I blamed everyone else. You know, everyone's fault but mine. I was speeding down the freeway to the graveyard. I had a problem, and something like that had to happen before I realized what I was doing. It was two years ago it happened, but I'm still adjusting. You don't ever wanna get where I'm at. Don't think I'll ever get completely right with it. Might get there when I die."

"Sorry to hear that," Harlan told him. "Well, it's the cards we're dealt, right?"

"Guess so."

"Nothing anyone can do about it."

"Just hope for the best."

"Sometimes that's harder than anything."

"You know, that's why there are drugs around. Gotta have something to get through this life," John smiled. "To make it up to ya, here's something for your trouble," John took one of the little bags of pills and gave it to Harlan.

Harlan gave the man a thumps-up. "Thanks, man! This will come in handy."

"Free of charge," the man called out.

"Best price I know."

"Indeed," he said. "Whenever you need more I got you covered. The guy who lives across from me, and his foxy chick make it in their garage. They have this whole fuckin' lab set up. It's pretty impressive, actually. The first time I saw it, I was shocked, never saw anything like that before. I asked him about the pigs, if they've ever been busted. He told me they hadn't been yet, so he was going to continue until that day comes. If you ask me, I don't understand what the real problem would be. The pills, they relax your mind, let you go on adventures."

"Those have a name?" Harlan asked.

"LSD. He told me what it means, but my mind's foggy right now. There are a lot of things that go into it, I can tell you that. You'd have to ask him the details. I just know they're good, good for a state of mind. First time I ever had one I had a half. Because, to be honest, I didn't really know what it was going to do."

"Thanks," Harlan said.

John continued. "You'll be good. Take the whole thing. Hell, take two. The fuck do I care? It won't hurt. They're made to help us, not hurt us."

"Right on."

"They haven't killed me yet. I'm still up, doing what I do best."

"That's what we all strive for, to be the very best we can, brother. We can only do so much with our time of this planet."

"That was my thought behind it."

Chuck ran over with a beer in hand. He said they were starting to play some drinking games and they should join. Harlan nor Rod were into playing drinking games. Rod joked that if they got him to play one of those games he'd die. A few other people tried to get them to play.

Rod said, "Are you guys trying to kill me? No way I can get into that. Would any of you visit my grave? When I go I guess you can have everything I own. It's not much. But, brother, I don't plan on going anywhere. I'm gonna be here until they shoot me dead. I don't give a fuck."

"That's the way to look at it," Harlan told the guy.

"That's how you have to handle yourself sometimes. Can't be a little punk, you know?"

"Of course you don't. I found that out when I was on the inside. In there, you have to always keep that in mind. You don't wanna get beat."

One of the guys came over. "Let's get this goin'! Push it to the fullest! What's it gonna be? The evolution of be-ings here, buddy!!"

A few others joined in.

Harlan laughed at them.

They were all joking around and acting like fools."

9

This one guy walked over to Harlan, and introduced himself as Tim.

"Good to know you," Harlan said.

Tim gave a nod. "You like the party?"

"It's not bad."

"Good, good. That's the way we do it around here. It's nothing but F. U. N. fun here. Stick around and you'll see. I assume you're a friend of Rod's?"

"We just met."

"I'm sure we'll get you into some wild adventures," Tim said. "You can never tell with this crew. One minute, you're having a straight conversation about this or that, next you're swimming somewhere in the clouds. You hope to climb down at some point. But, hey, nothing is set in stone," he laughed. "I just started driving trucks for Malvane. What do you do?"

I'm a janitor at the college here."

"That right?"

"For about a month now," Harlan told him.

"Hey, man, if it puts money in your pocket it's not all bad."

"That's what my thought is."

"If it works for ya, there's something to that."

Harlan said, "What kind of stuff do you guys haul?"

"All sorts of things. For the most part, I do loads for retail stores. All kinds of things."

"Sounds like good work."

Tim shrugged. "It has its good points. Get to drive a lot. Be on highways and freeways. The down-side is the thing that makes it great; You have to be on the road, away from your home a lot."

"Does it pay well?"

Another shrug. "I'm doing okay. I'm not getting rich or anything, but I'm doing pretty good. Bills are paid and I'm left with enough for booze and dope."

"That's something."

Tim raised a brow. "So, whenever I come to town I land here for a bit. This time around I have four days off. Now, I'm not gonna spend all that time here. But for now, I'm here until the party stops or I get so blasted out of my mind that I can't even think straight."

"I dig it, I dig it."

"But I just may have to step it up."

"You gotta do what you have to."

"Thing is, I wanna get so fucked that I can't recall any of this. That's the way to be."

"Right on!."

"The whole thing is outta sight, you dig?"

The two talked for awhile longer over a beer.

Someone came over to chat him up about some sweet drugs.

Harlan was fascinated by all the interesting people he'd met. Everyone seemed cool to him. He knew if he wanted to stick with the crowd he'd have to really impress Tiffany—after all, she was the main reason he was there.

Some more people came by. Everyone seemed to have some sort of drug. As they passed Harlan talked to them, and like good people they offered him whatever they had.

He took it all.

He was feeling pretty good.

At some point he found himself talking with the original group he started with. John said he had to leave, that he had to catch his ride home. As he wheeled away this one guy said he was taking him home. When John was rolling across the living room a sadness fell over him.

Another guy, Jay Fisher, a shaggy-looking guy, said John was full of it, and you couldn't believe a single word he said. Jay said the guy John was talking about did get busted and went away. He told Harlan that he got the pills from a robbery.

"That guy, that guy, he's just a fuckin' drunk," Jay said.

"That so?" Harlan asked.

"Oh, yeah, I know one of these days he's gonna really do it to himself."

"You think? Someone needs to help him, no?"

"He doesn't want any. Believe me, we've tried."

"That's not good."

"You got that right," Jay said. "Of course, you can't tell him anything. That guy there, he's gonna do what he wants. He's as bull-headed as he is stupid. If he doesn't watch it he'll find himself in a shallow grave some-where."

"No one can get through to him?" Harlan asked.

Jay shook his head. "If you think you can talk him into something, go for it."

"Some people, hell, you just can't help."

"They like playing victim to whatever they think of, what they have roaming around that stupid melon of theirs."

"I can see the truth in some of it."

"It's less than they let on."

They talked more about the guy in the wheelchair.

Harlan continued walking around, talking and joking around with everyone. There were plenty of drugs and beer. He found himself involved in a conversation with a man who told him he needed to get into the adult film business, and that he had the looks for it. Harlan shook his head and told him that wasn't his thing. The guy told Harlan that he was going to New York to film adult movies. He kept telling Harlan how much money he could make. Still, he wasn't interested. A guy and girl walked in carrying two big bags of cocaine. Everything became blurry to Harlan as he continued indulging in party favors. Some people broke out guitars and started singing songs. Some of the people started dancing in circles, hooting and hollering at one another.

At some point, Rod told Harlan if he wanted to take Tiffany to one of the back rooms it would be fine with him. He added that she lived there, so she'd probably want to go to her room, somewhere she'd feel more comfortable.

"She lives here?" Harlan asked.

"She moved in about three months ago."

"You guys an item?"

"No, no, no, nothing like that, man. I was friends with an ex of hers. They broke up and she had no place to go. Felt sorry for her and the situation. I told her she could stay with me. Now, believe me, she told me we weren't gonna sleep together. I tried like crazy."

"I don't blame you," Harlan chuckled. "She is a goddess. Can't believe she isn't married with ten boyfriends, you know?"

"Yeah, that's about it. Women like that, they're rare."

Harlan told him he had to see about Tiffany, that it was his duty for all human-kind.

Rod smiled. "If she lets you, gotta get the gold. Walk up there, take your chances, spin the wheel, see what happens."

"Sounds good to me."

"That's what I'm sayin'"

Harlan walked over to Tiffany. She was talking to a girl about whatever until a guy came by and scooped her up. Tiffany smiled at Harlan. She asked if he wanted to see her room.

She took him by the hand and led him to her bedroom. The room was plain, with a bed, a dresser, and a few bags full of stuff.

"Nice room," Harlan looked around.

"Thanks," she said. "It's my comfort place. Sometimes I just need a break from all the parties that go on here. It's a piece of my peace, I guess."

"There a lot of those?"

"Almost every night."

"Really?"

"Yeah."

She shut the door behind them.

He stepped closer to her. "What does Rod do for money to afford that?"

"I'm not sure he'd want me telling you, but he deals drugs along with a few other things."

"Drugs?"

"It was just grass, lots of it. But he just recently got into cocaine."

"Oh, I see."

"He's been making pretty good money at it."

"I heard that happens."

"Yeah, it's pretty sweet."

"You may get busted by cops. But, hey, there are risks in anything, right?"

She gave a shrug. "The thought of jail, that's one thing that's scary. I don't know how anyone could do it. I'd just die in a place like that."

Harlan proceeded to tell her about his past crimes, and that he spent time in prison. She really didn't seem to care. She told him she liked him and wanted to know more.

"I'm an open book," he told her.

"I'm the same way."

Harlan said, "Rod told me about your situation, about how you came to live here."

"Yeah, I'm not really one to dwell on the past. I don't want people to feel sorry for me."

"I understand."

She sighed. "I just do what I can to get by. I mean, yeah, it's a tragic story but I wanna get passed that. Sure, I grew up without a father, but I learned to deal with it. My mom, the bitch, told me he ran out when I was really young. Last she knew he was shacked up with some girl in Oklahoma. She told me he wrote her a few times."

"He never saw you after he left?"

"She sent him some pictures. I guess he wasn't interested."

"I'm sorry."

"It's okay."

"That's pretty mean of him. Well, he doesn't know what he missed. I'm sure if he knew he would've never left."

"That's sweet of you to say. Anyway, after awhile she got too demanding and I had to get out of there. I think a lot of it had to do with him."

"Damn. Did you ever learn his name?"

"Mort, Mort Bosworth."

"I'm sorry to hear that, Tiff."

"Oh, that's just part of life. It's just one strand that this fucked world has to offer. Well, I shouldn't say that, there's good in it, too. Like us meeting. Like if none of that had happened I probably wouldn't be here talking to you."

"Good point."

She took off her blouse and skirt in front of him. "Like what you see?"

"You have a nice body."

"I stay fit."

"It shows."

"Thanks."

He walked closer to her, placed his left hand on her waist. "This is nice."

"Yes," she said softly.

He took off his pants and shirt. They looked at each other's naked form. They looked into each other's eyes. He stepped closer to her. With his fingers, he slowly reached down and put them inside her. She sighed and lightly moaned. He fingered faster and harder. After a bit, she reached out and took his dog in her hand. As she yanked him he became harder. After some more moaning she took her other hand and started to caress his balls. Before too long she got on her knees and put his dog in her mouth. He lightly ran his hand on top of her head. She sucked until he came. She stood and pushed him on the bed. Her nipples were hard. She crawled on top of him and put his dog inside of her. It was warm and wet. She proceeded to ride him. She got faster and faster. Her firm breasts bounced to the rhythm. She felt his release shoot inside her, then she fell on him. The two spent the next few hours smoking dope and having sweaty sex.

The next day they woke, cleaned up, and continued partying with the others. They were still having a good time two days later. At some point, Harlan remembered he had to go home and face his girlfriend. He was a little nervous not knowing what she would say or do. For a minute he thought about escaping with Tiffany, going someplace where she'd never find him. In the end, he thought it would be best to face the music.

10

It was night when Harlan approached his house. The light outside was off, so he thought that was a good sign. He knew his girlfriend would be mad. He opened the front door, trying to keep the creaking door as quiet as he could. It was pitch black when he closed the door behind him. Everything was silent. As he made his way slowly across the living room a light flipped on. Harlan was frozen. The light was from the lamp beside the couch. Gretchen stood from the couch with her hands on her hips. They argued for a bit. He laid the blame on Denny, telling her they just lost track of time, that they got into the party favors pretty good. He apologized and she forgave him. He told her that he'd try to not let it happen again. She could tell in his eyes it was going to happen a few more times. She knew him too well. As he talked to her all he was thinking was how grateful he was she didn't have a clue what really happened.

As he got a shower that night all he could think about was Tiffany. He liked her and knew he wanted to try to get to know her more. And the sex, the sex was amazing. The thought of talking her and Gretchen into a threesome crossed his mind, but then, he figured neither would be into it. There was some sort of connection he had with Tiffany, and he had a good feeling about her. He wanted to sneak out and see her. When Gretchen went to sleep he went into the kitchen and poured himself a whiskey. He rolled a joint, thought of Tiffany, and finished his drink. He didn't want to break things off with his girlfriend, but he didn't want to end things with Tiffany. He loved them both. The possibilities with both were limitless. In a spark of genius, when he was pouring more whiskey, he stumbled around and found some paper and a pen, and he sat at the kitchen table and wrote a poem about the new woman in his life. He'd found something magical and didn't want to lose it.

The next day he went to her house. They had a nice day hanging out. He enjoyed getting to know her more. She seemed interested in him. He loved her beautiful blue eyes. He wanted to have both women.

A few days later, at Dough-for-Dough, over a slice of pepperoni, he told Gretchen about buying her a ring. He said eventually they'd get married.

She said, "Ah, baby, that's a nice thing. You don't have to spend all your money on me. It'd be nice to save some. I dunno, maybe you could invest it? A new car, maybe? You've worked hard for it."

"But I want to," he told her. "I want this more than anything. I don't want a new car. I want you, is that so hard for you to understand?"

"You really don't have to buy me anything."

"I wanna do it, though."

"Come on, I know where your heart is. I don't need a stupid ring to know how you feel. We know what we have. Nothing is gonna get in the way of that."

He took a sip of soda. "I realize that. It's a symbol, a symbol to let the whole world know you and I are going to be forever."

She swallowed. "That's a long time."

"I know. Well, with good company it shouldn't matter how long it is. It won't be like we'll get bored of each other. We can talk all day."

"Yeah."

"What, don't you think so?"

"We need to talk," she folded her arms on the table.

"Everything okay?"

"Depends on how you look at it."

"We are talking?"

"Not here."

"Why?"

"I don't want to," she said, as she took a drink. "Sorry, I brought it up. Let's just go. I don't want to make a spectacle."

He looked around at the other tables. "What? What's wrong?"

She sighed. "Can we just talk about this at home?"

"I am your home."

A little smile fell on her face. "That's nice of you to say. But we need to talk about this back at the house, okay? I don't wanna do this in public. You want me to be a bitch in front of all these people? I can that then some."

"No, no, no, I don't wanna hear that. Whatever you have to say, tell me now. I don't wanna wait."

"I know, but I think we should talk about it at the—"

"Just tell me here."

"I can't."

"Why?"

"Too personal."

"Get outta here," he said. "Too personal? Whatever it is you can tell me. I won't get mad."

"Don't say that. You don't know what I'm about to say."

"Tell me."

She stared at him, a small tear rolled down her cheek. "I don't... I don't wanna get married."

"Why?"

"The time isn't right."

"When is it gonna be right?"

"Not sure."

He frowned. "I guess I can wait."

"I don't wanna get married to you."

"How come?"

"I just don't."

"Oh, come on! What the fuck? What did I do?"

Gretchen said, "Our time has come to an end. It happens. I'm sorry you can't take it."

He just shook his head. "I'm not buying it. I'm thinking there's something else going on here."

"What would that be?"

"I'm not sure yet."

"That figures."

He stopped in mid-thought, and pulled back what he was about to say. Words seemed to escape him. He hit a brick wall. He didn't have anything to say. He had a speech ready to go.

The two, not wanting to say anymore, left the pizza place. When they got back home they continued the discussion. Their voices started to scream. Dishes were shattered and doors were slammed. She told him she couldn't live with him any longer, that she would feel a lot better about things if he wasn't there anymore. He asked her why. All she could muster, all she could tell him was she had fallen out of love with him.

"I told myself," she said, "I didn't want to hurt you. I hope you can understand."

"I don't get it. There another guy? You been fuckin' someone behind my back? I've always been good to you. Was it when I was still on the inside?"

"I haven't been fucking anyone else."

"Sure about that?"

"Pretty sure."

He threw his arms in the air in frustration. "I don't know why. There has to be something. No, no, no, you stupid bitch. There has to be a reason. You're keeping something from me. Tell you what, if I find out it's another guy he's fucking dead. I'll blow his fucking head off with a shotgun. I'll do worse to you, bitch! I don't give a fuck about prison. I wasted all this time on you."

She gave a stern look. "That's a threat. You're lucky I don't go to the cops."

"Go hide, run to whoever you're sleeping with."

"I told you I wasn't sleeping with anyone."

"I need some sort of an explanation."

She shook her head. "I never meant to hurt you. It's just life. I've realized I don't want to go that next step in our relationship. And I can't just stay on pause forever. I need something else. Things change."

"Like what?"

"Not sure."

"Sounds like you want someone else to me."

"Think what you want. And I'm sure I'll get someone else. I just need time for myself right now. I'm sorry."

"Whatever. I don't get any of this shit. Why would you wanna do this? I guess you don't want anyone to love you. I mean, you say you do, but it won't happen. It will never work with anyone else."

She said they were finished and kicked him out.

"Where am I gonna go?" he asked. "You're just going to kick me to the street like a dog? How do you think that makes me feel?"

"I don't care how you feel."

"Yeah, I see that."

"Oh, you'll bounce back. You'll probably have a new girl by the end of the week."

"I just want you," he told her. "Everything we had together, you're just going to let that die?"

"You're gonna have to get over that one, honey. Just get a hooker, you'll forget all about me."

"I never pay for sex."

"There's a first for everything."

He shrugged. "You're crazy."

"Takes one to know one."

"And you aren't going to reconsider?"

"Nope."

He pointed a finger at her. "You knew this whole time you were gonna do this? Why the hell didn't you just come up there when I was in the cage and tell me? Talk about being stabbed in the back! I can't believe this. You're something else."

She said, "Just tell yourself this is the next chapter of your life, a clean slate."

"Sorry, that's not the way I'm seeing things."

"That's not my fault."

"It should be."

She said, "I'm still young and I want to see what all is out there. I want to experience different things."

"Meaning you wanna fuck other guys."

"Maybe."

"Well, you can just go fuck yourself, stupid bitch! Just go out, spread your legs for every guy who walks by. Just let them into your sloppy snatch. I should've known it was going to be like this. My friends said not to trust you, that you'd do something like this."

She just stood in front of him, speechless. She started to cry. Harlan told her to get a life, and that he never wanted to see her again. And if she saw him at a distance in public she better turn, and walk the other way. He told her she was a dirty whore.

"How dare you call me that! If anything I should call you the whore, you fuck. I don't know how you can live with yourself, asshole."

"Easily," he told her. "I don't live my life in regret. If you want to, that's your business."

"I don't... I don't see how you can say something like that to me. And just to think, everything I've ever done for you was all for nothing."

"Sorry, you feel that way."

"You're the one who needs to be sorry."

"I'd disagree."

"I'm sure you would."

He glared at her. "Guess that's not your problem now."

"Got that right."

"I can do whatever I want."

"I don't really give a shit."

"Good."

"That goes for me, too."

"Hey, do what you want."

When she stormed off to the bedroom he went into the kitchen and started throwing dishes around. He didn't care anymore. She yelled out of the room, and told him he better leave or she'd call the cops. He figured there was no point in fighting anymore and walked out of the house.

All he left with was a bag of clothes and one full of personal items. He walked to his car, got in, and sped away into the night. He didn't really know what he was going to do. When he stopped at a gas station he used a pay phone and called Denny.

11

Denny told Harlan to meet him at Red's for a few beers. Denny told him he needed a drink, and that he gathered Harlan could use a few as well. When he arrived Harlan was already waiting by the door.

"Hey, hey, hey," Denny said to him as he approached. "Look who it is!"

"It's always a pleasure," Harlan said.

They shook hands.

"Thanks for answering," Harlan said.

"Of course. Don't be crazy."

They continued to make small talk as they walked into the establishment and took stools at the bar. They ordered a couple of beers.

Denny said, "I'm buying, so drink up."

"That's a true friend."

"You'd do the same for me."

"Sure, if I have the cash," Harlan said.

"That's what I'm gonna build."

"What's that?"

"A bar in the backyard."

"Really? I can see that. Man, we could start our own brew and shit."

"I dunno about all that."

The bartender put mugs of beer in front of them.

"It means a lot you were there when I called," Harlan told him. "I don't mean to get all sappy or anything, I just had to say you're a good friend. You're the best. They should give you an award. Someone needs to write a book about you."

"It'd be short."

"Oh, don't sell yourself short, man."

"Same here. If anyone tries to tell you that you're shit just tell them where to stick it."

They knocked their mugs together.

They discussed Harlan's problem. One beer led to another, and another after that. The guy behind the bar told them they had burgers if they wanted. The two men just shook their heads. Denny told him that beer was all they needed. The guy walked away.

Harlan said, "That girl, I dunno what to do about her. She's a fuckin' crazy one."

"Who says you have to do anything?" Denny said. "Sounds like you guys just need to go your separate ways. It happens to the best of us. You can't always see how things are gonna go. Just have to dive in."

"I just feel I have to do something."

"Like what? You can't win her back."

"I know."

"Okay, then."

"If I could go back I'd do some things differently."

"Like what? Hell, man, don't dwell on the past—that'll fuckin' kill ya faster than any bitch can. Just have to get over it. Best thing I can tell ya, a sure way to get over a girl is to get a new one. Shit, there are plenty out there. You're a good-looking guy. You can get any girl you want. Hell, before you and Gretchen got together you had all those girls wanting you. They were lined around the block."

"You're right."

"Of course I'm right. Been down that road many times. You have, too. Just have to take the hits and move on. Hell, you remember when Mallory and I got together? I told her it was a good thing she scooped me up when she did. A bunch of girls wanted me."

"That wife of yours, I should get with her sister."

"She's single. She goes on dates but nothing lasts for

her. Over at the house the other day, she was talking about needing to find a rich guy, someone with enough money to buy her everything she wanted."

Harlan said, "That's not me. I'm as broke as they come. I don't even have a home to go to. Probably find myself roaming the streets, sleeping in ditches, eating garbage."

"That won't happen," Denny told him. "You have the job at the college. It'll all find a way in time. Sometimes you have to step back from something, examine what went wrong. After you have the information make sure it never happens again. It's a learning process. All we can do is live."

Harlan told Denny about the people from the college he hung out with, about Tiffany and everything that happened. Denny clung to every word, wanting more, thinking they might be his sort of people as well. Harlan told him he'd introduce him the next time he got the chance. He went on to tell Denny he was going to leave the janitorial job at the school. He explained the only reason he took the job was because of Gretchen. His friend asked him what he was going to do for money, how he was going to pay the bills.

Harlan let out a sigh. "These classes we'd go to on the inside, they'd always talked about all kinds of things. All about reform, keeping your nose clean, doing your best to stay out of trouble, all that happy bullshit. We'd be asked what we were going to do when we get out. They were testing us, making sure the plan we had didn't involve going back."

"What did you say?"

"I'd just say I didn't wanna go back again. I'd say I'd take any job anyone would give me. Told them I needed something to occupy my mind."

"Money's money. It all spends the same," Denny took

a drink of beer.

"Very true."

"I hear myself tellin' people that a lot."

"It sums it up, though. You need cash to do anything. No one should be able to tell you how to get some. If it's illegal, hey, I just turn my head. I never saw anything. I'm no fool, I know what happens to you when you rat."

Denny chuckled, as he lit a smoke. "I wouldn't advise it. No matter how tough you think you are there will always be someone out there stronger and more determined."

"I'm not scared."

"There's no shame in it."

"Not going down like some pussy, I can tell you that." The bartender came back. They got some more beer.

"Not to kick you while you're down or anything, but I don't think it was smart asking her to marry you," Denny said. "Me, I wouldn't have done it."

"I appreciate your candor," Harlan said. "Maybe it wasn't the smartest thing I've ever done, but you can't tell until after. She still pisses me off, though."

"I can imagine."

"Makes me so mad I could kill that cunt."

"Really?"

"I wouldn't do anything like that. Fuck it. She's not worth it. Bitch is probably out there right now fucking two guys at once."

"Damn."

"Or a few chicks, that'd be cool."

"Hell, yeah, it wouldn't be all that bad."

"That's something I wouldn't mind seeing, actually. She'd never do that when we were together. I mean, when I was away I can't really say what happened."

"I never heard anything like that going on."

"Doesn't mean it didn't happen."

Denny said. "Anyway, what were you saying about what you were going to do?"

"I was sitting in class one day listening to the guy go on-and-on about some bullshit, that's when I got this idea to make money. Basically, it's preying on the naivety of people."

"That should be easy enough."

"That's what the goal is."

"Explain your plan."

"Oh, it's a good one."

"Great."

"We'll go down in history."

"I always wanted to be famous."

Harlan dug his cigarettes from his pocket, took one out, and lit it with a Zippo, "So, you have all these people, they're all looking for something bigger, something bigger than themselves, something they can believe in and feel good about. Everyone always talks about believing in a higher power, whatever that may be. You have those who believe in God and those who don't—that's where I come in."

"In what way?"

"I'll put on this façade of someone who is powerful, someone of importance, something to be remembered for. They all want something to follow. I'll give it to them. The tale of God and the Devil is something that's carried on throughout time. It's been and always will be a constant battle. Good against evil. You can't have one without the other. People will get behind it. I'm gonna start a church."

"A church?"

"Yeah, yeah, I know that might sound out-of-character for someone like me."

"Yeah, you think?"

"It's all gonna be an act. See, I figure it like this: You

have all these people out here, and they're all searching for something to believe in. Why not give them what they want? So, we'll start a group, a religious group promoting God and Christianity. We'll start with tent revivals and rallies then go from there. Tell people if they wanna join us they have to make a donation of some kind. You tell 'em what they wanna hear and they'll do anything. I'm thinking about getting a compound built. People will live there. And after that, with any hope we can build more. It'll be like a franchise. We can make business cards, hats, everything. We'll have posters and banners."

Denny said, "How big would you want this? Like every state?"

"Really hadn't thought about every state. I just figured we'd do a few. I'm not a contractor. Not sure how long any of that would take."

"You'd want people who knew what they were going. Don't need idiots on something like that."

"Yeah, I don't have a clue about that. Along with the compound, there will be a church. I want a big one. Something that stands out."

"Sounds like you'll need a lot of money."

"If things work out the way I want, shouldn't take too long."

Denny took a drink of beer. "I have to ask, do you believe in God?"

"Not really. If there was a God he gave up on me long ago. Everyone gave up on me long ago. I don't blame them. If I weren't me I'd give up on me, too. I came to terms with this life of crime when I was on the inside. It's the story of the frog and scorpion... Can't change who I am. I knew eventually after I got out I'd be up to my old ways. Gretchen, I was just doing what she wanted me to do, the bitch. I gave her the world and she does me like that in return."

"It's not right."

"It's not," Harlan said. "I just have to be a man, deal with it and shut my mouth. Don't need her making lies about me, trying to get me thrown back in a cage."

"Think she'd really do that?" Denny asked.

"Not sure. Hope not. But after this I wouldn't put anything passed her, the bitch. Still can't believe she did me like that. There had to be another guy."

"Not that I ever saw," Denny told him. "I would've told you if anything like that happened," he lit a smoke. "I can check, see if she said anything to Mal? But I think I would've heard about it."

Harlan said, "If I knew the truth I'd more than likely do something I regretted. I don't need to go back to that shit I was in."

"Hell, no," Denny said. "You have to start a church."

"I need to start makin' some real money. Figure I can't do that as a janitor."

"Maybe if you were a good janitor?"

"Fuck you."

Denny laughed.

"If I put my mind to it it'll work," Harlan said. "It may take some time, but we'll get there."

"We?"

"Yeah, I just figured you'd wanna get in on it."

"Man, that's a crazy idea," Denny said. "Have to be convincing. Yeah, it could work. Got a few kinks, but... So, what are you gonna call this?"

"I thought a lot about it, racked my mind for some time thinking this whole thing up, and I'm gonna call it Church of Modo."

"Modo? What does that mean?"

Harlan shrugged. "I dunno. It was just something I thought of. You know, when you're in a cell with nothing to do your brain goes to places you couldn't imagine. It sounded like a groovy name."

"Name sounds a little silly, you think?"

"Maybe. We'll see how silly it is when we start making cash. I'm envisioning a big plot of land. Not sure where it'll be yet. If I had my pick I'd want it somewhere outside of Bencroft, out by all that land."

"Sounds good," Denny told him. "For what you want it's gonna take a lot of space. It'll cost a lot of money, too. I'm not sure who owns that land."

"I'd just have to call the city."

"They'd know."

"You might want to think about getting a loan."

Harlan shrugged. "I'm not too sure about that."

"What would the problem be?"

"You'd have to pay back a loan."

"Sure. But they give you enough time to get it together. Don't have to pay it all at once."

"Don't they need to know what it's for, though?"

"If they ask just tell them it's for a big house, that's what it's for."

"Good idea."

"It's the truth. I wouldn't lie to you. I have no reason."

"Thanks for that."

"What are friends for? Someone has to have your back in this crazy world."

"Sorry about that. Guess I still have Gretchen in my head."

"Most likely, that'll be there for awhile."

"It's just strange how fucked things can get sometimes."

Denny took a drink. "Well, my friend, there's gonna be a lot more of that over time."

"Guess that's the way it's gonna be?"

"Pretty much. You just need to pick yourself back up,

get back on the horse. I could see about one of Mallory's friends?"

"Sure."

"She has some nice friends."

"Cool."

"I've thought about getting with a few of them."

"That wouldn't be wise."

"Hell, Mal would cut my balls off if she ever found out about that. After she cut them off she'd kill me."

Harlan smiled. "Yeah, you don't wanna do that."

"I love her too much."

"Love is good."

"Couldn't see it any other way."

"Wish I had that."

"It'll happen."

"Yeah."

They sat awhile longer and had another beer. Harlan told him more about his plans. Denny told him he could crash at his place until he found something else.

12

Mort sat in the dark theater as he watched the big screen. The movie was *Rollercoaster*. He picked it to watch because he liked riding rollercoasters. He needed another victim. He thought about going to the drive-in again, but then he imagined they might have an eye out for him. They didn't know what he looked like, but they could still have the cops on the hunt. When he saw the story of the drive-in in the paper, the work he'd done, he was pleased with himself. He marveled at his accomplishment.

As the movie was playing he looked around the seats to see who was in attendance. After awhile, he spotted a couple in the front row. From what he could tell they were young. The two looked so loving together. Due to the fact the auditorium was dark, he couldn't make out the color of the man's hair. He could tell the woman was a blonde.

The lights came on when the movie was over, and everyone got up from their seats and started to walk out. With the lights on he was able to get a better look at both of them. The girl looked young, early twenties, blonde hair, ruby lipstick, and a red dress. The guy, looking the same age, wore a pair of blue jeans and a green t-shirt. He had short brown hair. Once the two walked out the doors of the theater they turned right and headed down a sidewalk. Mort made sure to keep his distance as he followed. After passing a few storefronts the couple turned down an alley where their car was parked. Mort made sure no one else was around when he approached the guy.

Mort said, "Hey."

The girl walked to the passenger's door.

"Hi," the man turned to Mort.

"You guys doing good tonight?" Mort asked. "Nice out, isn't it?"

The man nodded. "Can I help you with something?"

"I like that," Mort said. "Someone who answers a question with a question, that says a lot about a person. Tell me, buddy, do you dream of the purple horse skipping across the sky?"

"What?" the man said.

Mort gave him a funny look. "Nevermind. Maybe you're the type that likes to taste the colors of the universe, you dig? Things are mixed up right here, buddy. If you saw things right you could see through the blue water."

The guy started to laugh.

"I see, you don't believe me. So, what are you guys doing tonight? Big date?"

"Went to a movie."

"I know."

"How do you know?"

"I noticed you two in there. I'm a bit of a people watcher. Hope you guys don't mind but I followed you out. You like the movie?"

"What? Oh, it was okay, I guess," the guy said.

"That's good."

The guy said, "Why did you follow us?"

Mort didn't say anything.

The woman asked if they could help with anything.

Mort said, "Thanks. Guys look like two upstanding people. Don't see that much these days. Usually, people just wanna screw you over. Doesn't matter what you say or do. It's like the nicer you are the more they fuck you. I was wondering if two fabulous people such as yourselves may have some cash you wouldn't mind parting with?"

The man and woman looked at each other.

"I can pay you back," Mort continued. "I just happen to be a little short at the moment."

The man reached into his back pocket and got his wallet. "How much were you needing."

"A few dollars."

"Would five be okay?"

"Sure."

"Hey, I know how it can get out here sometimes. It's a crazy world."

"Got that right."

The man handed him five dollars.

Mort said, "What's your name?"

"Eric," the man said.

"Eric?"

"Yeah," Eric said.

"Got a last name, Eric?"

"Deaver."

Mort looked at the girl. "And you?"

"Anna," the woman said. "My name's Anna Matis."

Mort said, "Good meeting the two of you. It's not every day you come across kindness. Guys are just enjoying the night? In the sweet embrace of love. Just two young people ready to face the world—that's enough to give people hope. They write stories about that type of thing. Just young and taking it in. Taking away a piece of life. The world's yours guys, do with it what you will. And if you're gonna have a party you have to invite me. Hey, I'm fun at a party."

"Well, that's nice of you to say."

Mort added. "And I think you two have a bright future in front of you. In a lot of ways that's all you can hope for in this life."

"Thanks," Eric said. "Well, listen, can we help you

with anything else? We're here to help, anything you need. Need a ride somewhere? You live around here?"

Mort looked up and down the alley. "I'm good. Thanks."

From the car, Anna said, "Let me give you our address so you can mail the money back. You were gonna pay us back, yes?"

"Couldn't live with myself if I didn't, ma'am. My mother, she wasn't much but she brought me up right. She was a hillbilly woman who lived in the mountains. She really didn't have much, but she taught me a lot about how to treat people. The contrast to that, my dad, he was a mean guy. He always beat her and I. When she started hookin', he told her he'd kill her. I knew I had to get out of there."

Eric and Anna looked at one another in confusion.

"That's not good at all," Eric told him.

"It's not," Mort said.

Anna started to write the address on a piece of paper.

The kid looked down at his shoes as Mort looked at the girl. She handed him the address.

"Thanks," Mort said. "This is gonna come in handy, you have no idea."

Anna said, "We just like to help."

Eric said, "If we can do anything else for you just let us know. We're actually starting a foundation to help people in need."

"Really?" Mort glanced behind him, then back at Eric. "That's a pretty good thing. Well, I wish you luck with that. I couldn't do it."

Eric continued. "It was something we'd been talking about for awhile. We bought a warehouse by 58, and we're gonna convert it into a shelter. We're planning on setting up a few other programs, too. If you're interested in helping I can use it. Or we can give you a call when everything is set up. We'll need everyone we can get at that time."

"For now, I think I'm gonna pass. I need to get myself straight, then I can focus on others."

"We understand that," Anna said.

"Not sure how long that'd take. I'm pretty mixed up. My mind, oh man, it's a scary place. If you could be in there for a few hours you'd go in-fucking-sane," he held up the piece of paper. "I'll make sure to send it back. That's one thing you can say about me, I always pay my debts."

"That's a good thing," Eric said.

"It is," Mort told him. "It's important. One way or another people are gonna talk about you, might as well have it be in a good light."

"You make a good point."

Mort told them that he was sure they could get a big blessing for their good deed. He assured the two he wasn't going to waste the money on booze or drugs. He asked how long they had been an item. Eric told him that they'd only been on two dates before that night. Mort said they looked good together.

"You sure you don't need that ride?" Eric asked. "I can go wherever. It's no problem."

Mort shook his head. "I don't need anything like that. Have to wander off to who-knows-where, get into some sort of understanding, defining myself, you know?" he laughed. "Plus, you love birds have to find your own oasis in your minds. I'd hate to keep someone from doing that. You don't need me in the way, buddy boy, you don't want that. Don't worry about me, man, I'll find myself somewhere."

"We don't have anything going on," Eric told him. "We were just going to go back to my place."

"Ah, the romance... That's what it's all about, man.

That's what keeps it all moving."

Anna said, "He's a good guy, you know? Yeah, I think I have something good with him. He's good to me, treats me like a queen. We're both happy."

"That's all you can ask for," Mort said.

"I tend to think so."

Eric nodded.

Mort looked at the girl in the car, then turned to Eric. "You mind if I talk to you?"

"That's what we're doing."

Mort laughed. "I know, I know. But I need to discuss something with you, and I'd rather not do it in front of your beautiful girl. She's a prize! And I want to be a gentleman, I'm sure you can understand? Why do little midgets talk in a circle? We serve the pretty girls. We delight in the wonder of them. So many of them, they're just so damn foxy."

"Sure."

"Won't take long," Mort told him.

Eric followed the man to the back of his car.

Anna heard the conversation and turned to the back of the car. She wondered what the guy wanted. She wanted to get out of there.

"Want something from my trunk?" Eric asked.

"Nah, nah, nothing like that," Mort looked over at the girl still sitting in the passenger's seat. "So, here's the thing, you carrying?"

"What?"

"Holding anything?"

"Holding?"

"Come on, come on, you know what I'm talking about. Look, man, I'm no cop."

Eric said, "I'm not into that type of thing."

"That so?"

"Yeah."

"Good for you. That's the thing about that, you don't wanna start because you'll never stop. It'll turn your brain to nothing. It gets its claws in you."

"I could've told you that."

"Save a lot of bread that way."

"I know."

"You need to spend that dough on that pretty girl in your car."

Eric said, "I like to buy her nice things.'

"Just remember money doesn't buy you love."

"That's what they say."

Mort let out a big grin. "You learn those things along the way in life. Hell, man, this one time when I was a teen my mom told me about money not being everything. We were pretty poor in those days. Yes, she worked the streets, selling that body she had. We still didn't have much money. We did whatever we could."

"That's unfortunate," Eric said.

Mort laughed. "Yeah, yeah, it was. But we got by. You suffer, and you learn to deal with it. Make everything easier. Once you understand these things, the better off you'll be. Trust me on that."

"I can see that, sure."

Mort looked out to the street, then back. "Check this out, man, I have a surprise for you."

"Yeah?"

"Your girl will love it."

"How's that?"

"Oh, you know."

"What is it? A sex thing or something?"

Mort laughed. "Don't be crazy. Nothing like that."

"Never hurts to ask."

"Is that what you're into?"

"No."

"Then, why ask?"

The man nodded. "I'm not sure. You run into all sorts of things out here, you know? It's a madhouse. Everyone seems to be on dope or something."

"Do you take dope?"

Eric laughed.

"I say something funny?" Mort asked.

"Not at all."

"Then why laugh?"

"I'm not a burn-out."

"How do I know that?"

"Because I'm telling you."

"Just because you tell me something, it doesn't make it so."

Eric looked at him funny. "What is it to you?"

"Me? Nothing. I was just wasting time before I hurt you."

"What?"

Mort drew a switchblade knife out of his pocket. When Eric turned back to run to the door of the car Mort hit him in the side of the head.

Anna jumped out of the car. "What are you doing? You're a maniac."

"I've heard that," Mort said slowly. "Stick around and find out. It'll give you nightmares."

When Eric regained his balance he turned to Mort just as he got stabbed in the chest. He dropped to the ground. As soon as Eric hit the ground bright lights came rushing over from the street. A figure jumped out of the car, ran over to Anna and shot her with a shotgun. She dropped. Mort noticed the figure was Forrest. Neither of them said a word as they both jumped into Forrest's car and sped away.

They were a mile down the road when Mort looked back. "No pigs!"

"Good," Forrest let out a deep sigh. "We don't need that mess

"The fuck did you come from?" Mort asked. "I almost killed you, too. Need to watch yourself. I could've ended you quick. You wouldn't know what hit ya."

"You don't have the balls," Forrest told him.

 Mort said, "That's what your mom said about you. Now, where the fuck did you come from?"

"I was driving along. Saw you from the street. Looked like you needed help."

"I had it under control."

"Oh."

"I mean, thanks, though."

"Just glad I was there."

"Why were you there?"

"Had a bit of business. I was leaving, and as luck would have it I drove by where you were."

"I figure we can read about it in the paper tomorrow," Mort looked out the passenger's window.

"I wouldn't doubt it."

"Always wanted to be famous."

"You've been that for the wrong reasons."

"I know," Mort looked and frowned at the shotgun in the floorboard. "Why'd you have a gun?"

"It's a good thing for you I had that."

"Yeah, yeah, yeah, I told you I had things under control."

"I was hunting, if you must know."

"Hunting? That's what you call it?"

"Stirring the pot? A little anarchy? I need to keep sane somehow?"

"Who were the marks?"

Forrest kept his eyes on the road. "Long story short, I went out with this girl a few times, and her husband found out we were going out. She asked if I'd take care of him. That's where I was. She told me he'd be off work tonight. She went to visit her brother and wasn't home. I thought about my plan, how I was gonna do the deed. Then I just figured I'd just fucking shoot him. As soon as he opened the front door. Plain and simple. Fuck it! As soon as he hit the floor I was gone."

"Gotta do what you gotta. Who would've thought?"

"How's that?"

"You with a girl, man. That's something that doesn't happen often. I know you were heartbroken because your cousin got married."

"Fuck you."

"Try me."

They got on the highway.

"Where are we going?" Mort asked.

Forrest flipped on the radio. "My place."

"Isn't that the other way, though?"

"My other place. Thought I told you about it?"

"Guess I missed that."

"Yeah, I bought this a year ago. Just a place to get away from everything. The guy who sold it to me, I was able to talk him down from the asking price."

"You can never argue with a good price."

"That's what I thought."

13

They got to the house. The place was a dump, Mort thought. A car rested in the driveway. Forrest told his friend that they would take the car when they left. He didn't want to take the truck for fear the cops would be looking for it. The place looked like a big shack, all black and brown. The windows were dirty. The door looked like it had been replaced. The roof looked as though it was going to collapse any day. The wind chimes that hung from the little front porch only had two chimes. But it would have to do. All Mort needed was a place to sleep and take a shower. It was a place to crash, a place to hide. Everything inside was wood and dusty. The living room had a fireplace, a television, and a table against the side of the wall with two chairs. The kitchen was small, but it had everything you needed; a fridge, cabinets, and an oven and stove.

"Welcome to paradise," Forrest laughed. "It's not much, I know. But it's a good getaway. It's just what we need. Away from it all."

"It's fine," Mort told him.

"Glad to hear you say that."

"It's a good place to re-group, that's all I really need."

"Yeah."

Forrest asked his friend if he wanted anything.

Mort asked if there was anything to eat. He said that he hadn't eaten all day.

"Hell, man," Forrest said, "can't have you dying on me. They'd say it was intentional. They'd fry me."

"You wouldn't want that, no way. You think I'm gonna die over there with ya you're fuckin' nuts."

"You'd already be dead."

"I'd what?"

"You'd be dead of starvation."

"Oh... That's right. You know, yeah, you're making a lot of sense, I dunno what I was thinking. I do that sometimes. Not sure what it is."

"Do what sometimes?"

"Make no sense."

"Oh, that happens to us all at time. Don't even worry about that. Just learn to go with the flow."

"Yeah."

Forrest opened one of the cabinets to see what they could cook. All they had were beer and cans of beans.

"Good enough with me," Mort said. "I don't need anything fancy."

"This isn't fancy by any means."

"If it was nice I might start liking it too much."

Forrest got a pot from a cabinet. "That's the thing about guys like us, we don't need things to be perfect. I'm fine with just the bare necessities to get by. I've never been much for liking rich people. Just seems that most times when a man becomes rich he loses who he used to be, what it was like before the money. They think their shit doesn't stink, that they're better than everyone else, you dig?"

"Oh, yeah, I know exactly what you're talking about."

Forrest said, "Because the day is gonna come when money will be useless. Then all those stupid fucks are gonna be looking at folks like you and I, asking what they should do. I fucking say they should just put a motherfucking gun in their mouths and pull the trigger. My bet, people wouldn't even give a shit."

Mort laughed. "Why would money be useless?

"The end of the world is approaching. An Apocalypse will turn everyone into mutant animals. It's gonna be interesting to see what happens. It's coming little-by-little, every few months we get closer to the end. The fear, people won't know what to do. They'll all be lost souls."

Mort laughed. "Think that's the case already."

"You know how it's gonna happen?" Forrest asked. "These stupid idiot politicians, they're the ones who are destroying this country. Just look at all that's happened over the past few years. Our resources are depleting like crazy. The gas crisis, pollution, consumption."

Mort shook his head. "I get what you're saying."

Forrest cooked the beans and they drank beer. He floated the idea to Mort that they should go on a state-to-state killing spree. He told him he thought they should go down to Texas, see what sort of action they could get into. After some discussion, Mort agreed. Forrest said they'd give it a day then leave.

"Change this up a bit," Forrest said. "I need to get out of here. The heat is on, and I wanna get out of the way. And I bet you could benefit from that, too?"

"Oh, yeah," Mort said. "I feel like the pigs are gonna break down my door every day. They'd love nothing more than to put me away for good."

Forrest said, "Can't have my buddy going away. If it comes to a shoot-out or anything, you know me, I'll do my best to kill as many of those fuckers as I can. See, that's why we need to get away, stir up more craziness. Hell, man, we'll hit every state. After we're done here we can go up to Canada—fuck those fuckers, man! I figure we can stay there awhile," he laughed. "Shit, we'll hit every country."

"We'll get everyone on Earth. After Earth, we can go to a different planet."

Forrest waved him off. "That sounds a little too crazy. We'd have to build a rocket."

The two talked more about their murder plans.

Two days later they hit the road. They made two stops for gas before they crossed into Texas. The two talked and listened to loud music on the way. A lot of stuff was talked about on that trip, a lot that neither knew about the other.

Feeling weary from the road they stopped at the Sandford Inn for some rest and relaxation. The girl working the front counter was this curly-haired brunette. She told them her name was Bonnie.

Mort said, "I noticed there aren't many cars out front, is the place empty?"

"For the most part," Bonnie said. "There's only one room taken."

"That all?"

"Most people skip this place. They wanna stay somewhere nicer," Bonnie smiled.

"Oh, well, the place looked okay from the road. We don't need anything that lavish."

"Thanks for saying that," she said. "Over the past year or so we've been losing business."

Forrest said, "Guys need to do something to spice things up, entice people to come in."

"We're gonna start remodeling next month."

"That right?"

"Gonna start doing brunch. Gonna expand the lobby, make things more inviting. The boss wants to do some upgrades. And he's talked about doing a few other things around here."

"What the fuck is brunch?" Mort asked.

"A combination of breakfast and lunch. You know, you have a variety of things to choose from. Light breakfast and lunch foods. Anyway, we still have to plan a menu. We talked about changing it every two weeks or so."

Mort said, "Sounds good. I'll have to check it out. Think of all that food... Who invented that?"

"You'd dig it," Forrest told him. "Not sure who came up with the idea, but I bet he got a blowjob out of the deal."

"You can come back in a few months, see for yourself," the girl said.

"We might have to do just that," Mort said. "If you're gonna still be here we'll have to see how that goes. We could have a good time. Just think about it."

The girl laughed. "You guys on drugs?"

"We are," Mort said. "You want some? We have a bunch. You seem like a cool person."

"That's okay," the girl said. "I have a job to do. Maybe if you're around later we could do something."

They stood around and talked to her for a bit. She told them she was going to community college in the fall. They told her that was a good thing, that it's only too late when you're dead.

The two took the stairs to the second floor. As they walked to their door another door flung open and a woman ran out screaming. Before they could ask what was wrong she was gone. The men looked in the room and saw a guy with a shotgun.

"You okay?" Forrest asked.

The man didn't say anything. He had short brown hair with no shirt. Forrest asked him two more times. Mort looked at Forrest, said that the guy must be high.

"Bitch stole my money," the guy finally said.

"Who?" Mort asked. "The girl who just ran out?"

The guy shook his head. "I should've shot the whore. took two hundred from me. She had no idea what I had to do for that. Don't know how people can do stuff like that and live with themselves. Does she think it's easy? I mean, the drugs pretty much sell themselves. But I still risk getting busted, have to hustle that shit every day. It's good money, but she wants more. I don't get it. Women, they're a huge pain in the ass, you know?"

"It's tough out there," Mort said. "I'm with ya, brother. Strange days we live in. Things escalate. Matters like this, they get out-of-control whenever drugs are involved. Now, don't get me wrong, we have nothing against drugs. We don't judge. Hell, we use them ourselves. The thing you have to do, you have to put bitches in their place. They think they can run all over guys."

"You would think I should know that by now."

Forrest said, "I'm sure we can persuade her to give the stuff back."

"How?" the man lowered the shotgun. "She's not the most understanding."

"We have our ways."

"Okay, then. Do what you think is best. Just to let you know, that girl is one crazy bitch. She might try some shit. If you thump she'll back down."

Mort said, "She won't fuck with us."

"If she tries anything we'll shut her down," Forrest added.

"Really?" the man said.

"Oh, you know it," Mort howled. "We're some bad motherfuckers! You're gonna read about us someday. You won't have anything to worry about."

The man said, "Right on! Do what you gotta."

Forrest and Mort left the room and went downstairs. Bonnie was standing at the counter and asked if everything was okay. She said the woman ran out the door, saying the guy upstairs was crazy.

"We don't want any trouble 'round here. Don't have time for that mess. They on dope?" Bonnie asked.

The guys told her not to worry, that they'd take care of it. When they got out to the parking lot they saw the woman sitting in her car with the door open. She was smoking a cigarette.

They approached her.

She looked at them. "You guys security?"

"Nothing like that, ma'am," Mort said. "You ran out of that room like you were on fire or something. What's that about? I was just wanting to go and rest after the road. But now we have to deal with you."

"Yeah, sorry about that," she said.

"Yeah."

"Nobody said you had to interfere."

She had black curly hair, holes in her jeans, and a white t-shirt.

She said, "I guess he told you I stole from him? He gave it to me."

"That so?" Forrest asked. "What's his name?"

"Jim," she muttered.

"And yours?"

"Kayla."

"That's a pretty name."

"It's probably why my parents named me it."

"Might be."

Mort said, "The hell happened?"

She finished her cigarette, threw the stub on the ground, and lit another one. "I'm sorry about all of this. Everything started off pretty good. We first met each other two days ago where I work. Both of us have room-mates, so we decided to come here for awhile to get to know each other better. It started off good enough, got high, had sex, and then we did it all again. After awhile of repeating those things, he started to act a little crazy. Started to think I made a mistake getting with him."

"Where'd he get the gun?" Mort asked.

"He had it with him. It was in his truck, then, he brought it up to the room to show me. I thought it was kind of rad."

"I'm sure it was."

"Oh, yeah, I like all kinds of guns. I used to have one but it always jammed."

Mort walked closer to her. "So, what do you wanna do here? We're just trying to be healthy mediators."

"If he stops acting crazy I'll go back to the room."

"That all?"

"Yeah."

"Sounds reasonable."

The front door to the Inn opened.

The guys turned around to see Jim step out of the door. Mort walked over, told him to calm down, that they can handle the situation.

"She said this wasn't the first time you threatened her," Mort said.

Jim grinned. "You ever have a bitch steal drugs from you?"

"I understand how you feel, but she's a woman. You don't treat women like that."

Jim said, "You guys can go about your business. I have this."

Forrest said, "We're making this our business."

After a few harsh words, Forrest and Mort had a discussion. They decided they had enough of all the foolishness. Both men went to their car and came back with guns. Before the guy and girl could get a word out they got hit with shotgun blasts. Bonnie ran out the door and yelled at them when she heard the shots. The two men walked over to where Bonnie was and cut her down. They went inside and took the money from the register. They raced out of the Inn and jumped into their car and sped away. They knew the cops would be called soon enough. A few miles down the road they stopped at a station for gas. After paying for the gas Forrest shot the guy behind the counter. After the guy fell Forrest jumped the counter and robbed the place. A little further down the road, they saw a Sun Inn. They got a room without incident. Both men enjoyed a nice meal and a few drinks at the bar. They asked the bartender where they could go to cut loose, and have some fun.

14

Later that night the two hit the town. They had to wash themselves of what happened earlier. Mort and Forrest asked a person on the street if they knew where the hookers were. The guy said they usually congregated three blocks away by a motel.

"Hey, man, tell 'em I sent you," the guy told them. "They love me. Oh, yes, they love me."

Mort said, "What's your name, friend?"

"Chris Vulure."

"Good to meet you. Well, if we go over there and tell them you sent us is it gonna work out for us, or, are they gonna tell us to take a fuckin' hike?"

Chris said, "That all depends on you, brother. If you have it in ya that's what it's all about, right?"

"I guess."

Chris was in his thirties with long brown hair with a white hat.

They were standing on a sidewalk in front of an older building named Crazy Zone. Chris said they were having a party for a friend of his. Both killers looked at each other because they didn't hear much noise coming from the building, a few muffled voices. Mort said something about not even hearing any music.

After a bit, Chris asked the two if either of them had a cigarette.

Mort gave the man one out of his pack.

"Thanks, brother," Chris said. "The world needs people like you around. Everyone out here roaming the streets, none of them have time for one another. It's like they hate what they've become, you know?"

Mort shook his head. "Couldn't tell ya."

Forrest asked Chris what he was doing. Chris laughed and told the two that he ran girls.

"There good money in it for ya?" Mort asked.

"Most times it's pretty good."

Forrest looked at Mort. "That's what we need to get into."

Chris laughed. "Shit, you don't wanna get in this. It's not all glamorous out here. Hell, these bitches out here, they're always tryin' to steal from me. Doesn't matter what I do for them."

"That's crazy," Forrest said. "The girls you told us about, they belong to you?"

"No, no, no," Chris told him. "They're not mine. I know the guy who's in charge, though. He's a pretty good guy."

Mort asked why Chris didn't offer them any of his girls. He explained they were all busy at the time, and afterward they had clients waiting.

"You guys wanna stay awhile for a drink or something?" Chris slapped his hands together. "Man, I feel it, brother, it's gonna be a good one tonight, boy. Man, look here, I tell ya what, if you guys wanna come in, hang out for awhile, I'll give you a free hit of LSD, you dig?"

Mort said, "We're gonna have to pass on that party. Ordinarily, You wouldn't have to ask me twice, but, tonight we're on another kind of trip."

"A trip to get pussy," Forrest stated.

Chris looked the two men over. "Oh, that sweet pussy awaits you. Don't let me get in the way. What kind of fella would I be if I kept you from getting that sweet thing?'

As things go, they stood around for another hour or so talking to the man. When they parted ways Forrest told Mort that they should've attacked Chris took his money.

"Can we do it tomorrow? I'm ready to get a girl."

"We might not see him again."

"Well, we can't do it right now. There are too many people. If you wanted to do it you should've just done it while you had the damn chance, you fool."

"I know, I know. I might have fucked us on that one, but we might find something better."

"I hope."

Forrest and Mort figured out they were staying at the motel where the girls were hanging around.

"Hell, there you go," Mort said. "Beauties by our room. The night looks bright, my man. When we get there, it'll be smooth sailing. Of course, with hookers, it isn't that hard to do."

"Got that right. I figure it like this, if they want respect they need to get in another line of work. People aren't stupid, they know what hookers do. You gotta think they wanna be a part of that lifestyle."

"We should give them what they want."

Forrest said, "They need to make money some way. They probably make more than we do."

"Without a doubt."

"See, we should've gone in the pimp business."

"Hey, man, there's still time. Not getting any younger. We're not dead yet, brother. We can get one or two at first, see how it goes."

Forrest said, "These chicks, how much you think they make selling their shit?"

"I think it just all depends on how much they charge. Not sure if the girl or the pimp decides the amount. I assume looks play a part in it. No one wants anyone who looks nasty. They have to have a little respect for themselves. But then if they had that sort of respect they wouldn't be whores in the first place."

"I know that's right," Forrest said.

They drove back over to the motel and went around the street. They saw a group of sexy girls. They approached them.

"Ladies, lovely evening, isn't it?" Mort said.

One of the girls said, "It is, isn't it?"

She had red curly hair, and luscious lips. She had long legs with a sparkling blue dress.

"What's your name, darlin'?"

"Buttercup," she said. "Guys wanting something?"

Mort said, "Glad you asked. He's Forrest and I'm Mort."

"Nice to know you guys."

"We're looking for some dates," Forrest said.

"You came to the right place, honey," Buttercup looked over at one of the other girls. "We can make everything come true for you, babe."

The other girl introduced herself as Cherry.

The guys asked how much.

After telling them the price and they were good, she told the others they'd be back later.

They took the girls back to the room.

They had two beds.

The girls were hopping from bed-to-bed for the next few hours, finishing with one and then going to the other. At one point Mort suggested they bring the other girls up to the room for an orgy. Buttercup wasn't interested. They smoked some grass and got drunk. Both men had a good time.

Mort woke in the middle of the night. After giving a heavy sigh Mort got out of bed. He looked at the beauty sprawled out on the bed. He walked to the bathroom. After peeing and splashing water on his face he walked out of the bathroom. As soon as he walked back to bed he stopped, motionless. He didn't know what to do.

The girl who was sleeping beside him turned into a white cat. The cat jumped off the bed and walked over to him. Mort remained motionless. He couldn't move. He wanted to run out the door, hop in his car, and speed the hell out of that place. He couldn't tell anyone, they wouldn't believe him. They'd throw him in the local crazy house.

"Hey, you," the cat hissed. "Look at you, wasting time with these girls. Things like this, they're pointless. Mort, where have you been? What have you been doing?"

"What do you mean?" Mort asked.

The cat got closer. "We had a plan, Mort, did we not? We had a plan outlined. It was to be so easy, Mort. Do you recall? You ruined it. Why would you do such a thing? What did I ever do to you?"

"Well, Forrest, he wanted to—"

"Don't blame anyone!" the cat snapped. "We had a plan. You had a mission."

"I know, I know," Mort cried. "It was all Forrest. He wanted to work together. I told him I didn't want to. He wouldn't have it."

"We had a deal," Dobbs said. "If you want to go back on your word, it won't end well for you."

Mort took a hard swallow. "I don't want that. Can we work something else out?"

"You have to go your own way."

"I can't just leave him."

"You must," Dobb's eyes widened. "If you don't we'll have to kill you. You don't want to die, do you? You have to kill, kill, kill, kill!"

"I don't."

"Come on, buddy."

"No," Mort shook his head.

"You know what you have to do," Dobbs said. "Do it, DO IT, DO IT!"

Mort was frozen.

The cat looked at the bed where the others were sleeping. "You need to get rid of them. They're slowing you down. You have a goal. You can't reach your goal if you are with him. It needs to be taken care of."

"And if I don't?"

"You don't want to see that. You're evil. Do what must be done."

Mort shook his head.

Dobbs' mouth opened wide, showing fangs. The cat jumped at Mort's face.

Mort screamed, and his eyes got big. He swung his arm out, hitting Buttercup, knocking her off the bed, and throwing her face-first into the edge of the nightstand. Mort instantly reached over to make sure she was okay. She turned and gave him a hard slap. The other two woke in confusion. Forrest jumped over to his friend to calm him down.

"She was the cat!" Mort yelled. "Holy shit! Why? She was the fucking cat!"

Forrest slapped him across the face. "What did you do? What?"

"The cat! It's the cat! You understand?" Mort said. "I don't know how else to say it. Oh, no, what did I do? I dunno what happened."

Forrest gave him a funny look. "What are you talking about? That's not even real."

"Oh, yes it is."

"You told me you made it up."

"I know, I know. I can't explain it. My subconscious came true or something. Dobbs was with us the whole time. I know it sounds crazy."

"What?"

"Before I went to the bathroom she was asleep on the bed. When I came out of the bathroom she was Dobbs.

She was the cat the whole time."

Forrest said, "You're really off your rocker. You've spun off the deep end of whatever is crawling around your mind. It's the drugs, you've taken too much of that shit. You need to slow things down. I know I can't really say much, but at least I keep mine under control."

"No, no, no," Mort said. "I'm not tripping on anything. I promise. She's some sort of shape-shifter or something. She could be a witch. She could be an old one that's been roaming around for thousands of years."

Forrest said, "What about her friend?"

"She's probably a witch, too."

"That's insane."

Mort hit the woman to the floor again.

Buttercup picked herself up from the floor. "We aren't witches."

"Says you," Mort said.

"I'm telling you we're not. That's one of the most dumbest things I've ever heard."

"You're a liar. Question is, should we burn you and see?"

"What do I have to do for you to believe me?"

Forrest and Buttercup argued for a bit longer. Cherry joined in the argument. Fearing the girls would run and get the motel manager Mort walked over to Buttercup and punched her in the face a few times. When she was on the floor he dragged her to the bathroom.

"What are you going to do?" Forrest asked him.

Buttercup was moaning.

Cherry started to cry.

Mort looked down at Buttercup. "This is what it's come to. You can take comfort in the fact this was going to always happen. Nothing would've prevented this. I bet you're regretting meeting us, aren't ya? You stupid bitch-cat. You're nothing but a stupid skank," he walked over to the toilet and knocked on the tank lid a few times.

Forrest started to laugh.

Cherry looked. "No. Please. Don't."

Mort looked at Cherry. "Say goodbye to your friend, darlin'"

"Oh, man, oh, man," Forrest muttered.

Mort picked the lid off the tank. He walked over to Buttercup, lifted it over her and slammed it down. He picked it back up and slammed it down again. He did it two more times. Forrest knew Cherry would start to scream, so he tackled her to the ground. He strangled her to death.

After the two took showers they decided it was best to move on down the road. They were still debating if the two girls were witches or not. Mort said they were. Forrest said they weren't.

"Well, you know," Mort said, "the one way you can tell is if you burn them."

Forrest looked at him. "You wouldn't do it."

"Oh, I bet I would."

"You're one sick fuck, you know that?"

"I've heard that before, sure."

"Let's go before you burn the place to the ground."

15

It was around eight in the morning when Harlan woke up and went to the kitchen. He started the coffee. He was looking out the window above the sink while the coffee was brewing. It was a clear morning. The old guy across the street was out mowing his grass. The garbage truck roared up the road, stopping at every house, as a guy jumped off the back and dumped the cans. A couple of kids rode by on bicycles. Harlan turned the water on at the sink and splashed some on his face. He and Denny got into a good night of drinking the night before. After a night of heavy drinking he always told himself he was never going to do it again, but, that promise only lasted until it happened again. He looked in the cabinets to re-trieve some headache medicine.

Mallory came down the hallway in her blue bathrobe. Her brown hair was still a little wet from her shower. The robe was cut off at mid-knee. She smiled at him. He told himself that Denny was one lucky guy. He was one lucky man, indeed. Mort knew he couldn't touch her. She was Denny's girl. And he couldn't do that to his friend.

"Hey, Mal," Harlan said.

"Nice morning, isn't it?" she said.

"Yeah."

"Had a lot of those lately."

"Nothing wrong with that."

"Not at all," she took a seat at the kitchen table. "Thanks for putting coffee on."

"The least I could do. I woke up with a big headache. Guess I drank a little too much last night. Oh, man, I don't need to do that again."

"I tried telling you guys."

He took the seat across from her. "Can't tell a guy something like that."

"We can still try."

"Good luck with that one," he said. "Just wanted to thank you again for letting me stay."

"Think nothing of it," she said. "You'd do the same for us."

"Still, it means a lot."

Mallory said, "You can stay as long as you need. I know Denny won't mind."

"And you?"

"Of course."

He stood and got a few cups from the cabinet. "Gotta start the morning off right, you know?"

"Absolutely."

"You can never go wrong with it."

"That's what I think."

Harlan poured coffee into both cups.

She thanked him, and they started talking about some things, about Harlan's situation, about what his next move would be.

The two talked about Gretchen. Harlan asked if she knew of any guys Gretchen had cheated on him with. Mallory told him that was a silly thing to ask, that she wouldn't have done anything like that.

Denny came into the kitchen. Mallory stood and told them she'd make them all something to eat. As the day grew on, Harlan talked to both of them about needing to get some fast cash, about doing a robbery. Mallory, she didn't like it at all.

"What happens when you get locked up, who's gonna get you out?"

Harlan said, "We aren't gonna get caught."

"If you do you'll go away for a long time," she said.

"If I go away, that's how that goes. But I'm not going to get caught. I have too much on the line. If I go on the inside again I think it'll be for the long haul. Hell."

Denny said, "I got your back. Nobody is gonna catch us. If they get us, we won't go down easy. We got some cool guns."

"Thanks."

"That's what we do, we look out for one another."

After some more convincing, Mallory gave her blessing to have Denny join his friend in the robbery. She knew no matter what she said he was going to do it anyway. Her only stipulation was that they go somewhere out-of-state. She didn't want them to get traced back to her home. They asked her to go along, but she said she didn't want to, that she wanted to hang around and go to a party with her friends Mitzi and Harriet.

"You're a drag," Denny said.

She stuck out her tongue at him.

They decided they needed Mallory for what they were going to do. The thought was she'd be a perfect detraction for what they were going to do. After all, she was thin and had perfect tits. Harlan always told Denny he lucked out when he found her. He would joke about how Denny was ugly and Mallory was the only woman who would take him. Everyone else he hooked up with eventually left him for somebody else.

On the road, after some talk, the three agreed they'd go to Texas. They figured they would pick a town when they got there. The plan was simple: in, out, nobody gets hurt. The easiest thing they could think of was to do a bank robbery.

When they got to the town of Gilbert, they stopped at a burger place. They dined on burgers, fries, and soda. One of the things they noticed, there weren't many people in the place. The place was small. After they were done with their meal they left. About ten minutes later Mallory walked through the front door to the counter.

"Welcome back, ma'am," the guy behind the counter said. "Can I help you?"

She studied the man for a minute. "You can, actually. Well, I hope so."

"What do you wanna order?"

"Nothing like that. I hate asking, but do you know anything about weed?" she licked her lips at him, leaned against the counter. "You wanna fuck me?"

The guy turned his head, looked at the other two working at the grill and fryer. "Gonna take a break, guys."

Mallory said, "Know where we could go to get high? You got a car or something?"

"What about those guys you were with?"

"Oh, I just met them. We aren't together."

"Oh, well, that's good for me, then."

"Yes, it is."

"That mean I might get lucky?"

"Honey, there's no 'might' about it."

"I like the sound of that."

"I knew you would."

He got a big smile on his face. "Yes, yes!"

She started to laugh.

"We can do a lot," he told her.

While Mallory was busy with the guy in the car Harlan and Denny, armed, walked into the burger joint. When the men working the kitchen saw the two men they ran to the back. Denny and his friend ran after them. When they caught up to the men Harlan took his gun and hit one of the guys with it, knocking him on the ground. Denny tackled the other one.

He yelled. "The fuck you want!?"

"We're just here for money. You won't get hurt if you tell me where the safe is."

"Fuck you do to Ben, you kill him?"

Harlan said, "He'll be okay. Now, where's the safe?"

"It's in the back office," the man said.

Denny picked him up off the ground. "Lead the way."

"You kidnapping me?"

"You have the combination, shithead."

The guy shambled back to the office as Denny kept his gun trained on the back of his head. After he got the safe opened he was instructed to get two bags for the cash. The guy who was hit with the gun started to move around.

Harlan said, "I'll give ya another crack, you fuck!"

He raised his hands in the air. "Please don't, I have kids."

"And your point?"

He looked at Harlan.

"I'm just fuckin' with ya," Harlan told him. "I'm not gonna kill ya. Tell me, the guy out there on break, what's his name?"

"Leonard," the man said.

"Oh, boy," Harlan looked over at Denny. "Hopefully Mallory isn't fucking the guy in the car. He's a Leonard."

"Oh, damn," Denny said. "Guess we should check on then."

"Sounds too much like 'nerd.'"

Denny laughed.

"What should we do with these two?" Harlan kept his gun pointed at the guy he hit.

Denny looked at both men. "Bet you guys didn't expect this today. You guys come in here like any other Thursday, making burgers, fries, shakes, and then the next thing you know you have two crazy guys with guns in your faces. There's a way you can still get out of this in one piece. You have any rope around here?"

They said the rope was in the supply closet. All four men walked over to where the closet was. The one guy opened the door, and after looking for a bit they discovered they didn't have a rope.

"Thought you said you guys had a rope?" Harlan asked.

"We did," one of the men said.

The other one said, "But we don't know. I guess someone took it," he shrugged. "Maybe someone wanted to hang themselves?"

Harlan said, "You're a funny guy, buddy."

"I've been told that before."

"I'm almost sorry I hit you with my gun."

"Oh, that's okay. Stuff happens."

They had to figure something else out. They shoved the men in the bathroom, beat them around some, and then took the store keys from one of the guys—he had them in his pocket. When Harlan and Denny were outside they locked the front door and threw the keys down a sewer grate along the side of the street.

"Kind of mean, don't you think?" Harlan asked.

His friend said, "If you want something bad enough there's always a way."

"Can't argue with that logic."

When they approached Leonard's car it was clear they were still inside. Denny opened the driver's door. A cloud of smoke floated out.

Leonard turned and looked at him. "Sorry officer, I wasn't doing anything, man. We were just doing—I don't know."

"Time to go back to work," Denny said.

"Oh, no, not yet. See, see, this chick right here," he pointed at Mallory. "She was going to give me a handjob. If you wait she might give you one, too. Said she was pretty good at it."

Mallory said, "Sorry, hon, I should've clarified: I never said I was going to play with your dick."

"But you said 'handjob'"

"I did. But I meant my hand across your face," she slapped him hard in the face.

Denny said, "Come on, baby, leave this cat alone."

"Why'd you do that, stupid bitch?" Leonard bellowed.

Denny pulled the guy out of the car and hit him. "Is that any way to talk to a lady? You need to learn some respect."

Leonard asked where his friends were at. Denny told him they were in the restaurant. Mallory got out of the car and joined the two men.

"Damn, girl," Harlan said, "how much did you guys smoke?"

"Two joints," she said.

Leonard asked if his friends were still alive.

Harlan said, "Of course. Who do you think we are? We aren't some crazy killers or anything."

"Then what did you do?" the guy asked.

"We just got a shitload of money," Harlan told him. "Now, I know we put a little kink in your day, and we apologize for that. But it's all over now, and you have to get back to making burgers. Just go in. The place is un-locked."

The three told him to have a nice day, hopped in their car and tore down the street.

"How much did you get?" Mallory asked.

"We got every penny in the place," her husband said. "Yes, ma'am, every three thousand dollars of it."

"Holy shit!" she looked into the bags. "This is a lot. I mean, this is really a lot. And just from one fast-food place."

"It's pretty wild," Harlan said. "I didn't expect that place to have that much. I'm not complaining, though."

"Pretty good score," Denny said. "Those don't fall in your lap every day."

"You can say that again," she said.

"Whatcha think, Mal, wanna do some more stealing?"

She laughed. "Maybe."

"I can always go for some more," Harlan said.

"I could've told ya that," Denny pressed harder on the gas. "We'll have to talk about that idea you had. Things could work."

"It's gonna take dedication, that's for sure. It's gonna set me for life. Depending on how you guys wanna get into it, it can be profitable for you."

Mallory asked what they were talking about. They told her she'd find out when it was time.

They hit a few other fast-food places.

On their way back to Arkansas there was a lot of talk about a better life, a life where things can be easier. Mallory asked if they should rob another place.

16

Harlan continued doing a good job at the college. His bosses told him if he kept up the good work they'd give him a raise. All Harlan could think about was what he and his friend were about to do, the crimes they were about to commit. He couldn't wait. There were still details he had to hash-out. And he still wasn't sure if Mallory would be on board or not. Just because Denny was going didn't mean she would.

He was sitting at a picnic table outside of the Administration building eating lunch when he saw Tiffany sitting at a table down from him

He walked over to her. "Hey, there!"

"Hi," she said. "How are you?"

"Not bad at all," he sat across from her. "I was thinking about you."

"Oh, yeah? That's nice to be on someone's mind. It's pretty flattering," she placed her book bag on the ground beside her. "You on break?"

"I was just taking a little smoke before I took my official break."

"I see."

"How's your day going?" he asked.

"So far? It's been good. Found out I have an English test next week."

"That should be easy enough. I mean, you already speak the language."

She laughed. "I wish it was that simple."

"Regardless, you'll do fine."

"Thanks."

"I was never one for college. But I think you have it in you to go far."

"It takes dedication."

"Anything that's worth it is."

"Yeah, you know, after I get my degree I shouldn't have trouble getting a job."

"I hope that's the case."

"All the time I've spent doing this, I'd cry if it doesn't pay off."

"It will," Harlan told her.

"That's what I keep telling myself."

Harlan said, "Sometimes you have to look at things, sit back, smoke a joint and watch things flow on their own. Too much stress can kill you."

"Yeah, that's why I smoke weed."

"That'll do it."

"If it goes the other way, guess I'll just have to deal with it."

He gave her a look. He loved how she looked. He knew he'd have to put in some serious time with her if he wanted to know every little detail, and he did. Her eyes were the shade of blue he wanted to swim a lifetime in. He wanted to hold her in his arms every day, to feel her soft pale skin on his, to taste every inch of her. He was very lucky he met her. After what happened with Gretchen he knew he had to play things very carefully. He didn't want to lose her. It surprised him, actually, how well their courtship had gone until that point. They lit cigarettes and started to discuss their day. She rambled on about her classes and the English essay she turned in that day. The topic of the essay was the works of William Shakespeare, and how they impacted the world of literature.

"I bet that was boring," Harlan told her.

"I like some of that stuff," she said. "But I didn't like having to think of why someone wrote something. Hell, we weren't alive back then. For all we know he wrote all that stuff to get girls. I'm sure even back then women creamed themselves when cats wrote anything."

Harlan laughed. "You should've wrote about that."

"I'm sure that'd go over like a lead balloon."

"Never know until you try."

"Guess you're right."

Both of them chuckled.

She went on, and told him about the rest of her day. He loved the sound of her voice. He wanted to tell her that he really loved her, but he thought that'd scare her off, that it was too soon to drop that sort of information.

"I have to tell you about Rod and the others," she said.

"What about them?"

"They all got busted yesterday."

"Cops?"

She nodded. "Yes."

"You weren't there?"

"I was with a friend. She was about to drop me off, we were on my road and we saw the cops. We didn't wanna get caught so we just rolled on by."

"That's smart. You don't just wanna hand yourself over like that, it'd be like, 'Pardon me, sir, but you need to lock me away as well, to file anything you find under my name'"

"There was a lot of stuff in the house. There's no telling how much time they're gonna get. If they're smart they'll say it was all Rod's, let him take the fall. I mean, hell, first chance he got that's what he'd probably do."

"What makes you say that?"

She shrugged. "He just seems like he'd do something like that. I can see it in him. His attitude."

"I guess you know him better than I do."

"Yeah, he's a snake. I just hope no one says anything about me. I don't need all of that."

"I would think the cops would've seen your room."

"I thought about that."

Harlan said, "Where have you been staying?"

"At my friend's house."

He tossed the cigarette stub in the ashtray on the table. "You think someone ratted?"

She shrugged. "Had to be. Can't say who. I have a few ideas, but it doesn't really matter. Whoever it was, they're probably in jail, too. I mean, that would be the only reason to tell the cops on someone, if they got caught, wouldn't you think?"

"I can see that."

"That's just what I figure."

Harlan said, "Anything in the house you need?"

"My stuff is there, yeah."

"I was just thinking, we could sneak over there at night and get your things?"

"Wouldn't they of taken it already?"

"Hopefully not."

"Guess we could give it a shot. Just have to not get caught."

"That's where I shine."

"Isn't that why you went to prison?"

He shrugged. "I wasn't on my A-game that night. It could've happened to anyone."

She laughed. "If that's what you tell yourself, you should stick to it."

"Oh, nah, nothing like that. I got in a fight with this guy who was hanging out in he backyard."

"What was he doing in the backyard?"

"I think he was planning on stealing something for himself. My friend, Denny, he was supposed to be there that night."

"Why wasn't he?"

"Told me he forgot."

"You believe him?"

"Not sure," Harlan said. "I'm not sure what to believe anymore. People say what they think you want to hear."

"But I think that's for people's benefit."

"How do you figure?"

"I think people do it because they don't wanna hurt anyone. But, then, like you were saying, you really can't trust those who do that."

"It's not good."

"You'd think it would change."

"Maybe. I wouldn't count on it."

Ten minutes later he went back to work. At the end of his shift, he took Tiffany with him back to Denny's house. He told her that she'd like Denny and Mallory, that they were good people. Later that night they drove out to Rod's place. The street was silent and no one was in sight. A few houses had lights on, but they weren't really worried. They parked across the street from the house. After making sure no one was coming they ran to the back of the house. The house had police tape all around it. They wore gloves so they wouldn't leave any fingerprints. As quietly as they could they wedged the back door open.

Denny said, "Think there's still drugs around here?"

Harlan shrugged. "They probably took everything."

"That's a shame," Denny said.

Tiffany said, "I know they had a lot here. I had some in my room. I'll see if it's still there."

Denny said, "I hope it is."

"That would be groovy," Mallory told them. "They aren't gonna miss it. If they find anything they'll sell it anyway. No harm done."

"I don't think that's right," Denny told her.

Tiffany and Harlan went to her room and the other two stayed to keep an eye on things. Mallory and Denny stood in the dark for almost twenty minutes while they were back in the room. They didn't want to attract any unwanted attention by making noise. The two finally came out with some bags full of stuff and a suitcase.

They went to the back door and started to open it, then they heard something. Something was outside. It was two police officers. They couldn't hear what was being said, but after a minute they left. The four waited another five minutes or so, to make sure no one else was around. They quickly and quietly got on the other side of the door and ran across the street. After they piled into the car they rolled away. As they went down the road Denny asked about any drugs.

"That's a big fat negative," Harlan said.

Mallory said, "That's a drag."

"Good thing we still have stuff at home," Denny added.

Tiffany said, "Thanks for doing this. I know we could've gotten caught."

"Oh, that's alright," Mallory said. "We're always glad to help."

Denny said, "We weren't gonna do anything else tonight. We're always lookin' for a good time."

On the way home they talked about Tiffany staying with them. Denny said they had no problem with it. He said since Harlan was staying there they had room for another. The topic of Harlan's plan came up. Both girls were on board. Tiffany said it could get interesting. She started talking about the path her future was going, and that she really wasn't sure what she wanted out of life.

17

A couple of days later, Denny and Harlan started the task of recruiting people for their heist. The first guy they went to, Clint "Hammer" Martin, had been a friend of both men for a few years. Clint met Harlan when they tried to steal the same car. After a brief fight, Clint agreed to give Harlan a lift to where he was going. Harlan told his new friend about the guy he worked for, and that he paid for stolen cars. The driver liked the sound of that. Harlan introduced everyone and Clint went to work. Both men were good at what they did until they got arrested. Soon after they got out of jail they decided to stop stealing cars. That's about the time Harlan and Denny started breaking into houses. When Harlan called Clint about the new venture Clint was excited about it.

They were sitting in Clint's living room drinking beer as they were talking through their plan..

Clint had been waiting for something big to come along for awhile. He needed some sort of score that would set him up. A girl by the name of Sydney Cross left him two weeks prior. She met some hip cat at a club, Zap. The two ran off out of state somewhere. Before she ran off she managed to take all of his money, everything he had stashed in the bank and around the house.

"What do you think, Clint?" Harlan asked. "Just think of the nice payday for you. Just think of all the things you can buy with all that money."

Clint grunted. "How many do you wanna do? We gonna act like a music band or something? How long is it gonna take? I mean, I don't have a problem with it. I just wondered how long this whole thing is gonna take."

"As many as it takes. My thought behind this, right

now we're just on the ground floor of this thing. We keep with it, the back end is gonna be huge if things go the way I want. And they will."

Clint let out a sigh, held up a finger as he leaned back in his chair. "What happens when we get busted? No one's gonna start a church if that happens."

"That's the risk we'll have to take, I guess. Nothing is ever promised."

"You're right about that."

Denny said, "So, you interested? We understand if you need some time to think it over."

"I don't need any time," Clint shook his head. "I need something that'll keep me busy, none of this bumming around business. I'm in. I'm just tired of being poor all the time. I need this."

"Right on, man!" Harlan gave Clint a thumbs-up. "Groovy, groovy, it's all coming together."

"How is the bread gonna be cut, man?" Clint ran his fingers through his shaggy beard. "Just thought I'd ask. Gotta get back to where I was. That bitch took every-thing I had."

"I understand that. We have to discuss that when we get the others to join."

"How many more were you planning on getting?"

"A few."

Clint said, "If it's too many the cut won't be as big. But you also say this is gonna be a long-term thing, right? Yeah, I can see it. We're talking about some good weight."

"That's right," Harlan said. "If things go the way I'm thinking, it's gonna be years."

"Hey, nothing's holding me back," Clint laughed.

After Clint assured them he was on board they sat around drinking beer and talking of days past.

"So, tell me, how does it feel being outside of prison?

I know the first day I was out, it was the happiest thing."

Harlan said, "Yeah, I bet. Feels great. Some things have changed, others haven't. It's been an interesting ride. A lot of catching up to do. I'm never going back to that fucking place."

"That's what I said the last time I got out."

"And this will help keep you out."

Clint shook his head. "After the last job I pulled with Mike it's been a little slow. Has to lay low. I was told the pigs were snooping around."

"Those asshole like doing that," Denny said. "All those sneaky eyes, I've seen them hanging around my street. I know what they want. Those dirty motherfuckers won't get me without a fight."

"Last time I was inside they tried to get me to rat. Those are my friends. I'll never rat on anyone. Hell, they may as well shoot me themselves if I do that. The right people find out, I'm fuckin' dead. It's not my time yet."

"I hear that, brother," Denny lit a cigarette. "I don't wanna have to take my piece to any of those people. If it's me or them, it's gotta be them. I'm not gonna let anyone take me out like that."

Harlan said, "That's what I'm saying, with this there won't be any more violence. I mean, technically, this is a crime, sure. But no one has to die."

"But if things get out-of-hand we'll have our guns," Denny added.

"You guys see that Volkswagen bus in the drive?" Clint asked. "We can use that to drive around."

"Thanks," Harlan said.

Denny said, "I was gonna buy me one of those. Knowing my luck, though, it'd break all the time. Mallory would be giving me the business about it."

"That's pretty funny," Clint said. "How's she doing these days? Hadn't seen her in awhile."

"She's okay," Denny said. "She complains a lot. The trade-off is she lets me fuck her. Things could be worse."

"Tell me about it," Clint said. "You could be single, have no one. In this dizzy, crazy world we live in it helps. Anything to get by days. Here's the thing, cops always wanna come after us for breaking the law, they need to go after all of those damn politicians. Hell, they start wars and kill people all the time with whispers behind closed doors. Not to get on a rant, but we had a president who broke the law and nothing was ever done about that fucker. The shit-show was before then, and it still goes on. Odds are it'll continue for the next fifty, sixty years."

They all went on to talk about that stuff for awhile, about how the country was sinking.

Clint asked how he came up with this idea. Harlan told him what he told Denny, about the forces of good and evil and everything. He thought Harlan had to be tripping pretty hard to come up with an idea like that. Harlan admitted it was a crazy plan. But like he told him, some of the craziest ideas are the best.

Clint asked the guys if they wanted to get stoned.

"Maybe later," Denny told him. "We have a few more stops to make."

"I have the good stuff, man. A friend of mine grows his own. I have to admit, at first I was a little leery about buying it. Thought it might've been shit. But I wanted to help my friend, so I bought a bag. I was surprised. It was good stuff. I went back and got a few more bags. Gotta stay stocked."

"Oh, no, you can't run out of that," Harlan took his last drink of beer.

The next stop on their recruiting journey was Zed Levis. Zed was a thief who had yet to be caught. There were a few times his luck almost ran out. He knew eventually he'd be caught and have to do time like his friends. Zed was a short quiet guy. He had a wire frame with shaggy brown shoulder-length hair. He was smoking a fat joint when he answered the door. Like any good host, when he saw them he offered a toke.

"We're fine," Harlan told him.

"That's okay," Zed told them. "I'm all about sharing the love and harmony."

They walked into the living room.

Denny said, "So, what are you doing with yourself these days, Zed? It's been awhile. For a minute I thought you might've left town."

"Not me. Just whatever I can do," he staggered over to the kitchen. "A nice cheeseburger always does the trick. You guys want one? I have plenty. Can't have my guests going without. Don't need you guys dropping like flies. Can't have something like that hanging over my head."

The guys said they didn't need anything.

"Guys want something else?" he asked. "I have all sorts of food around here. My girl should be back soon. She went out to get some booze."

"I'll never turn down those important things, man," Denny told him. "We have a few things to do, but we can always make time for that."

"Nice," Zed told them. "Hey, man, before I forget would any of you want to buy a bike?"

"A bike?" Harlan asked.

"Motorcycle. Yeah, a buddy of mine bought one. But his old lady told him he had to get rid of it. She told him she didn't wanna see him get killed on it."

Both men told him they didn't want it.

Harlan and Denny thought he was a little strange. Zed's girlfriend, Annabel Ward, used to be a hooker. When Zed found her she was down on Hulas Ave. trying to get a date with a drug dealer. Zed told the man if he didn't leave things were going to be really ugly for him. The guy, not wanting to bother with Zed, walked away. At first, Annabel wasn't sure what was going on in Zed's mind. She thought he was some sort of loon who escaped from the asylum. She yelled and hollered at him. Zed had it in his mind he could change her. She agreed to go out with him. They dated for a few months, then, got married a few weeks later. Soon after, she went back to working the streets. Zed didn't like it but liked the money it brought. Friends asked him why he stayed with her, and he would just tell them he loved her. She meant everything to him.

While Zed got the meat out of the fridge for the burgers Harlan and his friend glanced at the TV. An episode of *Sanford and Son* was on.

Denny nodded at the set. "This show's good. The dad, he's a funny one. Gets me every time."

"Never really watched," Harlan said. "*All in the Family,* that's what I like.*"

"That's a good one, too. Thought it'd be cool to be on one of those shows. You get on one of them, that's where the money's at. Wouldn't have to worry about stealing and shit."

Zed turned on the stove. "If it gets me a better place to live I'm all in. This place, I gotta tell you guys it's a dump. Hey, and if it's my place, if I own it, we can party like there's no tomorrow. We can break the walls if we want."

"Didn't know you rented this place," Denny told him. "For some reason I always thought you owned it."

"No, no, I still have to put up with a bullshit landlord. Guy comes in, this guy tells me I'm the reason the faucet keeps leaking."

"Those guys can be a pain," Harlan said. "Last one I

had, we got into a fight."

"That hasn't happened here yet. He call the cops?"

"I told him if he did I'd beat him. We didn't have a problem after that. Of course, after that we moved."

"Oh, I see."

After a little bit, after Zed cooked the burgers, Annabel got back with the booze and other stuff. She had a bottle of whiskey and a bottle of rum.

"Just in time, honey!" Zed gave her a hug. "The burgers are done."

"That's great," she said. "I knew there was a reason I keep you around."

Everyone laughed.

Zed said, "I've had ideas from time-to-time on how to make money."

"Like what?" Harlan asked.

"I thought about starting a newspaper or a magazine."

Denny shook his head. "That's a good idea."

"But you have to have start-up cash for something like that. I'm broke."

"I hear that," Harlan said.

Denny agreed. "I think a lot of folks can relate."

"Well," Zed said, "we can always start small, that's how every big company started. You have to be somewhere, start from scratch."

"I still have to pass. I'm gonna be wrapped in this thing for awhile. No telling how long this will take."

Zed looked surprised. "If we're gonna be on the road, what are we gonna do for gas money? I mean, it's not like we can just come back home every time we need gas money."

"Exactly," Denny said. "That's why we have to get creative. We have all the guns and stuff to do jobs."

"That's interesting," Zed told them. "It'll be the excitement, the rush I need."

"See, it won't be all bad," Harlan said.

"There's good in everything if you think about it," Zed told them. "It's how you look at things."

Denny said, "Those are some true words. Don't think I could've said it better myself."

"Don't know until you say it."

"That's interesting."

"I'm full of that mad knowledge."

Harlan and Denny ended up having some burgers. They had a long discussion with Zed and Annabel about what they were doing. Both of them were intrigued and wanted to do it. They even offered to use their camper.

The next couple people they saw, Chester Cobb and Eric Beck, were pretty easy to persuade. They weren't doing much. The only thing they asked was if it was okay if they brought their girlfriends along. They all knew one another from high school.

18

They packed into Clint's red Volkswagen bus and Zed's camper. Harlan and Denny brought their cars. They brought all the weapons and supplies they needed. The plan was to conquer one state at a time, one town at a time. Harlan told them the secret was to make them believe their madness. He gave a speech about how from that point on they were part of something big, and how important it was to keep it alive. Even though they weren't doing the most ethical thing.

They started with Arkansas, going to every town, wherever they could preach and get people to listen. They started at street corners in Bencroft. Only a few people stopped that first time. One of the guys who stopped asked if they had any flyers or anything, and at that time they didn't. They were busy doing things and flyers hadn't crossed their minds. They drove over to the store, got supplies and made flyers by hand, then, they went to a place and had copies made. The next place they went was the parking lot of the store where they got the supplies. The thought was that there were a lot of people a the store, and on their way to the car they would stop and listen to what was being said.

Harlan and Tiffany got out of his car. Denny and Mallory joined them. They were out there for about thirty minutes. People listened and took the flyers. They stopped and talked to them, laughed, shook hands, and told them to have a nice day. A few of the managers came out of the store and told Harlan and everyone else to leave.

The next stop down the road was Cabot, Arkansas. They found a piece of land to park at in the parking lot of a grocery store called Snyder's.

Everyone got out and looked around.

It was sunny out. People were going into the store. A few were hanging around outside. Some were huddled together jabbering away about this or that. A few coughs and cackles came from the group. One of those groups you saw and wondered what they were talking about as you passed. There was a special spark in the air, fast and fresh, one of those that only come when everyone's energy

Harlan said, "I'm kinda thinking we need to get mics, amps, stuff like that. We have a lot of people out here. I really wasn't expecting this size."

"Further down the road," Tiffany said. "We seem to be doing okay so far. You have to start thinking about money, babe. We aren't rich."

"Maybe you're right," Harlan told her. "We don't have much to spend as it is. I think we need to talk about that later. Get that thing going."

Denny snorted. "I hear that, brother. Sounds like my type of game. I dig that."

Mallory agreed. "We need to spark some sort of action over here. I mean, yeah, the mission, the mission, that's the most important thing, but we need some fun around here. It's like we're just on a road trip, and not that glamorous of one. I mean, we're just in Cabot. I don't even think those who live in Cabot wanna be here."

Harlan said, "I hear your pain. Well, you never know what people are gonna connect with. Have to hit all the spots. I don't like this place much either."

"We should double on one of the other spots and skip this one."

"I almost got arrested here once."

"Almost?"

Harlan looked onto the lot. "Yeah, it was this bar fight. Pigs were called and they almost put me in cuffs because they assumed I started it. I was just defending myself. Yeah, man, I thought they were gonna take me away."

"That would've ruined your weekend."

"I know."

Denny looked at her. "Baby, we're on the road. Nothing gets by you, does it?"

Mallory gave him the middle finger. "Right there, buddy! We're still in our prime," she laughed. "We could start a circus? As long as we're traveling we can do that, too. Hell, the sky is the limit."

Tiffany said, "I like that idea. We should do that. We can make both works. And we could double our money, get more people to join."

Harlan grabbed her waist. "Only problem with that, we don't have any rides or anything. There's the tent, but that's it. We have all these weapons we could have shooting contests."

"We don't have any prizes," Denny told him. "We'll just have to send them on their way. Word will get out. People won't participate."

Zed nodded. "I can juggle. It comes in handy sometimes in conversation."

"Really?" Denny said.

"Picked it up about ten years. Took me awhile to perfect it, but I have it down. But, you know, it'd be cool if I could get paid for doing it."

"I dunno about all of that."

"Hey, it's one of those things people don't think about."

"Yeah, yeah, I hear that."

Clint came over and started to talk to them about the route they were taking. They talked for awhile about it. Clint didn't think Harlan had a clue about where he wanted to go next. They were all stoned at the time. In the end, he told Clint that he had faith in going any way he wanted.

Harlan and Tiffany started to talk over a few things.

"What are you thinking, babe?" she asked him.

"I'm thinking it's gonna be a good crowd."

"I like the way you think."

"Have to look on the bright side."

She kissed him.

"It still gets me," he said.

"What's that?"

"That people will listen to me."

"I guess they're all looking for something."

"I don't blame them."

Tiffany LeeAnn Bosworth wanted everything Harlan had to offer. She was always searching for a place she knew as home. As a teenager, Tiffany rebelled against her mom every chance she got. Her mom blamed it on the fact that Tiffany's dad wasn't in the picture. When she was seventeen, after graduation, her mom couldn't take it anymore and kicked her out. Her mom told her it was time to make her own way in the world, and she didn't want to pay for her any longer. She moved in with, Beth, a friend of hers. She stayed with Beth for about six months before she found herself homeless again. She met a guy named Jeff and moved in with him. For the next ten months, things were fine. She caught Jeff cheating on her and split. It was around that time she met Rod. They were at a party and became friends. After she told him a little about herself and what was going on, he asked if she wanted to move into his house. He assured her he wasn't up to any funny business, and that he was seeing a girl. She didn't have any other place to go, so she moved in with him. Things went well, she met a lot of people and went to a lot of parties.

The first few times she was with Harlan were fabulous. At a certain point, she knew she wanted to spend the rest of her life with him. He was excited and knew. No one can predict the future, but she was going to do everything in her power to make him stay with her. The thing she liked about him, he was very passionate about whatever he did. When he first told her the idea of starting a cult she was speechless. She was in, anything to be with him. As Harlan was talking to the people about converting to Christianity she thought how it would change everything.

19

Harlan said, "Don't worry brothers and sisters, I have a way to make it through. My friends and I are starting a nation-wide family. We need all the help you can get to rid the world of the demons. We are gonna have a compound of our own. We plan on having living quarters, so if you and your families wanna move in you'll be able to do so. All I ask of you is just a small donation. If you want to live in peace and love, away from all the hatred, away from the disgusting stench of the world, come join us. At my place you'll be able to praise God all the time without interference from those that don't believe, those who wish to waste their time on things that don't matter. To be honest, I'm not sure what those people are thinking. Whenever I see these people I walk up to them, ask if they wanna talk things over for a bit."

A few cheers came from the crowd.

Harlan continued.. "As I look out on all of y'all, I see a lot of younger men and women. Maybe you're living with parents, maybe not? Maybe you're lost and need to be found, got twisted-up somewhere along the way? Believe me, I'm not here to pass judgment of any kind. I know what it feels like. I know how it feels like to be left out in the cold, to feel like you have nowhere to turn, to have that dead feeling inside, to feel like there's no end. I'm here to help. We all want the same thing here. Come with us and see. You can live at my house until we get the compound ready."

Some guy in the crowd yelled. "I got kicked out of the place I was at. You can count me in, fella. I have nothing. When do we move in?"

Another guy in back of the crowd said, "I need something. I wanna be a part."

"Can I bring my dog?" another asked.

Harlan said, "You can all come today, brothers and sisters. Just donate what you can. You can come with us today. We have a bus, truck, camper, and two cars. If we have to, we can always look into other accommodations if the construction is gonna take too long. We're on the bottom floor with this thing. You can be a part of history. In twenty or thirty years you can look back on this and be proud that you're doing something, something important. I know, I know, you must be thinking I'm out of my mind, right? Like I've gone crazy or something?"

Some more people in the crowd nodded and shook their heads.

Harlan continued. "I want you all to know, I want you to know we're about peace and love. You know, in the past few years this country has been through Hell. We had all the assassinations in the 60's. It was a divisive decade with the civil rights movement, our involvement in the Vietnam War, and then came the protests. I'm sure I don't need to go down memory lane with you guys. Hell, a friend of mine, I remember he told me how he was at the protest at Kent State when those shots were fired. He said he couldn't believe it. Told me how he'd never seen a dead body before. Shit, man, we just got out of that insane war a few years ago. What was it all for? Have that Nixon fucker, don't even get me started on him. What a demon that guy was, right?"

A few people started to cheer. A few people, at the sound of Richard Nixon's name started to verbalize their disguised. Some people hollered and yell in defense of the ex-president. A few in the crowd started to argue with each other about who the better president was. A woman yelled that the best thing to happen is when they killed Kennedy—some agreed, others didn't. Some of them were saying they shouldn't be talking politics.

"Not here," one of them said. "There's a time and place for everything, and you shouldn't say things of that nature in a place like this. Now, if you were to accompany me to Don's Tap House afterward that'd be a horse of another color, a knife with another blade."

Tiffany came up in front of the crowd where Harlan stood holding a Bible. He took the book and gave her a kiss. They loved one another.

He said to the crowd. "See everyone, it pays to have a good woman by your side."

"You got that right!" Tiffany said.

The crowd cheered.

Mallory walked over. "I say, love can cure all. We all need more love here. You can never have too much. We need to drive away the evil things."

"No, you can't," Denny joined her. "It's not that hard at all. Love is free. Love all the people you can. Nobody wants any of the nasty vibes of the world. Come on, we're starting here. We aren't going away. They may try to deny, but they can't push away the truth forever."

Mallory yelled. "Yes, yes! Listen to what my husband said. We are gonna improve your life."

Harlan held up the Bible. "In here, in this book is a blue-print to life. Some may call them stories, fables, parables, whatever you wanna call them. Thing is, they're said to be written by Jesus' followers. I can't say if that's true or not. I wasn't there. As far as I know none of you guys were there either. But it all comes down to faith, and if you have any," he patted the Bible with his hand. "This book has a lot of heavy stuff in it. The stories are great. It's history. The foundation of everything pure in the world. God is love. Love is God. And I don't know about you guys, but I know we need all the God we can get right now. Things get darkest before the light shines, and this is one of those times. We need one another more than ever. I'm not a know-it-all or anything, but I can tell you this: I don't wanna be stuck outside alone. I wanna be inside, inside with peace and love. I don't wanna be left out in the cold, and I know you guys don't want that either. We all have a mission, we have to support those who we love in this life."

A few more cheers came from the crowd.

Denny roared. "The revolution starts here, baby! You know it's coming. There's something in the air. Do you feel it? It's going to be our reality."

Harlan said, "We have all this stuff pulling at us, going in any direction, digging its way into our lives. Don't get discouraged by all the bad things. There is still good out there. We have to fight for what we want, though. God gave his only son to die for you, it's the least you could do for him. He cares about you. He made you. We are all his creations. Why wouldn't he want the best for us? You fight for what you love. It's about the burden of obligation. Some may say it's not a burden when you love the person. That's a lot like a church, he has this building so his friends can feel free praising and wor-shiping him."

Another person in the crowd said, "If he loves us why does he let harm come to us? Why does God kill us? The whole thing, it doesn't make sense to me. I know if I made something I wouldn't want to destroy it."

Tiffany said, "That's the Devil at work. See, both of them are angels. Early on they started fighting each other. Satan was known as a rebel, always disagreeing, always arguing, wanting the thrown for himself. They continued fighting. Finally, God created Hell and threw him in for eternity. The whole thing is this: Both sides think they're right. Satan has God working overtime, trying to convert whoever he can. He's a master manipulator. He'll do anything he has to. He has to get those numbers up somehow. Now, it's up to us, children of God, to spread his word of peace and love. It's really pretty simple. When God created everything he did it out of love, and when Satan saw what was going on jealousy and rage got the better of him. When push came to shove God created Hell just to toss him in. Now, it's a power struggle. It's war and the battle ground is here. Two armies, only one can win. Which side do you wanna be on? I don't know about you guys, but I want to be on a side that loves. It has been said in legend Hell is full of pain and hatred. I think he, after being cast away, did nothing except wallow in pity for himself. His house became fire. He turned cruel. He uses his evil ways to get people on his side, to fight for him. We can't let him win. It's our job to convert his followers to our side. Remember, God loves all of us. Even those who deny him, he loves you, too. He turns no one away."

"How do you know this?" someone asked.

She said, "You must have faith. Look, we don't have all the answers. All we can do, all you can do is praise God the best way we can. We've sinned in the past, you've sinned in the past. But there's always time to turn it around. He forgives. God understands no one's perfect. Now, sinning in his name is not bad. If our sins are for the greater good, I don't think he'd have a problem with that. Vietnam, people did what they had to in order to survive, the same with the second World War. We won't get cast into Hell for something like that. Many have died throughout our history. But there's many of us who can still rise and defeat the evils of this world. I'm not perfect, and I know you guys aren't either. We all have things in our closets we're not proud of. He doesn't care.

I'm gonna let my main guy take things over again."

Harlan walked back over. "I know, I know, you guys must think we're a bunch of freaks, right? Well, if you think that, it's okay. Some people have to see to believe instead of believing to see, in that case you can see what we're all about and join later. I know what it's like to have your dreams shattered to pieces. When I was inside there was a time I thought there wasn't any hope. After a period of time I saw the light at the end of the long tunnel. I knew I had a new calling after reading the Bible. I was laying in my bunk one night when God started to talk to me. He told me it was my mission to bring people to him. I'm the new chosen one, a messiah, if you well. I'm a solder of God's to stomp evil, cast it away to nothingness. If you'd like to spread the word we'll welcome you with open arms."

Clint came over. "Yeah, man, I've known Harlan for years, he wouldn't do you guys wrong. He's a good guy to have on your side. When he first told me about this, I really didn't know what to say. I was on board with whatever he wanted to do."

"I have to agree," Denny said. "Of all the things in the world, there's no place I'd rather be. I can see all the energy you guys radiate. It makes me glad to be a part of this. Once you guys dedicate yourselves you'll see."

One of the guys in the crowd said, "You guys talking about a commune? I can dig that. We need a lot more. It's just what the world needs, people out there taking a stance, feeding the good beast."

"Brother, what's your name?" Denny asked.

The guy said, "Chad Hill."

"Well, Chad," Denny said, "tell me, do you wanna be a part of our little party?"

"Sure. Can I bring my wife and kids?"

"Sure."

"The kids won't be much trouble. Just as much as any other person's kids, I guess. I'm all about getting in on a good cause, you dig?"

Denny laughed. "Yeah, that's fine. We welcome everybody, no matter age or gender. And actually, as I'm sure you can guess, younger people are good for this. As years pass it'll be the younger generation that keep this going when we're gone. The plan is to always have this."

The guy shook his head. "I'll tell my girl. I'm sure she'll be thrilled."

"Where is she?"

"Work. She's at Silver Dog."

"Oh, I see."

"Hey, money is money, it all spends the same. She should feel lucky."

"I know."

After some more talk the crowd broke apart.

A few people came over and gave Harlan some cash to join. They wanted to ride in the camper because they had never been in one before. They said they thought it was neat, like a house on wheels. They had to go to their houses to pick some things up. Harlan and everyone thought it was crazy that they would stop their whole lives just because some people asked them to. But they figured that they were the ones who wanted to change the trajectory of their lives, that it was their choice.

When they crossed into Texas they found a mall parking lot in Wonaing. The sun was bright, and the day was clear. Forty minutes into him speaking, a few people approached Harlan and wanted to join the cause. As they were leaving cops started to converge on the scene. Someone had complained. Harlan and Denny would say they didn't know why people didn't mind their own business. It was a sad state of affairs, they thought.

When they got on the road they decided they needed more money. They discussed options: beg or steal. They took a vote and decided the best way to go about getting money was to rob something. After some more talk they came to the conclusion that you could get more money from robbing a bank. When they got to Green Stone, Texas they stopped at a place called Spotted Eagle for lunch; they served fried foods. The hostess sat them at a big round table and got drinks for them.

"We gonna do this here?" Zed asked Harlan.

Harlan nodded. "You have any objections?"

"No, no, nothing like that. I was just making sure we were on the same page."

"Yeah, that's the plan."

"Have to make sure we do it right."

"Of course. You doubting me now, Zed?"

"Just don't wanna see any problems."

Denny said, "I don't think anyone wants that. We'll talk more about it outside."

"Too many ears in here," Harlan added.

"Understood."

"You can never tell what's around the next corner. People, they'll tell you a lot of things," Harlan told them.

20

After they paid the bill they walked outside to the vehicles. Harlan told the new recruits, Mark Green, Roger
Ellis, Mary Sharp, and Shannon Willis they had to participate in the robbery. He said he had to test their loyalty.
Harlan assured them they wouldn't be caught, that they
were doing God's work. They protested at first, saying
that wasn't what they signed up for. After some more
back-and-forth they agreed. After they located where the
bank was they laid out the plan.

Clint said, "Should be easy as pie. Nothing to it."

"What if we get caught?" Roger asked.

"Then you go to jail," Clint said.

"Never been there before," Roger said. "I can't do
that. Never been in trouble."

"If you get pinched that'll be a new experience for
you. Everyone can use those every now and then."

"Oh, no! I can't have that happen."

Clint laughed. "Trust me, no one will know it was us.
They won't know what hit 'em."

"It'll be okay," Harlan told him. "It'll be such a
fuckin' rush you'll be glad you did it. Guys will look
back on this and laugh."

"Really?"

"Trust me."

Roger said, "I'm ready for some action. It'll be perfect. Look out people! We'll go in there, they won't even
know what the fuck to think. You know, one minute
they're going about their normal day, no big deal, the
next they have loaded guns pointed at their heads."

"I'm with you on that one," Mark said. "I don't wanna
have to take someone down, but if that's what happens,

then that's what is gonna happen."

Harlan said, "Love the enthusiasm, guys. Keep it up, you'll go far in this life."

"What life is that?" Mark asked.

Harlan looked at him. "Survival."

The guys looked at the gun supply in the camper.

"What do you wanna use?" Denny asked.

Harlan said, "Think this is a shotgun job."

"You got it."

"With something like that, they wouldn't dare try anything. The threat of death if they do, they won't want any of that."

Roger said, "I'm not afraid. I can handle anything you throw at me."

"Sounds good," Harlan said. "Okay, then, let's just go and see how this will work."

"Let's go."

"One last thing, don't do anything stupid."

"Got it," Roger said.

"If you get locked away I'm not visiting."

"Understood."

"If they get me in there they probably won't let me out. They'll throw the book at me."

Roger said, "When I get out I'll be sure to come by. I'll bring a date."

"Thanks."

Roger nodded. "I'll talk some girl in coming with us for you. I'll make sure she's foxy."

"Have to do it up big"

"I'd have it no other way. We'll have a bunch of grass and booze. It'll just be a big party."

"That's the only way to do it. When you're gone, you aren't coming back."

"You're right," Roger told him.

They were parked beside the bank. They sent one of

the new guys in to check things out, to see how many people they had to deal with. Mark came back, told them there were six people in the bank.

Harlan told everyone to be careful, and that if they could help it try not to kill anyone. He asked if they were okay, and that if they felt sick at all they should sit that one out.

Everyone was fine.

They threw on their masks and rushed into the bank. Harlan took the lead, firing the shotgun into the ceiling after he burst through the door.

Everyone looked in his direction in a panic.

Some of the people screamed.

One of the patrons started to say something to Harlan, but he told the guy to shut-up.

Roger, Denny, and Zed ran around to all corners of the area to see if anyone was hiding, and to see if there was any loose money laying out anywhere.

A few people had to be reminded with guns pointed in their faces that they better not say a word.

Harlan told them to remain calm and no one would get hurt, and for no one to trigger the alarms for the cops. As Roger was standing there he couldn't believe what was happening. He never robbed a bank in his life. Sure, he shop-lifted a few times, but nothing major.

After a few minutes, when they got the sacks of money the crew ran outside. Tiffany was behind the wheel with her foot ready to put the petal to the floor. Within five minutes they were on the highway.

21

They looked on the map and decided the next stop would be in a town called Wallion. They found a nice piece of land on Main Street. As a few people came around to see what was going on Tiffany was the first one to greet them. Everyone seemed to like her personality.

"We're here to spread peace and love," Tiffany said. "I hope all of you are having a fantastic one, I know I am. It's nice all of you are interested in hearing what we have to say. See, it's things like this that give me hope, hope for a brighter future, a fresh day. If you see someone not having a good time just smile, it means a lot to so many. I know, those who need it most never say they do."

Harlan said, "We're here to enlighten your minds. It's a free world! Times, they are here, brothers and sisters. Time to rejoice in the love of Christ. His love is immeasurable. He wants you to do the same."

A few mumbles came from some of the spectators.

Tiffany said, "We'll try to make this as quick as we can. It's hot out here! I thought Arkansas was bad. I don't know how you guys do it, honestly."

A few people laughed.

Someone said, "You'll get used to it, honey. You just have to stick around a little while."

"Someone can show you a good time, girl," another said.

An overweight guy said, "We can find plenty to do."

"Thank for the invite, guys," Tiffany said, "but we have more places to go after this. We have a time table to keep to. Maybe next time."

A woman in front said, "Just let them continue."

"Everyone needs to shut-the-fuck-up," a big man called out.

"Fuck off!" another said.

Some more people started to shout. For a minute things were getting heated. Some people left. Other people thought the ones that left were rude for showing up in the first place.

Harlan just kept looking around at the crowd. "Well, well, alright then. Is all of that out of the way? Can we get on with this thing? I know, at least, some of you came to hear what we had to say. Sorry, I'm not the best public speaker, but I'm getting better with each one of these we do. I'm getting better," he laughed. "I'm not sure, I hope we can continue for a long time."

Denny said, "This is still a little new to all of us. We're in this together."

"I'd just like to give thanks to all of you," Clint told them. "You're here, that's the first step. You've already gone far. You need to thank yourselves."

Mallory said, "Oh, yes!! We're here."

They started their speech. The crowd was more engaging than any of the ones prior. As they talked a few people asked questions, questions concerning whether they had the faith they said they did.

Harlan said, "Look, I know you guys probably look at us and wonder why you should listen to us, am I right? You may ask yourself what makes me so special, right? Who am I to stand here, talk to you about God and sin? What kind of credentials do I have? What qualifies me to talk to you guys about this? Well, I'll level with you guys, I've lived a life of sin. I just got out of prison after being in for two years. Before I was on the inside I was a bad guy, someone you didn't want to be around. I lived life on the edge. In a lot of ways I'm glad I went away. If things didn't go down like they did I might have found myself dead somewhere. I don't know if you guys have ever been to prison, but I can tell you it's a pretty dark place. You're basically on your own. No friends or family are with you. It's a very sad place."

A few in the crowd started to whisper among themselves.

"I know what you must be thinking," Harlan continued. "Yes, I'm a felon. I've seen the light. I've reformed myself. If you're like I was I wanna tell you that there is hope. Yeah, the road you were on may have been a scary one, but as long as you're still alive there's always time to do the right thing."

Some guy in the crowd said, "I know, I know. I heard your little talk the other day. I was thinking, I was thinking I need to join you guys. I need something other than what I have now."

Harlan said, "I know where you're coming from. Trust me. I've heard of it all. Everyone is always welcome to be a part of this."

"Thanks," the guy told him. "It sounds good."

They asked how Harlan was able to change.

Harlan said, "When I got in there I had to develop eyes in the back of my head. You have gangs in there, killers, you have people who'll do anything they can to make your time a living hell. And those in there for the rest of their lives, they don't care if they kill you or not. They're already in there forever. They don't have anything to lose," he glanced over at Tiffany and the others.

Tiffany blew him a kiss and the others gave him a nod.

Harlan continued. "But back to the question. Sorry. So, when I first got in I spent the first week not really talking to anyone, then, on the second week I met this one guy when I was eating lunch. You know, I didn't think much of him—this older black guy with a back problem and a limp. He introduced himself. He asked what I was there for, and I told him robbery. He was in there for murder. Anyway, we told each other about our pasts and stuff. He tells me I need to channel my emotions and calm down, because I was pretty angry. He'd tell me if I didn't want to keep returning that I needed to make changes in my life. We would have these sessions, and they were a huge benefit to me. One thing he would tell me, he'd say I need to stop hanging around the people I was, that they were a negative influence—which, yes, I agreed. I had to rid my life from all of those evil things that were keeping me from leading a pure life. He gave me a Bible and told me to read it. As I'm going through it I start to like it. Soon after, this guy who I'm not going to share his name, was sent to the hospital. He was having some health problems. Two weeks later he was gone. And everything he told me stuck. So, I just kept my head down, did everything I was told, didn't cause any static with anyone, and finally my release day came. I can't tell you the happiness I felt. It was glorious. I felt like a new man, like I had a new lease on life. I was proud of myself. When I got back home I kept reading this Bible. It interested me. After some time passed God started to talk to me. He told me I needed to start a church, a church to bring more people to his grace. No matter what you did God forgives. He forgives all. Even if you think you're doomed forever, he forgives. I know some things may seem tough, but it's true. You just have to put faith in something."

People asked what his favorite scriptures were. He rattled off a list and they seemed to enjoy his answers. They discussed the verses. He asked what some of their favorites were. Some of them hadn't read the Bible, others hadn't even heard the book they were talking about.

Other people had questions for him. He said if they want to turn their lives around they needed to join him and his friends to fight sin and the Devil. They talked for another hour or so about it. They recruited ten more people.

A long-haired hippy named Laralyn said, "You guys seem totally boss. I'm in," she forked over some cash. "I've been looking for something like this for awhile. I need a new home. I've just been bumming around."

"Laralyn," Clint said. "I'd like to welcome you to our little family. Good thing for you, we are boss, very boss."

She laughed. "Right on! It's all about good vibes, right?"

"Absolutely," Clint said. "I couldn't imagine it any other way, you know? It's refreshing to know we're doing good in this crazy world—well, trying to anyway."

"I know what ya mean."

"It's the least we can do."

"Every little bit helps, I guess."

"Yeah."

Harlan looked at Laralyn. "Would you wanna join us on the road?"

"Sure," she said. "Do you know how long you guys will be on the road for?"

"At this point, I'm not really sure. We still have a few places to hit."

"I'm fine with that. I don't have any place to be. And I can help with whatever needs done."

"That's good," Harlan smiled. "We have a lot to do."

"Good. I won't let you down."

"I know."

The two walked over where Tiffany was. He introduced them. Harlan could tell they had a good connection. As Harlan explained to them, it's important to get along with those you spend a lot of time with. They all laughed and joked.

Laralyn said, "I actually have a farm with an old school bus on it. It broke down, so the school got rid of it. I bought it, and along with a few friends I fixed it up. We can use it if we need to. I don't have a problem with it. I'm in this to help. To be part of something like this, it's what I've been looking for. It's all about peace and love, right?"

Harlan said, "Where's the farm?"

"It's not that far away."

Tiffany said, "It'll be nice having another girl join us. We can never have too many."

"We have to balance things out somehow," Laralyn laughed.

"You'll dig the other girls with us."

"I'm sure I will."

"No lie."

"That's good."

"I love meeting new people."

"Me, too."

"I can tell we'll have a great time."

Laralyn laughed. "See, we already have that in common."

They laughed.

It was perfect.

Some of the others came over and introduced themselves. Laralyn seemed to like everyone, and everything liked her.

Harlan and Tiffany held hands and kissed.

Everything was working the way he planned.

They all went out to the farm and spent the day there. The bus was faded yellow. They got an idea to paint flowers and symbols of peace and love on it. Harlan asked if she could drive it.

22

The other people on the highway had no idea they were sharing the road with a bunch of crazy people going from point A to point B. If you were cruising through around that time you might've passed them on your way to work or a friend's house. They did their best not to stand out. Some would recall years later seeing them bumming around the open road. They did their best to go the speed limit. They couldn't afford to get pulled-over and hauled into some police station where no one would hear from them again. The vehicles stayed connected by Walkie-talkies. They laughed, joked, and had a good time as they trucked down the road. A few of the new people wondered how they were going to hold rallies when they just finished robbing something. Denny and Harlan said that's what the masks were for, so no one could see their identity, so they could go on about their day. Harlan told them with any luck as they continued this tour they wouldn't always have to stop and rob, that eventually they would have enough money gathered they wouldn't have to do those things.

While in Texas they made a total of nine stops, getting new people at each one. They came from all walks of life. They all had a story, a story of how they became the person they were and how they got there. It was all interesting to Harlan and the original crew. They thought it was sort of funny so many people joined them. Harlan didn't really figure many would take the bait, but they took it. They were all looking for something. They wanted to be involved in anything, and from the looks of it no one really gave them much of a chance.

Laralyn said, as she drove. "Just remember, we're try-ing to make the world a better place."

"You wanna change it?" one of the guys, John, said. "I'm not sure about all of that. It's a big place out there. A lot of people to talk to."

Laralyn said, "Come on, it can be fun. No one knows if we can make it that far."

John Mirman was a guy with slick hair and looked like he'd walked out of the 50's, but he was only eighteen. His parents had kicked him out a few months earlier; they told him he needed to learn to live on his own.

"Well, like Harlan was saying," Laralyn said, "can't expect change to happen overnight. Nothing good ever came easy. It takes time to make a significant impacted. He was saying when the church gets built he was going to start broadcasting the sermons."

"To where?"

"All over the country. You need a big net to catch just a few. You never know who you're going to have an im-pact on. It's a mystery what the world has in store for us. I can't wait to see what the next chapter is gonna be. You know, he was telling me a little about the compound they're building, it sounded pretty sweet. Like every-thing we need in one place... I can't wait to see it."

"Really?"

"Aren't you?"

"Not really," John said. "I don't understand why we're still doing this. I thought they'd lose interest after a while. Thought he might've thought about this on an acid trip or something."

"That might be true," she said. "One never knows what goes on... It's crazy when you think about it, life, this revolution, whatever it is. I just know I needed a lit-tle direction and this was a perfect answer. I was stand-ing there listening to Harlan speak, and everything he was saying just seemed to make sense."

"He has that down pat, you gotta give him that."

"It's inspiring."

"You think so?" John asked.

She pressed harder on the gas. "Tell me, what's the issue? You have beef with someone."

"Nothing like that."

"Then what?"

"This is turning into a job. I just thought we were gonna do this for a week or something. This Church of Modo thing, what's that all about? I bet he was tripping hard when he thought of that."

"Maybe."

John said, "Nah, I just need to get myself together. It's been something I need to find within myself. I need to travel the jagged road alone."

"So, you gonna just flake-out on us?"

"When you put it like that, it sounds—"

"Do whatever you want. I can pull over, let you out right here."

"I don't want you guys getting mad."

"Hey, buddy, it's your call."

"Think Harlan will understand?"

"All I can do is ask him," Laralyn said.

"Well, see what he says."

"Not sure what he'll say."

"I'm sure he'll understand. He's a person just like we are. If there's an issue I'll tell him what's what."

"I love it!"

He laughed.

She got a hold of Harlan and told him John wanted to leave. Harlan told her they would turn off as soon as they could. They all talked about where they were going to stop, and they saw a sign for a park in the area and decided to stop. A few twists and turns later they found themselves on a long road with the public park at the end.

As they pulled in it was clear the place was empty. They all turned their motors off. They got out and gathered together. Harlan and Tiffany came over to join them.

"How's everyone doing?" Harlan said to the crowd. "I hope the road isn't too much for you guys. We've been covering a lot of ground, it can get one twisted if they aren't careful. We have a situation. It appears one of you doesn't want to be a part of this anymore. This person wants to wonder off to that great unknown, still slipping through the cracks of life, digging themselves deeper in the dark core. I ask you, why would anyone wanna do something like that? This person, they want to betray you."

No one said a thing.

Harlan walked over to John and stood in front of him.

John said nothing.

Harlan said, "So, John, what's this all about?"

"I just think it's time for me to leave."

"Why do you think that?"

John shrugged. "I just think it's time for me to leave, that's all. What's the big deal? Isn't this America, where I can come and go whenever I want? Why do you care?"

"In a perfect world, yes, you're right," Harlan said. "Thing is, you told us you wanted to be a part of the family, that you were dedicated to the cause. Now, you say you want to leave, go back to your lonely life doing nothing?"

John kicked some dirt at his feet. "What does it matter, man? You have enough people to continue with."

"We're all out to change the world, it's a shame you don't want to continue with the quest. This is better than me and you. We're doing God's work, partner. You even get a ticket to see this great country of ours. You don't like being here?"

"I didn't want to do it for this long."

"Well, it's pretty simple. I can't let you just leave."

"Why not?"

"You know too much about us, about the other things we've been doing."

"I won't tell anyone," John said. "I promise."

Harlan shook his head slowly. "We can't take that risk. You could end us all."

"I won't tell on you guys. I need to leave. I have my life to think about. If you wanna keep doing this, that's fine. I have to go my own way."

"Go your own way, huh?" Harlan Stared at him. "If you want to be against us, if that's your last stance on the matter, I guess we'll have to let you go."

John smiled and shook his head. "Thanks. There are a few things I wanna do. Glad you understand. No bad feelings, right? We'll look back on this one day and laugh."

"I understand you're a fucking demon posing as a man. You got by us all. I don't know what I was thinking letting you join. You're evil," Harlan took out his knife and stabbed John in the chest. John fell to the ground and Harlan stabbed him a few more times. "I can't have that. No one's safe with you here."

John's blood crept from his body..

Harlan bent down close to him and slit his throat, and the red paint flowed like a river.

"Is he dead?" Roger asked.

Harlan said, "What do you think?"

Roger looked down, kicked some dirt with his shoe. "This isn't good."

Another person said, "This guy isn't fuckin' around. What are we going to do?"

Some people covered their mouths with their hands. They didn't sign on for murder. They didn't want to test Harlan's temper, so they didn't talk to him for the rest of the day.

Harlan told someone to get a sheet and cover the body. He said they'd have to wait until it was dark, dig a hole in the woods and throw the body in.

A lot of the people were shocked, frozen, unable to move. After things calmed some he told everyone that he had no choice but to get rid of him.

"I have to apologize for what happened," Harlan told them. "But he was trying to destroy what we are doing. I couldn't have that. There was no other way. He goes off on his own, tells the cops on us, it's all over. See, it's people like that who work against us. It should serve as a reminder to all of you there's evil forces at work at all times. I urge all of you not to go down the path John did."

He told everyone to relax and enjoy the afternoon. Someone decided they'd go out and bring stuff back for a picnic. They told themselves they didn't want to do anything to get under Harlan's skin. For most of them that was the first time they ever saw Harlan's darker side. Some of them talked among themselves, and they came to the conclusion they didn't want to end up like John, getting killed on a beautiful day.

Harlan had them right where he wanted. He knew they'd be too scared to flee. It was turning into the per-fect con. Harlan was happy with everything. As the oth-ers started making food for the picnic Harlan went to the restroom to clean-up.

After they ate, Harlan and Tiffany took a blanket and walked to a secluded area. They laid the blanket on the ground and made love on it. He made her have three or-gasms that afternoon. As they were putting their clothes back on she asked if she should be worried about him.

"Why do you ask?" he said.

She was sitting on the blanket slipping on her panties. "Babe, I just saw you kill someone."

He glanced down at her panties. "I love when you don't wear those."

"I bet you do," she laughed.

"Hey, hey, what can I say?"

She threw on her shirt. "No, seriously, do I have to worry?"

"Not at all, babe. Never about me. Mainly did that to make things more believable."

"Oh, I see."

"Yeah."

"Did you have to be that extreme?"

"It worked."

"I'd say so. I don't think he'll be coming back."

"If he does we'll all be in trouble."

"We'll have a zombie on our hands, on top of everything else."

"We don't need that."

"Got that right."

"But if something like that were to happen we'd be famous. It would make headlines, dead guy comes back to life."

"And when they find out how he died you'd get arrested."

Harlan nodded. "Yes, you do have a point."

"And then you may as well forget about all of this. You'd be in that place forever."

"Yeah, that'd be bad."

"You think?"

He laughed.

She took a smoke from her pack, lit it. "So, let me ask, do you believe in God? I mean, this whole thing might be a big con, but you spend the whole day talking about it."

"I know. To be honest, I'm not really sure. I know I believe in something, I just don't know what that is. For me, I have to see something before I believe it. You?"

She said, "Never gave it much thought. Without my dad around my mom wasn't the best parent. She never seemed to be at home Sundays to take me. People would talk about it, and I always wondered what it was like."

"Guess we'll both learn together," Harlan told her.

"Sure I'll figure things out one of these days. For now, I'm just loving livin' life to the fullest."

"Me, too," Harlan said. "I just look at these past few years and have to be very thankful. When I first got out of prison I didn't know what I was gonna do. Crazy world we live in, am I right?"

"I know what you mean."

"It's strange when you think about it. I just roll a joint, crack a beer, and sit back and watch it all glide by. There's a lot you can find out about someone by just watching them do nothing."

"That's deep."

"That's how I do things. You have to go further in someone's mind to find out what they're all about. You can't just be on the surface all the time."

"You're wild."

"That's what some have said."

They talked more before going back to the others. A little after midnight a group of them got together, dug a hole, and put John in it.

23

The next day they were taking a break at another
park when the subject of Harlan killing John came
up. A bunch of them were laying and sitting on the
grass. A few of them were talking about leaving,
about how they didn't want to be around a psy-
chopath. A few were saying how they had to call
the cops.

 "We should tell someone," a guy named Stephen
said.

Another guy, a long-haired guy, Jay, said, "We'd
be incriminating ourselves. We aren't exactly
saints, you know? We have just as much to lose as
he does. What? You wanna go to prison? I don't
think so, man. I can't get with that scene. If I
wanna kill myself I'd rather shoot myself."

"We can leave out those details. No reason we
should all go down."

"You can't have it both ways. You're talkin'
about this and hadn't thought it through yet. You
need to think before you talk."

"Oh, I've thought about it," Stephen looked at
him. "When he talked at the rally he didn't say anything about violence. That wasn't what I wanted for
myself. I can't do this. I'm gonna have to leave."

"What? You wanna go home?"

"I dunno yet. Yeah, I wanna be a part of this but
to hell with the rest of it. I can go back on the road.
I can't go on knowing he killed."

Jay shook the idea off. "Nah, you aren't gonna do
anything, man. You're all talk. You don't have the
balls to do anything. You're just singin' in the

breeze, man."

"Who?" Laralyn jumped from the grass. "You wanna go to the cops?"

Stephen said, "I'm just saying what we're all thinking. I mean, I don't think I'm over reaching when I say this."

"You go to the cops you might as well throw your whole life in the trash, and ours too. You tell, they find out about all the crimes we've been doing, it's over for all of us. Do you want that on your shoulders?"

Stephen shook his head. "No."

Laralyn said, "They might find a cell to throw you into, too. You know, if we can't trust you you'll have to be the next to exit, to pay the price. All I have to do is tell Harlan. He'll put a bullet in your stupid fucking head. We'll just leave you in a ditch somewhere. That the way you want things to go?"

"No, you don't have to do that."

"Good," she said. "I like you. I'd hate to see anything happen to you. Anyone else have a problem with it?"

Stephen smiled at her.

Everyone else sitting around looked at her for a minute. She just knew someone else was going to chime in. She told them since no one said anything that the debate was over. If anyone else uttered anything she was going to snap at them. She had a habit of being a little crazy. If you asked some of them, they had stories they could tell you.

Jay said, "Well, I look at where I'd be if I didn't join this thing— I'm good with it. Just have to be tolerant of stuff. I've learned to live with a lot of stuff in my past. I think more of you guys need to be grateful."

Another guy, Stan, laughed. "Ah, get your little thoughts in the way, that's not what the world wants. Just dream of what tomorrow can be."

"How does that go?" Stephen asked.

"There are many schools of thought. But the one I look at is this, we need to make the change. If Harlan doesn't wanna change we have to be that change. He needs us as much as we need him. Sure, he may not admit it but it's there in black and white. I look at him close and I can tell he has things to hide, things he doesn't want anyone to know."

"You don't say?"

"There was more at work here, more than we'll ever know. It would be our gift to him."

"Interesting."

"You'll learn."

"Okay, then. Who taught you about it."

"Life taught me. You can learn more out here than they can ever teach you in school."

"I liked school."

"I didn't. Finally, I just stopped going. My folks got super pissed."

"I bet they did."

Everyone got quiet for a bit.

While Laralyn was laying on the blanket she closed her eyes for a few minutes. The guys looked her over. Jay, in particular, had a strong feeling toward her. He wasn't sure what she thought of him. He thought that if he played his cards right he could win her over. The others liked her a lot.

She knew they liked her and considered it a complement.

They weren't what she was after.

They talked and got to know one another better.

For some of them, they made life-long friends on that trip.

Before that day about the only thing they knew about one another was that they were a part of a group that liked to commit crimes, liked smoking dope. They continued talking about everything, about their stories and the things that drove them there.

If you were to ask them if they liked being on the road all the time. Most would say they made great friendships along the way. Those friendships were what pulled them through the dark days that were to come with Harlan.

About an hour later some of them continued the talk from earlier. One of the guys, Edwin, said, "Man, just look at this day. The sun is out. It's a great day to be alive. I dig the road. Why are you guys sitting around talking about this depressing stuff?"

"I'm just saying if it happened to him the same thing could happen to us," Stephen said. "We have to watch ourselves out here, no one's gonna do it for us. The way I see things he doesn't care about us. He just cares about this cause he has. We have to watch our own backs, guys."

Stephen continue the conversation with others about Harlan, and about what they were going to do about the situation.

Laralyn looked at him. "He doesn't care? Why would you say that? If it weren't for him you would still be out roaming for whatever. We would all still be lost. He saved us all."

"Maybe," Stephen replied.

"Nothing's keeping you here. If you want, you can always go somewhere else. Plus, aren't you having fun? I'm getting to meet people I would've never got to meet."

"I guess you have a point. I'm just not sure about all of this."

"I understand how you must feel," Laralyn told him. "You should just relax and enjoy it. I have to tell you, you're making me a little nervous. All you keep doing is saying the same shit. Aren't you tired of the same thing? I don't wanna have to say any- thing to Harlan."

"Don't worry. You won't have to."

"Glad to hear it. I like you. It would be a shame if you go."

"Yes, yes, it would."

"I think we can do good things together."

"Maybe."

"Hey, good times, huh?"

"You know it."

Stephen and Laralyn talked some more. As others around them talked they went on a walk. Along the path they stopped at a shady area with trees and bushes and had passionate sex. Laralyn would later tell people the only reason she had sex with the guy was to give him a little comfort. Of course, she'd never tell him.

While on the road, to kill time, they played games, sang songs, and they talked endlessly about things they wanted to do in life. When they did their rounds in New York they went to Central Park. They loved it. They went there on a Monday and no one was there except them. They were smoking dope the whole time. They got bombarded by some cops who didn't want them there. One of them, Kitty, almost got arrested for arguing with one of them before Harlan intervened. The cops asked them a few questions then let them go on their way, telling them it would probably be in their best interests not to return. They laughed about it later.

When they got to New Jersey they stopped at another park. They liked the parks because they could enjoy nature, to be part of something so pure. There were a few families having picnics and walking around. Harlan's group decided to go on the other end of the park. They didn't want to scare anyone off. Most of them were aware of the fact some people looked down on those that didn't fit into their social class—or what they thought their social status was. A few others, they told Harlan if people didn't like them that's their problem. It wasn't the group's job to conform to what others thought they should be.

Harlan gathered everyone together. "I hope you guys are enjoying yourselves on the trip. You guys may not realize it but you are doing good work, God's work. When they see us working together, trying to fight the good fight, they'll want to join. When they see all of our smiling faces they'll want to join. Yes, sure, at first they might be a little skeptical but it's the job of all of us to welcome everyone with open arms. I'm proud of all of you. When we end this journey on the road we'll look back on all the good things. I think we'll have a lot to celebrate."

Someone asked how much longer they were going to be on the road.

Harlan told them they had a certain number he wanted to hit, but he didn't say what that number was. A few others had questions. After they voiced their concerns and whatever, Harlan told them to have a good time while he and Tiffany got some alone time.

"I just want you to know," Harlan told them, "I hope all of you have been having a good time. I know I am."

Applause came from the crowd.

A lot of the people liked Harlan.

There were some with reservations.

24

Laralyn found Harlan and Tiffany and told them about Stephen, that she felt he was going to do something. She told him he might tell on them. Harlan told her he'd take care of it. Laralyn knew what that meant, but she didn't want to say anything. She valued her life and didn't want him turning on her.

Harlan said, "Hate to do it. Sometimes you gotta do what you don't want to."

"You have to do what's best for the group," Laralyn told him.

"Glad we understand each other."

"I wouldn't want to do anything to get in the way."

"That's good."

"I'm here for a reason. I wanna do my part in all of this."

"I can't tell you what all of you mean to me."

Laralyn wanted to prove to Harlan and the others she was loyal and could be trusted. She always liked to impress people. She went back to Stephen, and the two made love again. The two talked about what their lives were like before they found Harlan. They smoked a joint and continued making love. While they were still in town they bought some drugs from two guys in a sharp-looking red car. After an enjoyable afternoon, they headed out to the next destination. In the back of her head, Laralyn felt a chunk of guilt about Stephen. She knew she signed his death certificate. She knew nothing she said or did would change Harlan's mind.

They stopped at a place in Pennsylvania, a place

that had beds and meals. Some of them decided to go further up the road to stay at a cheaper place. The next day, as they were driving through the town they came to an empty plot of land. They asked some of the locals if anyone owned it. They went to find out who owned it from the town leaders. When they told Harlan no one owned it he asked if they could set up their thing. Harlan told the folks all about it, and they thought it was a pretty swell idea. They told him he should be proud of the work he was doing. Harlan thanked everyone, laughed and joked with them before he left the office, telling them everything would be okay and not to worry about anything.

The next day they had everything ready to go. A little after noon Harlan started. By that time everyone was used to the same speech Harlan would give. A lot of them ended up just walking around or just talking with the locals. When they took a break some of them went to the store across the street to get something to eat, a little grocery store called Stacs. Stephen was one of the people who walked to the store. Harlan followed him. Stephen walked over to the meat counter. He wanted to get a few slices of turkey and cheese.

Harlan said, "We need to talk."

Stephen turned to him. "About what? Can we do it later? I need to eat. You hungry, too?"

"Afraid it can't wait."

"Well, let me get my stuff."

"It can't wait."

Stephen took a step closer to Harlan. "Just say what you have to say."

"Not here. Let's go for a walk."

The two walked out of the store.

Stephen said, "What's the deal?"

"I hear you have some concerns?" Harlan said.

"Who told you that?" Stephen asked.

"It doesn't matter. Is it true?"

Stephen shook his head. "Yeah. I have my reasons, knowing things I know."

"That right?"

"That's the way I see it."

"Think some would get upset if you let people know certain things."

"I really don't care."

"You don't care, huh? I find that interesting."

"That's reassuring. What are you gonna do about it?"

"Not sure yet. I'll have to wait and see what happens."

"About what?" Stephen said.

The two walked to the back of the store. The only things in the back were three stacks of wooden pallets against the back of the store along with broken wood all over. Harlan explained it wouldn't be in Stephen's best interest to tell the cops on him. He told Stephen if he kept quiet he would be rewarded.

Stephen said he still thought he should tell someone, that he didn't believe a word Harlan said.

"I'm sorry, then," Harlan told him.

"What are ya talkin' about?"

Harlan reached down, picked up a piece of wood and hit the man, knocking him to the ground. Harlan stomped on his head. He grabbed another piece of wood, saw there were two nails sticking out of it, and slammed it into Stephen's head six times.

Harlan looked at the body and saw all the blood and threw down the wood. He looked around, saw nobody was watching, and then walked away. He was all sweaty and needed to change clothes. He walked all the way back to his motel room to clean himself before he spoke to the people again.

When Harlan got back he saw everyone seemed to be in good spirits. That was good, just what he needed. Some of them noticed he had changed clothes but didn't say anything.

After Roger finished saying a few words Harlan came over. He spoke for about an hour.

They got ten people that day. Harlan felt good about what he was doing. Some of the crew noticed Stephen wasn't anywhere around. They asked but nobody knew. They asked Harlan but he said he knew nothing. He said Stephen probably got tired of all the fun and went home.

"I can't stop people from leaving," Harlan told them. "I can't force people to do something they don't want to. I can only hope eventually they find the right path. I wish him all the best."

If that's what Harlan told them they didn't think much about it. Why would he lie to them? What would he have to gain from any of it? They never thought about it.

Later that night at the motel room Harlan and Tiffany were laying in bed.

"How many people do you want?" Tiffany asked Harlan, as they were smoking a joint. "I need to get off the road for a while."

"I hear that," Harlan told her. "Just a few more stops, and then we'll head over to Louisiana. Never been. Heard New Orleans is a happening place. It's a non-stop party from what they say. All the smoke and booze you want, babe. A nice way to get twisted."

"Groovy. That sounds fun, baby."

"It should. By the time we get back, building on the church should be starting to take shape."

"I can't wait to see it all."

"You know, when you're fuckin' a lot of people over at once it'd be nice if they lived in comfort."

"You're crazy," Tiffany told him. "You don't feel bad about any of this? They expect you to be this messiah or something. How are you going to talk yourself out of that one?"

"Hell, babe, I never told anyone I was a miracle worker. I've heard the word 'Prophet' a few times from them," he shrugged. "Not too sure about that. But let them think what they want."

"When you tell them that God speaks through you, these people, they kind of get that idea."

Harlan thought about it. "I guess you have a point. I gotta tell ya, I'm surprised they all want more. I dunno, maybe the people that did join could see what I was doing, you think? I know if it were me I'd see what a fraud I am."

"Could be."

"Good thing everything is going as planned."

"So far."

"There's been a few things here and there, but for the most part it's all been good."

Tiffany took a big hit and coughed. "You sure have a way about you, I'll give ya that."

"Thanks. I do what I can. You know, you try to influence people, sometimes it works and sometimes it doesn't."

"Whatever happened with Stephen? That stuff Laralyn was telling us?"

Harlan laughed. "We had a little talk."

"And?"

"It's not gonna be a problem anymore."

"How so?"

"We came to an understanding. We won't be seeing him any time soon."

"Why?"

"He left."

"Where'd he go?"

"Guess he wanted to go back home. Looks like he didn't want this. Said something about missing his family."

She looked at Harlan. "Why didn't he just wait until we got back to Arkansas?"

"I'm not sure. He didn't say. I was surprised he didn't say anything before. I dunno, maybe someone did or said something to piss him off."

"You sure about that?"

Harlan shrugged. "Sure."

"I'm just thinking about what happened before. The guy you beat... What the fuck was his name? You know who I'm talking about."

"John? That didn't happen," Harlan pointed his finger at her. "Nothing like that. I promise."

"You sure there's not gonna be a write-up in the paper tomorrow, them finding a guy in a ditch somewhere?"

"That's not gonna happen."

"Sure about that?"

"Yeah, because I didn't leave him in a fuckin' ditch. He's behind the grocery store."

Her eyes got wide and she took another hit. "Are you kidding me? What the fuck, man? What's wrong with you? I hope nobody saw you."

"No one did. I made sure."

"Good. We can't afford to get in that sort of trouble."

"Got that right."

She giggled. "So, that's where you were when we took that break today?"

"Yeah."

"I was wondering where you went. I was talking to Mallory and Laralyn. I tried to find you."

"Guess you weren't looking in the right place."

"I know that now."

Harlan took the joint. "Honestly, I wouldn't let it bother you. I'm not concerned about it. by the time anyone finds out we'll be far from this place."

"Let's hope that's the case. Can't get arrested, go away for awhile. I won't do it. And you, you really don't need to get arrested again. Damn, think you're in competition with someone?"

Harlan laughed. "Yeah, that's a good one. I don't care what happens, I'm never going back there."

"That bad, huh?"

"When you go to that place, they tell you that your freedom has disappeared, doing the same thing day after day—taking orders, having people yelling at you all the time, humiliation, degradation, you never wanna go back."

"Doesn't sound good."

"I can think of about a billion things I'd rather do."

Tiffany said, "You ever think about escaping?"

"Thought about it, sure. Who wouldn't? Trust me, I thought about it every single day. Even though I wanted to the deck was always stacked against me. I would've been caught, got some more time, more time gone to waste. It wasn't worth it in the end. In addition, that extra time they would've given me, I would've invariably done some stupid shit to extend my sentence."

"If that happened we probably would've never met."

"I wouldn't go that far. I think if something was meant to be it'll eventually find its way."

"Maybe you're right."

"And if it doesn't it wasn't meant to happen."

"I see. Well, if you had stayed inside I would've probably been in at some point. Remember that big drug bust, they took my roommates away?"

"Yeah."

"There you go," she said. "That would've been me if I was there that day. But even before then, I was very fortunate they never took me away."

After they finished the joint he asked if she wanted another one. She told him she didn't and he lit a cigarette.

She grabbed it, took a drag then handed it back to him. "Think about it like this, it would've been his word against yours. And you have a lot of people here who would have your back. They probably wouldn't have believed him anyway."

"Except for the fact he's dead."

"There's that."

Harlan took her hand. "I think people would be against him if he was alive."

"Why's that?"

"I dunno, he was always a little odd, you know?"

"How so?" she asked. "I never really talked to him."

"He just always had this strange look in his eyes, like he was thinking of evil things or something."

"I never got that from him."

"I can't say for certain, but that's what I thought."

She laughed. "I know he and Laralyn fucked a few times."

"Really?"

"Yeah."

"Crazy."

"You're tellin' me, buddy."

"I've heard of stranger things."

"I know."

Harlan laughed. "Crazy world we live in these days. Some of these places we've been to, see things that aren't in Arkansas. All the different people, just make you wonder. Those people, the lives they've led, the experiences they've had. It's like when you're in a car, look at another car, see the plate from another state and come up with a story about whoever's in the vehicle."

"I never did that."

"Not even once."

"Never."

"You should try it sometime. You may surprise yourself with what you come up with. It makes time go by."

"I'll have to try."

He went on to tell her about how he wanted to get an early start on the road in the morning, and that they could try to beat the traffic. She nodded and asked if he had told the others about leaving early. He said he had. She said that the morning would be good. She thought it was best if they left in the morning because someone probably would've found Stephen, because even though Harlan said no one saw him someone probably had. And that person would've gone to the cops. The cops, that was something Harlan or the others didn't need. He'd hate to have everything he had worked for thrown away. After he finished the cigarette he lit another joint and they smoked half of it. They had sex. Harlan loved the way she made him feel. He could write all kinds of love poems and stories for her. She felt the same about him. She didn't know what the future held for them or anything. All she knew was they made each other feel good. For all she knew the both of them could get busted by police any day. She was too young and beautiful to live in a small cell.

25

Forrest was sitting on a barstool working on his third beer at a place called Mini Red. Mort walked out of the restroom and took the stool beside his friend.

"Where to now?" Forrest asked.

Mort said, "Not sure how you feel about it but I think we should go somewhere, do something else?"

"Like what?" Forrest asked.

"Any ideas?"

"Think we should do something that doesn't get us caught."

"That'd be nice. I'm sure if we sit here long enough we'll figure something out."

Forrest said, "In that case, we should order some food."

"That's a good idea. I've been hungry all damn day. Think some burgers might be in order."

Forrest slapped him on the shoulder. "Sounds good to me."

The tall bartender came over. They ordered more beer to go along with the burgers. The tall man went on to say if they needed something else to just ask.

"We're good," Mort said.

The bartender said, "Guys new in town?"

"Just passing through," Forrest told him. "We've been on a little road trip."

The bartender said, "Those are always good. Life's short and you need to take advantage of all this country has to offer. The sites, man, the sites... It's fantastic. No matter where you go, it's all breathtaking."

Mort snorted. "I dunno about that."

"My name's Eugene, and I can tell you a few places to go if you wanna have a wild time."

"Well, we're not gonna stay here too long," Mort said. "We might check them out, though."

Eugene folded his arms on the bar. 'I'm not gonna get killed by anyone's wife, am I?"

Both killers laughed.

"Neither of us have a girl," Mort told him.

The bartender laughed. "That's a horse of another color. I have a rule, never piss off a woman. Never know when you're gonna need a good one."

The men shook their heads. Eugene went on to tell them about two-night spots in the area—the first, a place called Disco Town, the owner didn't think much about the name, and the other was called BAM! Both places had groovy music and dancing. Eugene told the two killers that if they went to any of those two places they would find a girl and get laid, maybe even two girls.

They liked the sound of that.

"You ever get a girl at those places?" Mort asked.

The bartender smiled and pointed his finger at Mort. "Man, I don't even have to try. I just walk in there, and they rush me, wanting to spend the night. And let me tell you, they were staying the night but neither of us was sleeping."

They laughed. He told them everything was within their grasp. He told the guys he had to do his job, and walked away to wait on some more people.

A few minutes later a man in a white apron came over with the burgers. They thanked the man and he walked away.

"What do you think?" Mort said to Forrest.

"About what?"

"Wanna go to one of these places tonight?"

"Sure. Why not? What else do we have to do?"

Mort said, "We should go somewhere to clean up a little."

"Where?"

"I think there's a place a few miles down the road."

"That'll work for me."

"We'll just sit here and finish our beers and food," Mort said. "After a bit, we'll go over there."

"And see what sort of trouble we can get into."

"Yeah. Nothing like the crazy world, buddy. You know, I was thinking, at some point, we need to make our way over to New Orleans."

"Why there?"

"Heard it was a groovy place to be. Heard there was a lot going on there."

"We'll have to check it out. Some rest would do us good. It'll allow us time to plan our next move."

"The good thing about us is that they haven't caught us. We have all the power."

"I just wonder how long it's going to last? Nothing is forever. Everything has to end."

"We need to enjoy it while we can. No point in worrying about the future, trying to figure everything out. When it comes, it comes. If it doesn't, it doesn't. We need to live in the moment."

"Yeah."

"Of course."

They finished their beers and burgers. The bartender came over with their bill. They threw some cash on the bar. The guy took the money and told them to have a good night.

The two stood from the bar. Mort suggested they

should shoot some darts before they left.

"The fuck you gotta be?" Mort said.

Forrest shrugged. "Oh, shit, sounds like someone wants to get their ass kicked."

"You wish."

"There's no shame in it."

Mort laughed. "Fuck you, dude."

"Yeah, yeah, yeah, fuck you, too."

Both men laughed.

After a few games of darts, they went over to shoot some pool.

"Loser has to buy dinner tomorrow," Forrest told his friend.

"Get your cash ready," Mort said. "I want a nice steak."

"You better get a whore to buy you one of those. I'm not gonna buy that. I'm gonna win."

"Just keep telling yourself that."

"Oh, I see what you did there."

"Got that right, bubba."

"Pussy!"

"I am what I eat."

"That so? How'd your mom's taste?"

"Like paradise."

"I'll have to try that sometime."

"Guess you'll be going all the way to New England where her grave is."

"You get rid of her?"

"No. What kind of guy do you think I am? You'd have to be a sick fuck to do that."

"That's funny."

"Yeah, you like that?"

In the end, Mort lost. Forrest heckled him like crazy. Mort looked around the room, threw his pool stick on the table and stormed to the restroom. He came back a little while later and said they had to leave. When Forrest asked why he didn't get an answer. Mort told him to move out fast.

"Sorry about that," Mort said when they got outside.

"What was all that about?"

"You'll see."

"What?"

"Just wait."

"On what?"

Mort looked through the window of the bar. "I set a fire when I was in the restroom."

"What?"

"Yeah."

"You crazy?"

"Maybe."

Forrest shook his head. "I guess we need to go."

"I think that would be best."

The two jumped in their car and flew down the road.

"Why do you always do stuff like that?" Forrest said.

"I get bored sometimes. I have to do something that gets everyone going. Oh, yeah, look out world! Two of the roughest motherfuckers alive. You better watch out!"

"Heard that. Yes, sir. Town-by-town... What are they gonna do? No one can stop them."

"That's what I've been saying. They'll write books about us."

"Right."

"About the two that got away."

"Well, I guess sooner or later they'll track us down. We can't stay on this road forever."

"I have enough fight in me. Bring 'em on, I'm

Bradley Davenport

ready for anything."

The car flew faster down the road.

26

The two came to the motel and got a room. They got a shower, and put on some fresh clothes they'd bought the day before. They decided to go to BAM! They walked in and the place was crowded. They went to the bar for drinks. Everyone was coming and going. Music was blaring. Everyone was drunk and dancing around.

Mort looked around. "Look at how things are."

"Yeah," Forrest said. "I always loved this. Nothing quite like sitting back with a cold drink, bud in your mouth, girl on your arm. Man, it doesn't get much better than that."

Mort moved his head slowly up and down to the music. "Hey, if that's what you want, go get it. We can stay awhile. Might be a few days," Forrest told him. "We don't have to punch a time clock or anything."

"We needed to get off the road. I just hope no one finds us."

"We don't know if they're even looking. If they are looking they don't know who we are. Now, shut-the-fuck-up about it. We're resting."

"If I'd have to guess I'd say the cops, they have very little to go on."

"If anything."

"I'm sure we forgot something along the way. Honestly, I wouldn't doubt it. I tend to do that sometimes."

"Sometimes?" Forrest looked at him. "Hell, you do everything but sign your name and a picture."

"Sorry about that. No one's perfect. I mean, when

you're in the moment everything is a big rush. Your adrenaline kicks in, and that's all she wrote. You're off to the races. I have a great passion for what I do."

"That's what you call it?"

"You have to dedicate yourself to anything you do."

"I can't argue with something like that. I guess no matter how bad it is," Forrest told him.

The two continued talking and looking at everyone passing by.

Forrest looked down at the floor, then back at his friends. "I could just kill you, take all your money, buy the whole bar out and piss on your grave."

"That wouldn't be good for me."

"Wouldn't think it would be."

"Oh, boy."

They talked about some things they'd like to do when they finally left the country. They talked about going to Europe and starting a crime spree over there.

"Think of all of the possibilities," Mort told him.

Forrest said, "Are we gonna smuggle ourselves there somehow? The minute we get to the airport and they look at us, we're fucked where we stand. I do happen to know someone who owns a private plane."

"Think he'll give us a lift?"

"Maybe. I'll have to put in a call. Shouldn't be a problem. He goes a few times a month."

"For what?"

"That's his business."

"So, it's something illegal?"

"Pretty much."

"What is it?"

"Drugs."

"That's a good business to be in."

"Seems like it."

"We can get into something like that."

"Sure, I guess. It'll be a fresh start. The future before us, it'll be great."

"It would."

"How fast would it take, you think?"

"It would take some time to set it all up. If I had to put a time on it, I'd say a year or so."

"Why so long?"

"We'd have to pay off a few people, get fake lives. All of it takes time."

"Guess that's better than nothing."

"It is. And let me tell you something, don't start bugging me with your crazy shit. And don't ask him about it all the time."

"I wouldn't do that."

"Sure."

"Come on, give me a little more credit than that."

"I dunno about that."

Mort started to hear a little hiss in his right ear. He ignored it. Soon the hissing went to his left ear. He cocked his head to the side as Forrest was talking to him. The hissing got louder and in both ears.

"You okay?" Forrest asked.

"Sure," Mort said.

The hissing got even louder. As Mort blinked he saw the cat walk across the floor, the cat that he feared, Dobbs. Mort thought the cat was going to kill him right there. Dobbs walked to the center on the floor, stopped, looked at Mort and hissed. The cat shouted at Mort that he had to keep killing, that he started something and needed to finish it. The next thing Mort knew Dobbs was gone. He looked around the room and didn't see the cat.

Forrest said, "You sure you're okay?"

"I'm good. I guess I'm just tired, you know?"

"You just have to push through it."

"I know, I know. I have to soak it all in, you know?"

Forrest said, "So, what do you think of this place?"

"It's not bad. Good stuff."

"I think so."

"But you can't go wrong with a bar. All it has to have are booze, broads, and good music."

"Yes, sir."

After a few more drinks they went to mingle with some girls. They got a couple of girls and took them back to the motel. A few hours later they sent them on their way. Later that morning the guys got in their car and headed down the road.

When they stopped at a filling station they discovered a newspaper ran a story about them, about a couple they had killed a week before. They didn't know the names of the killers but they had the story. After they got the gas, to be on the safe side they killed the clerk. Nothing could be left to chance. There was no one else in the station. Before the men left they flipped the sign on the door to CLOSED.

As they continued down the road they ran across a man and woman standing beside their broken-down car. They stopped and got out.

"What seems to be the trouble?" Forrest asked the two.

"I'm not really sure," the guy said. "It just stopped, died on us."

"That's some shit," Forrest said. "It picked a bad place to do that at. You don't have anything out this way."

"Tell me about it."

The man looked to be in his early thirties. He had shaggy hair and a full beard. The girl looked to be ten years younger than the man. After talking with them they learned their names were Louie and Beth.

"Well," Forrest said, "do you guys have anyone you can call or anything?"

The guy said, "Do you know where there's a phone around here?"

"There's a gas station down the road," Mort said. "We just came from there."

"How far is it?" Louie asked.

"A few miles."

Beth looked down the road. "Oh, that seems a long way," she looked at Louie. "What do you wanna do?"

"Guess we'll just have to walk to the station," Louie told her. "I can call my brother. He should be back from fishing by now."

"You sure?" Beth asked.

"Yeah."

Mort said, "Would you want a ride there?"

The man and woman looked at each other. They agreed. The four got in the car and drove down to the gas station. When they got to the station they saw the clerk had been killed.

Louie and Beth were in shock.

Mort took his gun out and pointed it at Louie. "Do you wanna die today?"

Louie threw his hands up. "No, no, no, I can't die! I have a lot to live for."

While the man was held at gunpoint Forrest went out and got his shotgun from the car. When he came back he pointed it at Beth. She screamed.

"Don't hurt her!" Louie yelled.

Mort shoved the gun closer to his face. "No one's gonna kill anyone if you do what you're told. Here's what you're gonna do: You are gonna call your brother and tell him to meet you at your car. You're gonna tell him it broke down and you need his help."

"Are you gonna kill us?" Louie asked.

"We aren't gonna kill you if you do what we ask. See, as it turns out you guys ran into us today, which is very unfortunate for you guys. We're fuckin' psychos."

Louie picked the phone up and dialed his brother's number. Mort listened as Louie talked to him. Louie did what he was told. After he got off the phone Louie asked if they were going back to the car. Before Louie could say another word Forrest shot him with the shotgun. He shot him two more times. He turned the gun on Beth and shot her. When they saw that they were both dead the killers told each other they had to leave. Before Mort walked out he flipped the sign on the door to OPEN. The two jumped in the car and zoomed away.

"Man, that was a good time," Mort told his friend.

Forrest said, "That exact thing?"

A shrug. "We'll just see how it goes. Might wanna change things at the last minute."

Forrest said, "We were lucky we didn't get

caught that time. It was just our dumb luck no one came by."

"And your point?"

"We need to get away from this area."

27

Harlan's crew decided to go to New Mexico. They hit three cities and held five rallies. By the time they got to Arizona, they had a small army. The thought was to go to California, hitting everywhere in between. Once they finished in California they'd start with every state they missed. Along the way a few people trickled off, not wanting to continue the journey. Those people just had enough of the road and wanted to go home. The ones who left promised they'd still be part of the group when Harlan returned. They promised not to say anything about the crimes they committed.

Everything went off without a hitch. Every stop they made they got more and more folks to join them. There were times they had to run from the cops, not everyone appreciated the speeches they were making. They ran into cases where they were told they had to move on down the road because they didn't have the permits for a demonstration. The whole time, from state to state, they were smoking grass and having a good time. They got to know one another quite well.

Just before they crossed the state line into Louisiana they stopped at a filling station for some quick cash. Harlan wanted to go to New Orleans to party. He heard that it was happening over there. But first, they needed to get cash. With the donations they were getting, Denny and Harlan were sending the money back home. They found a bank and took it down. Some of them thought if they got caught they'd go away forever.

After a stop in Wally, where they recruited two other people, they stopped at this little stand that had burgers, fries, ice cream, sodas, and a whole list of treats. The guys who ran the thing told the gang they were brothers. Their names were Ned and Todd, and if they had a special request they could make it. They were a pair of old guys who looked like they were on their last leg, that the party ended for them years ago, but no one told them.

"Oh, boy," Denny said. "We hit the mother-load with this one. Oh, man, I can go for a nice burger. Oh, man, I wanna get into something like that. We can't help what we need, am I right? I know all of you are thinking about what I'm saying. When the feeling hits ya, you just gotta."

"I can get behind that," Harlan said.

Todd laughed. "Some of the best food in the state... I swear, you'll be back before you know it. And all of you, tell your friends."

They all told the guys working what they wanted.

Mallory said, "Nice day, isn't it?"

Ned smiled and looked up toward the blue sky. "Yes, ma'am, it is. It's truly a nice day whenever you're on this side of the dirt, that's what I always say," he coughed. "On a day like this, you need to take some food and enjoy the sunshine. Yes, indeed, the man upstairs sure has a great playground here. He's the best artist anyone can find, magnificent with a paintbrush. Nobody can compare."

"It sure looks good," Mallory said.

"Thanks," he told her.

"We always have repeat business. Word seems to get along fast out here," Todd said, as he cranked up the grill. "You boys wanna impress a fine woman? Sometimes all it takes is a hot burger and a cold beer. They'll be clay in your hands. Trust me on that."

Clint said, "Think I can speak for all my friends when I say that it won't be a problem for us."

Todd put some frozen patties on the grill. "Glad to hear you say that, boys. Not every day you hear something like that. Sure those girls would love that. You have to treat 'em good. You do good by them, they do good by you."

"Oh, enough of that, man," Ned slapped him on the shoulders. "They don't wanna hear that. They're hungry. They want their meat. No one needs you rattling on about that mess. Maybe if you said that to Molly she wouldn't have left you, took all your money."

"Hell, brother, they don't wanna hear that. Come on, you've been saying the same shit."

Harlan said, "I have to hear all about this."

Ned said, "It's a wild one."

Todd laughed. "Not sure about all of that. You just like teasing me."

"I'm just returning the favor."

"You're funny."

"I know."

"I'm still gonna kick your ass, though."

"I'll believe it when I see it."

Clint said, "You guys are cracking me up. Just two loons flipping burgers, I dig it. Man, it's laid back, smoking grass, making food for these humans. It's a pretty good thing you have here. You guys hiring?"

"Hell, boy," Ned said, "we barely have enough money to pay our bills."

Everyone laughed.

Todd joked that he might need someone else after he kills Ned. Ned gave him the bird and told him to go have sex with his sister. Todd told Ned he had wild sex with his wife the night before. He added that she was one of the best he ever had and that he was going to pay her a visit that night.

Ned told him to take a walk.

The two told the crew all about Todd's ex-wife, and what she did to him. Todd caught her in bed with her boss. They fought and she called the cops on him. She took all of his money and tried to kill him by burning down their house. After a six-month court battle, he told her that he never wanted to see him again. A few months after they parted ways her boss dumped her for a younger girl, who dumped him for another girl some months later.

"That's something," Zed told them. "I'd hate if someone did that to me. Think I'd go crazy or something. You have to watch yourself."

Harlan said, "Hell, the girl I was with, she ended things with me for nothing. I was going to marry her, but she threw that out the window."

Denny took his wallet from his pocket to pay for the food.

Ned said, "You guys new to the area? Passing through? There's a lot of things to do here."

"Just passing through," Harlan said.

"I see," the man said. " I'm sure you guys will enjoy yourselves. You guys have some sort of music group?"

Harlan shook his head. "No band."

"I asked because of all the vehicles."

"We're spreading the good word of God."

"Really?"

"Yes, sir."

"Well, son, that's the best news I've heard all day. Can't get any better than that."

They talked a bit about what they were doing. The brothers took a few flyers and said they'd think about it. After they were finished eating they returned to the road.

When they got to New Orleans they went to Bourbon Street to see what all the hype was about. They were surprised to see how many people were walking the street, going in and out of the clubs, smoking grass with music playing. Some people were on sidewalks playing instruments. Women walked the street trying to sell their bodies. Drug dealers roamed around selling deadly fantasies.

They had to find a place for everyone to park. The fact there were so many people coming and going, it took awhile to find parking spaces. Some parked in a garage across from the action while others had to scatter around.

Mallory's eyes were wide as she looked around. "Just look at this place. A girl can definitely have fun here."

"We sure can," Tiffany agreed.

Some of the other girls chimed in.

"It's so fresh out here," Laralyn said. "You can feel it, it's something strange in the air."

Betty, a girl they picked up in Ohio said, "Yes! Time to relax. I've been waiting for this place my whole life."

"You gotta dig the vibe, man," Denny said. "It's powerful. It's all-electric. The nerve here is pulsating. It's on, it's on! We should make it an all-night thing, baby! We need to get set to do this thing right."

"Let's do it," Zed told everyone.

Mallory said, "Do you think they give girls drinks for free?"

"That'd be nice," Tiffany said. "We'll have to find out. Sure they'll take a look at us and give them up."

Laralyn laughed. "That's reasonable."

Zed walked over. "You girls, always trying to get free stuff with your looks."

"Oh, you're saying you don't do the same thing?" Laralyn said. "See, if it was all women behind the bar you'd be doing the same fucking thing. We're just doing what you guys do. That's just how things go."

"I was joking. I didn't mean to turn it into a whole big thing. It's okay. I admit, if the shoe was on the other foot it'd be the same way."

"See, you just prove my point. And, hey, I know how things work, we're doing the same thing. That's just how things work around here. you can't stop it, I can't stop it."

Zed laughed.

Laralyn smiled.

They walked into a place called Sunrise Lounge. A painted sun was above the door. Harlan and company guessed the place got its name from the sun. The doorman was a big bald guy with big rings on his fingers. On the stage were a few guys who were playing smooth jazz. One of them was doing the singing, a slick young soul brother. Near the bar a few people had a card game going. The boys thought it would be nice to take in some gambling during the night. About five guys sat around the table trash-talking each other. They were all rolling smoke.

The crew got some drinks and stood for a few songs. Everyone around them was drinking, chatting loudly, and dancing, and some were doing cocaine at the tables. They had a few more drinks and then moved to another place called Black Flash. The music in Flash wasn't that great. It was made up of two guys with acoustic guitars going on about bad relationships. They stayed and applauded for two songs. It wasn't a good vibe in the place at all. Harlan heard a few of the people talking about going elsewhere, checking out other spots, and making sure they never came back. The group, they determined things might be better at night, so they left the area for awhile. They drove around, looking around the city. They met some new people along the way.

"What time you wanting to set up here?" Mallory asked.

Harlan said, "Before we leave tomorrow. This way, if we get a bad reception we can flee fast, and we don't have to worry about not being able to party."

"Makes sense."

Around six at night, they came back. A lot more people were roaming around. Loud music and neon lights poured out of the bars. They went into a place, Dinos, that was playing dance music.

"Oh, boy," Mallory billowed, "You can get your boogie on here!"

"They have good tunes," Denny said, looking at Mallory. "I'll have to show you my dance skills. Might even have to give it to ya here on the dance floor."

"You wish," she laughed. "They'd take us away

for that."

"Why? They shouldn't do that just for having sex. hey, they probably do it all the time."

"You're crazy."

Denny tapped his finger against his head. "Takes wild minds to make things go 'round. You'd be surprised, babe."

"Yeah?"

"Oh, you have no idea. I mean, if you did your head would explode."

"I don't want that to happen."

"Of course," Denny said. "That wouldn't be a hip thing to have. What we all do, you dig?"

She laughed and said he was crazy.

The place had a big dance floor in the center. People were having a good time dancing, singing, and doing whatever they wanted.

One of the casualties was Zed's girlfriend, she didn't want to continue on with the road. Instead, she was going to oversee some of the things going on back in Arkansas. Zed told the crew that as long as his girlfriend wasn't there he could cheat. He told them he was off to look for a fine-looking thing to get busy with, to give some of his love to.

Mallory said," She'll be a lucky lady."

Zed told her he would then give her a thumbs-up. He was off to see about getting a girl. They watched as he strolled up to a table and started talking to some women. It wasn't too long before he took one of the girls, a tiny girl with red curly hair, on the dance floor.

Tiffany looked at the dancing and led Harlan by the hand to the center of it. He grabbed her waist and pulled her close. She ran her hand over his chest. They kissed and rubbed against each other for an entire song before they started dancing. Harlan glanced at his gang. They were scattered everywhere enjoying the night.

After a few more songs Denny came over and tapped his friend on the shoulder.

"What?" Harlan asked him. "I'm doing something here, can't you see that?"

"I know, I know," Denny said. "I have something, didn't want it to pass us by. It's big, man. This will be good for a few days."

"What is it?'

"See that guy over there?" Denny pointed at a man sitting across a table from another man.

"What about him?" Harlan asked.

Denny said, "Guy said he can hook us up with a bunch of coke."

"You fuckin' kidding me?"

"Nah, man, nothin' like that."

"Why do you need permission from me?"

"I told him and his friend all about us. Well, not everything. I told them you'd be interested. They said they wanted to meet you. I figured you wouldn't have a problem with it."

"Fuckin' shit. The fuck you get me into?"

Denny said, "They wanna meet you, that's it. It's not like they wanna kill us or anything."

"How can you be sure?"

Denny shrugged. "Guess I don't."

"You think?"

Another shrug. "Well...."

"Never mind," Harlan said. "If it's gonna happen, it might as well happen here."

"That wouldn't be good for us."

"Hell, brother, you're the one who got us into this. Shit, no telling what's gonna go down. I'm gonna beat you for this."

"Seems about right."

"They'll throw us away."

"It'll be okay."

"Sure."

Harlan gave a nod, told Tiffany he'd be back and gave her a kiss. She asked if everything would be okay. He told her not to worry, that it was okay. They kissed again. He thought it was nice someone cared enough to ask things of that nature. He didn't want to see her disappointed. As they walked away she danced through the crowd, found Mallory and danced with her.

Harlan felt a little nervous about meeting these two men. He wasn't sure why they wanted to meet him. From what Denny said it sounded like he could make the deal himself. After all, Denny was his close friend. He wouldn't ever do a friend wrong.

As they got closer the two men at the table stood.

"Hey, the name's Morn Bosworth," Mort said. "We've heard a lot about you," he extended his hand to Harlan.

They shook.

The other guy said, "My name's Forrest Crumb."

They shook hands.

"Nice night to get your fuck on, right?" Mort said.

They nodded.

Denny said, "It's the only way to be, right?"

Mort looked at Harlan. "That fine fox you were dancing with, I'd love to take her back to my place. I'd fuck her until she couldn't fuck anymore."

Harlan said, "Sorry, we're together."

"That right?"

"Yeah."

"Well, when you guys call it quits I can take over."

"That'll never happen."

"Never hurts to try."

"Trying is all you'll do."

Everyone sat around the table.

Mort said, "We rolled into town the other day. We've spent some time on the road. Thought we'd check New Orleans out, heard a lot about it. Non-stop party!"

Denny said, "That was our thought. We just needed a break ourselves, bumming from place to place. So far, it hasn't been bad at all."

Forrest said, "I knew a dude that used to live out here."

"Never told me about that," Mort said.

Forrest snorted. "There's a lot of things you don't know about me."

"What happened to him?" Denny asked.

Forrest shrugged and took a drink. "He fell off the roof of his house. Was up there fixin' his an-tenna, lost his balance, fell backward into his car below."

"Damn," Harlan said.

"Well, what are you gonna do?" Forrest said. "You never know when the party is gonna end. Might as well live-it-the-fuck-up while you can, brother."

"Hell, yeah, that's something I always do," Denny said. "I tell people that all the time. Every-thing is just so inspiring. The way I look at it, I just say how bad I'd feel if I couldn't do everything I wanted."

"I get that," Forrest said.

Mort asked if he could buy them a drink.

"We won't turn down drinks," Denny told him. "Anyone wanting to pay the bill is good with me."

Mort called the waitress over and got his new friends some drinks.

After some more conversation, Harlan looked over and saw Tiffany and Mallory walking toward them.

Mort said, "Something is familiar about that girl."

"Who?" Harlan asked.

"Your girl."

"Oh."

"I can't seem to put my finger on it. Where have all the women gone? I dunno. Will you tell me, please?"

"Wish I knew," Harlan said. "Been trying to figure that out my whole life."

"But you found yours."

"Only after finding all the wrong ones."

Mort laughed. "I've met my fair share throughout the years. I couldn't even tell you how many."

Forrest said, "There are plenty out there, all swimming around, trying to suck on anything they can get. You can't respect those whores. I mean, you say you do until you get what you want. After that, fuck 'em. They don't deserve shit from me."

Tiffany and Mallory got to the table.

They introduced themselves.

Forrest said, "It's my pleasure. Hope you ladies are having a lovely evening."

They said they were

Mort looked at Tiffany. "You are a stunning creature if you don't mind me saying so."

"Thanks," Tiffany told him.

Mort said, "You're beautiful."

"Thanks," she said again

"Your mother sent me pictures of you, but they don't compare to seeing you in person."

"What?" She asked.

"You don't know?" Mort asked.

"Know what?" Tiffany got a confused look. "What do you mean? You okay?

Mort said, "I never knew when this day was gonna come. I played this out in my mind a million times. Guess you never know what's around the next corner."

"Fuck you talking about?" Tiffany glanced at her boyfriend, then back at this guy.

"You've caught me at a disadvantage, dear. I wish this was in a better setting. I'm your father."

"Huh?"

Everything became silent.

"I wasn't sure when I saw you from a distance. But when you came closer I knew it was you. You look so much like your mom."

Tiffany said, "You're freaking me out. I don't know what to say. Where do I even begin? Are you sure you have the right person? You said yourself you weren't sure."

Mort took a drink. "I know I said that. Yeah, I'm sure of it now. You look exactly like your pictures. I might be on drugs a lot, but I'm clear about that."

She sighed. "Well, then, looks like we have some catching up to do."

"What better way to do it than at a place where you party twenty-four hours a day."

"That makes sense."

"Naturally, caught me a little off guard. I wasn't planning on things happening like this. But things had to come to light sometime."

"I agree," Tiffany said. "This is a trip, I have to say. This is a nice little surprise."

They had an emotional exchange. After awhile, Tiffany warmed up to the idea of Mort being her father. They talked over more drinks. They all laughed and joked. Harlan asked the guys about the cocaine. Mort told him they could get to that later, and that if they wanted they could have some of his supply.

They hit a few more spots. On the street, they passed dancers and jugglers, street cons, drug pushers, pimps, and hookers. Two of the guys in the group, Roger and Mark, bought grass off of a guy who had a hook for a hand. Roger asked the guy if he ran girls, too, but he didn't. The guy told him if he wanted that sort of action he could just get one from the street. He walked over to a girl and talked to her. After a minute they went away to a hotel.

Mark said, "That's okay, I'll take my turn after he's done. There's more than plenty out here. You don't have to worry about finding a girl here. You basically have to beat them off with a stick. They're all dick crazy."

They all laughed.

A little while later Roger returned, and then Mike went over to her for his turn.

"Just like a door knob, fellas," Mark said, "everyone gets a turn...."

Harlan and company would discover later that Roger and Mark had known each other all their lives. They started out being neighbors for the first twelve years of their lives, and then they became roommates.

Laralyn came skipping over with a few other people, saying they got free drinks at the place across the street. All they had to do was do a little dance for the bartenders.

"If you got it, may as well flaunt it," Laralyn said. "There's no shame in it."

Tiffany and Mallory nodded.

Mallory said, "I want some free drinks."

Denny and her ran across to the bar. When they came back they were carrying two drinks a piece.

Mort and Forrest wanted to check out this strip club, so they all went. During the night, as drinks flowed and music was getting louder Mort and Tiffany were getting their first taste of a father/daughter relationship.

"Did you ever try to come back?" Tiffany asked her dad, as they walked on the sidewalk from the club. "Weren't you always missing something?"

Mort thought about the question and looked at her. "When your mom and I called it quits she didn't wanna have anything to do with me. She told me not to try and contact you. She told me if I ever did she'd shoot me."

"I don't think she would have done that."

Mort laughed. "Considering how we ended things, I think it's a safe bet she would. Things got complicated. She wasn't the biggest fan of me."

"It would've made things easier for me if you guys would've."

"I know, baby," Mort said. "Truth is, I did a lot of bad things when we were together."

"Like cheating?"

"Among other things."

They continued to talk as they walked the sidewalk. Tiffany was over the moon that she was talking to her father after all those years.

"So, this crusade you guys are on," Mort said, "how long have you guys been doing it?"

Tiffany said, "A couple of years. We've been going all over the country. I sort of feel like I'm in a music group on tour."

"How much longer you guys gonna do this?"

"Not really sure."

Mort told her he wanted to join them. He told her he thought what they were doing was a good thing, that they could make a change in this fucked world. Tiffany asked if Forrest was going to join the cause.

Mort said, "Don't know about that guy. I mean, he's a good dude but he can get a little too crazy at times. I'll see what he says."

"Okay."

Mort said, "I like Harlan. He seems to have his shit together."

He told her how much he liked Harlan, and that they needed to get married as soon as they got the chance.

28

They ended up at a place, Drop, where they took in a few more rounds. As the places started to close in the early hours of the morning, the crew was left to roam around.

Forrest looked up at the sky. "What a great way to end a night, you know?"

The sky was getting a lighter shade of blue as the crew walked down the street. A few were muttering about what the day was going to bring. They were all drunk fools searching for something to hold on to, something they could call their own. All walks of life were walking down the street together. Everyone with their pasts and experiences that the others never had. Yes, in a lot of ways they shared the same lifestyle, but, they had no clue exactly what the other had been through.

Harlan said, "Hey, man, during the blurriness over everything I forgot the cocaine. You still wanna make a sale?"

"Of course," Forrest said. "It's out in the car. Yeah, man, can't forget about that. That's what happens when you have too much fun, your mind slips, forget things. We're just the little people at work, my friend. The world moves as we stay in one place. Spend so much time dissecting ourselves we forget the outside wants to communicate. Crazy, huh?"

Mort said, "Everything's ready for ya. It's in the trunk of the car. All tucked away like a baby."

"Let's go," Harlan told them.

"Good. I just have to get something from my

room first."

"Okay."

"Don't go anywhere."

"I'll be here."

As they went to the elevator, down to the lobby, they were all talking, joking around. Everyone liked everyone.

Harlan told one of the other guys he'd be back in time for the rally.

Mort and Forrest told them they'd do the deal in the alley behind the motel. They told Harlan that he, Tiffany, and Denny were the only three allowed on the deal.

When they got out to the car they told Harlan to come around to the trunk. Mort and Forrest were standing on either side of him. Mort unlocked the trunk and opened it.

Tiffany and Denny came along with their car. They got out and walked to where the others were. Mort held out the coke for Harlan to see.

"Here it is," Mort said. "I hope you have enough to play in all this snow."

Harlan gave Mort the money.. "Of course."

"My favorite color," Mort glanced at the money. "That'll do it."

"You can buy yourself some more."

"Yeah."

"You can never have too much, right?" Harlan laughed.

"The price of this stuff, though, you have to start being picky. Makes me think I should become a smuggler."

"From what I hear that can be pretty profitable. Don't get busted, though. You'll be inside for the rest of your life. I know a few who can tell you about that."

Mort reached his hand out to give Harlan the bag, and as he did he took his other hand and crushed the bag. White powder fell to the ground.

Before Harlan could say anything he was hit on the head with a pipe, knocking him to the ground.

"There's your fuckin' coke," Forrest snapped. "Snort that shit like a pig! Snort that shit like your fucking life depended on it, bitch!"

When Denny rushed the man who hit Harlan he was met with a gun to the face from Mort. They told him if he knew what was good for him that he'd do nothing.

"Why?" Tiffany said to her father.

Mort said, "You should come with us. It'll be fun. We can catch up on lost time. We'll make a great team. Everything is at our fingertips, hon."

"I don't think so," she got a disgusted look on her face.

"Why?"

"I don't know you. You had your whole life to get to know me, but where were you? Nowhere to be found. Didn't even wanna fight to see me. Fuck you! If things were reversed I would've fought for you. Fuck you, asshole."

Mort pointed the gun at her. "If that's the way you want it, sure. That's the way things are gonna have to be, I guess. We can't risk you talking about us."

"Give it your best shot," Tiffany stated.

"Don't tempt me, sweetie. I've killed women be-fore. All kinds. The fuck do I care?"

Denny was able to hit Forrest to the ground. He hit Mort, making the gun fall out of his hands. Denny punched Mort two times.

Tiffany ran over to Harlan.

Denny picked the gun off the ground and pointed at Forrest, told Mort. "Say goodbye to your friend," he fired three times, killing the man.

He picked Mort up and hit him. Mort returned with a punch and Denny fell to the ground. Harlan stood. He grabbed a rock and threw it through the passenger window of their car. He took a jagged piece of glass, turned to Mort and shoved it into his chest. He pulled it out and stabbed again. He dug it as deep as he could. It wasn't long and Mort bled out.

Tiffany started to cry.

Harlan went over and comforted her.

She looked at him. "Why'd this have to happen?"

Harlan couldn't say anything.

As the bodies were on the ground the three just looked at one another. No one said a word. They knew they had to get out of there. They knew someone probably heard the shots and called it in. Tiffany said they could just claim self-defense. They told her that'd be okay but the fact they were criminals themselves wouldn't be good for them.

"What should we do?" Tiffany asked.

Denny said, "We need to leave as soon as we can."

"Need to get everyone to haul out," Harlan told them. "This is fucked."

"Tell me about it."

"I didn't count on doing this today."

"That makes both of us."

"It's over now. Nothing we can do about any of it."

Harlan went over to Tiffany who was crying. He wanted to let her know everything was going to be okay.

"You need a minute?" he asked her.

"I'm fine."

They got everyone together and sped away fast. They knew the people who worked at the motel would find out soon enough.

Harlan told Tiffany that he was sorry he had to kill her father, but he had to. Mort would have killed him. He still had things to do. Tiffany told him she understood, and that she didn't know him well, that it was fine.

Neither Denny nor Harlan knew the two men they killed were serial killers. They didn't know until they heard the report on the radio. When the guy on the radio said how many people the killers were suspected of killing, Harlan and Denny knew they had done a good deed. Tiffany felt a little bad when she found out the news. She cried a little. She didn't want to be anything like her father.

29

When they got back to Arkansas they were all exhausted. They landed back at Denny's place. Their time on the road had been a fruitful one. They'd recruited a total of eighty-five people. Harlan had hoped to get more.

Denny and Harlan were sitting at the kitchen table talking about the future of this thing they'd started, and what they were going to do.

Denny said, "I talked to Hank the other day. He said you should come by and check on things. Said he and his guys have worked too much."

"How'd he say things were coming along?" Harlan said. "The price tag is sky high."

"Yeah, he said it was going good. They're starting to do all the electrical stuff soon."

"That right?"

"Yeah."

"I'll have to head out that way," Harlan said.

"He said the guys were gonna be over there tomorrow. Think I'll join you when you go."

"Sounds good to me."

"Have nothing else going on tomorrow."

Harlan laughed. "I know it's gonna seem strange not being on the road anymore."

Denny went over to the fridge to get some beers.

The girls were outside messing around in the garden.

Denny came back with some beers and handed one to his friend. "You know, I keep turning around that day in my mind, those two sick fucks, The more I think about it, the more I think we did the right thing. At first, even when we found out who they were, I felt bad about it.

But people like that don't deserve to live. I mean, people killing folks for no good reason? The fuck is that about?"

"Know what you mean. I think it's the climate of the nation. It's like they're all upset and need to find an outlet for all their rage. The whole place is a ticking time bomb. And it's gonna blow sooner than later."

"I get that," Denny took a drink. "You know, when you first told me about this whole plan of yours, I was a little more than skeptical. I didn't think it was gonna turn out to be much. But you surprised me, this has surprised me. It's shaping up to be something special."

"That's what the idea was," Harlan told him. "I just knew I needed to do something big. Hell, at first I wasn't even this committed. But I tell ya, as days passed I started to reevaluate the situation. Tiffany asked a few times how long this was gonna go on. She finally told me I had her full support. In the end I can't blame her, someone comes along, says they love her and wants her to uproot her world for a few years on some sort of revolution mission: yeah, she's been a trooper."

Denny said, "You gonna marry her?"

"At some point," Harlan said.

"She's a good girl."

"She is. I have to say, I'm a very lucky dude."

"A woman like that, brother, you need to hold on to."

Harlan nodded. "Yes, sir."

Denny got up to get more beer.

When he got back he said, "After the compound is finished, what's the next step gonna be?"

Harlan cracked the beer bottle open. "We're gonna have a few days of people getting settled into the new place, and everything that is gonna go into that. One thing I was gonna start doing, I was gonna get with the local television station and start broadcasting sermons from the church."

"And then?"

"And then, if things go well we'll go international."

"Really?"

"Why not? This will be a business. Why not do the most we can? I dunno, maybe it won't be popular overseas? But that'll have to be a few years down the road. That one, it might be a little more tricky to pull off."

"Yeah, that's gonna be big, something like that."

After talking a little longer Denny asked Harlan how his girl dealt with the fact her father was a killer.

Harlan said, "It was a little shocking. She wanted to distance herself. She couldn't bear the idea that her dad killed all those people."

"Yeah, I don't blame her. That's a tough one. But you can't be responsible for the actions of others."

"That's what I was trying to tell her. After talking through it, though, she said how she didn't have a connection to that guy, so she didn't feel anything for him. It was all the victims she felt for. You know, all those families lost loved ones to those sick fucks. Nah, we did a good thing."

"Think anyone will be after us? The people who work in the motel could've told the pigs about us renting rooms, and they could track us down."

"I wouldn't worry about it," Harlan shook his head.

"Why?"

"I used a fake name when I got the rooms. We didn't leave anything behind."

"Good thinking."

"It'll keep everyone out of harm's way. And I'm not sure I even wanna go back there anytime soon."

Denny shrugged. "I could take it or leave it, myself. It was nice, but a lot of things were nice. The music and all the people, that was pretty cool. But, you know, just another place."

"Yeah."

"We can smoke dope and party anywhere."

"You make a good point."

Denny shrugged. "I do the best I can."

"I dunno, man, just call us old-fashioned."

"Know the feeling. You remember that second day we were back?"

"What about it?"

"Went over to Circle J, Mal wanted candy and a few other things. Anyway, I was walking out of the place with my stuff and saw a few guys standing around a car playing loud music. Now, I'm all for loud music but this shit was garbage. Guy told me the name, but I forget it now. The drinks were good. Although, drinks are good pretty much everywhere."

"It's the age."

"I feel it."

"Funny thing is, some days I feel it, but then, others I don't. Most days I feel like I'm in my early twenties. Hell yeah, I can party like it."

"That's the way it should be," Denny said. He said he had to take a leak.

Harlan told him not to fall in.

As soon as he shut the restroom door, Tiffany, Mallory, and Laralyn came in through the back door. Harlan nodded, asking if everything was okay. They said everything was fine. Tiffany went and sat in Harlan's lap. She had a happy glow about her. She and Harlan kissed.. When Denny came back to the kitchen he asked his lovely wife if they were going to be getting any tomatoes soon. They had their nice neighbors watch their garden while they were away.

"Doesn't look like it, babe," Mallory said. "Looks like we're gonna have to wait until next year. Can't win 'em all, I guess. We got a few peppers, cucumbers, and squash."

"That's good," Denny said. "When I go out tomorrow I can pick up some more seeds."

"That'd be great," his wife said.

"I might get some different things. I need to get some of that plant food, too."

"Anything helps."

"I have the money for it."

Laralyn said she had to run out to the bus for a few things she forgot. They all laughed and joked that she had forgotten the big bag of grass. Laralyn gave them the middle finger, telling them to stop making fun of her. When she got back from the bus she was carrying two bottles of wine and a big bag of grass.

They laughed.

Tiffany said, "See, this right here is what I like! All of us together, that's what it's all about."

Harlan said, "I may not have said this enough, but I have to thank all of you do a job well done. I couldn't have done it without all of you. People like you, you're good friends to have."

"Thanks for that," Denny said. "Things were sure interesting, that's for sure."

The others agreed.

Later on they made dinner, poured some wine and rolled a doobie, and then another doobie. After they watched television they fell asleep to dream of pleasant things.

The next day the guys went out to the construction site. They were glad to see things were finally coming together. Considering the building was going to be massive, it still had a ways to go before it was going to be completed. They spent the afternoon walking the grounds, talking about permits and other things they would need to install. Still, after seeing everything, Harlan was a little worried that things would fall apart at the last minute. That night, after they ate dinner and shared a joint, they went to Zagos to have some fun. After some drinks, they were all feeling pretty good.

Laralyn said, "I have to say, you guys, I'm glad I found you guys. My search led me to you. Honestly, I didn't know where I was going. I just knew I had to get out of where I was. I think I'm going to stick around for awhile."

"Well, thank you," Harlan said. "You guys are all family to me."

Tiffany agreed. "I feel the same. I love you guys. Tell us, something, whatever happened to that farm of yours?"

Laralyn said, "I signed it over to a friend of mine, Bill. I knew when I first started with you guys I'd never be able to keep up with all of that, taking care of all those animals and duties. He offered to give me half of the income, but I told him just to take it all. Let the past stay there."

"How did you come to own it?" Tiffany asked.

Laralyn sighed. "My parents had it. We all lived there before they went away."

"Where'd they go?"

"Don't know," she shrugged. "They just left one day. It was a Saturday. Said they had to take care of some stuff and I couldn't go. Said they'd be back a few hours later, but they never showed. I eventually had my Uncle John come and take care of me. He had to leave, though. A few weeks passed, and then this one day some cops came to talk to me. I thought I was in trouble. They told me what happened. My mom and dad were killed."

Harlan and Tiffany looked at each other when she said that name.

Laralyn continued. "I was in shock. I couldn't believe it. They never did anything to anybody. I asked the cops why they had to die. I was sad, mad, upset at the world, confused as ever. It hurt me I didn't have any answers. Anyway, soon after the cops came back and we had another nice long talk. They asked if I knew anything at all. I got the feeling they didn't believe me. Just how they acted, made me think that way. Then a few more weeks passed and they came back. This time they told me they knew who did it but couldn't find the guy. His name was Mort Bosworth. They asked if I knew him, but I didn't. They said they'd contact me whenever they found Mort. I guess he'd killed a few other people."

Harlan said, "Damn, that's a hell of a story. I'm so sorry that happened."

"That's some shit, girl," Tiffany sniffled a little.

"I've dealt with it," Laralyn told them. "Just had to come to the fact that it was part of my reality, nothing I could do about it. Damage was already done. Nothing anyone could do would bring my parents back."

Harlan said, "If you ever need anything you can always come to us."

"Thanks."

"That's what family is for.'

Denny said, "Exactly. There's nothing more important than the relationships we have with people."

Mallory kissed Denny and said she loved him.

Harlan and his girlfriend didn't know if they should tell Laralyn about the strange coincidence that connected the three of them. Would Laralyn get mad at them if they told her what they knew? Would she be okay with it all? When she slipped away to the bathroom they decided the best thing to do was wait until another time. They didn't want to ruin the night. They didn't want to upset her, possibly pushing her over the edge, and sending her in a fit of rage.

The night ran on and everyone was having a good time, dancing, chatting, doing drugs, anything they wanted. A guy came along who said they were celebrating a friend's birthday, and they were buying everyone drinks. Harlan and company weren't known for passing on free drinks so they indulged. They stayed at the club for a couple more hours partying the night away.

The next day Harlan started writing, writing what he called RULES FOR CHURCH OF MODO. For the next few days, he was working hard at the typewriter, writing notes, memos, flyers, and guidelines for how he wanted people to live. The way he saw it: After they wanted to join him, now, they have to comply with the lifestyle he designed for them. He wrote and made copies.

Three months passed, and then the compound was complete. A good chunk of time was spent moving people in. The compound was made of four big buildings along with a main one that housed the church. Along with the church on the bottom level it housed living quarters on the second and third floors.. The other four buildings were all three levels high.

The first bit of business they had to get to after everyone had moved in was to have the first meeting, the first of many. They ushered everyone into the main building that used the church. There were a total of five hundred people in attendance. Harlan, Tiffany, Denny, Mallory, and Laralyn sat at a long table in front of everyone. Harlan explained the people sitting at the table were the administrators and management; they were in charge of everything.

Harlan said, "I look out and I see all your smiling faces, it brings joy to me. I'm excited about this chapter in life we're starting together. All of this is God's doing. Because of him, we're all here together. I'm not sure how many of you remember this, but see, God spoke to me, saying I needed to start this church in his name, to praise everything he has given us. He told me my mission was to bring more people to know him. I took it upon myself to write some rules and regulations we all will follow as long as we're here. All of his is set in stone. If you choose to not participate in group activities you'll be banished, no questions asked. You have to be serious about what our goal is here."

As Harlan continued talking Tiffany started distributing all of the papers to everyone.

Harlan said, "While living here we'll spend a lot of time getting a better relationship with our maker. As I'm sure you've noticed around here, we've gone to great lengths to try and make this place enjoyable, full kitchen, and game rooms. Now, if any of you have any concerns regarding rules and regulations anyone in management can help you. And let me just tell you this: The rules for this place are meant to help and not hurt. As days pass this will all be normal."

He opened the room up for questions.

This girl, a redhead named Molly from Denver said. "I'm on board with you guys. You're the reason I'm here."

"Anything you want!" this guy with thick glasses said.

Another said, "We're ready for work."

"I'm happy to hear you guys say that," Harlan told them. "When I first had the calling to do this I had my doubts. But I asked God for guidance and it came."

An overweight gentleman in front said, "Yeah!! Yeah!! Yeah!! We're gonna fight, kick that motherfuckin' Devil dude outta here. We need to rid him from our lives! We've all had affairs with the damn beast."

The guy's name was David Hill and his mother was Susan Hill. When David was a child he was in a car accident that rendered him with brain damage, causing him to have to live with his mother for the rest of his life. David's father couldn't deal with the fact his son had a disability and left.

30

The last day of the 70s bought a big party. They had a lot of everything; booze, weed, and other drugs. It was a party of great importance, a celebration welcoming the future and saying goodbye to the past. The future looked bright for all of them.

Harlan and the others spared no expense when it came to the party favors—after all, it was the party that would end the decade.

The main building of the compound is where the party was held. They sent invites to the whole town. They wanted to be on the good side of everyone. A lot of people showed just because they were curious what Harlan Reeves and the Church of Modo was all about. They had live music, dancing, food, drugs, booze, and all the fun you could stand, and then some.

"I'd like to thank all of you for coming," Harlan said. "As we say goodbye to a year and welcome a new one. Yes, and I hope it's as good as the others. See, ladies and gentlemen, we are embarking on something really special here. I have to thank you, thank all of you for your determination and your willingness to expand your horizons. I hope our time together will be profitable. For those of you who came here out of pure intrigue, I hope you like what you see and hear. There are flyers and pamphlets all around. And if any of you have questions as to what we're about you can ask one of us."

Some commotion came from the crowd, a few hollers and cheers. He ended his speech by telling everyone to have a great time.

The band started to play as the booze began to flow and everyone started to mingle. Harlan and Denny were talking over a drink when Tiffany came over. Harlan and her hugged and kissed.

"I ran into a friend," she told him.

"Oh, really? Who would that be?"

"Remember that guy, Rod, I used to live with?"

"Yeah," Harlan said. "He got busted for drugs, no?"

"Well, he got out two years ago. We were talking and I told him what we were doing, and he said he wanted to help."

"In what way?"

"I'll let you talk to him about that."

"He still here?"

She pointed at a group across the room. "Over there."

He walked over to Rod.

Harlan said, "How's it going, Rod?"

"Hey, Harlan, long time no see. How have things been?"

Harlan nodded. "It's all good. Everything is as co-pacetic as can be, all smooth sailing."

"Good to hear, good to hear."

Rod told the people he was talking to he'd be back shortly. He and Harlan walked outside and looked onto the open field. Little beams of light shot from cars as they traveled down the highway that led into Bencroft.

"Quite a party," Rod said.

"Have to make a statement somehow," Harlan said. "Have to let them know I'm here."

"I think you've accomplished that."

"We'll see. We do what we can, partner."

"Ain't that the damn truth."

Harlan said, "You still at the place you used to be?"

"Had to find a new place. I was just renting. When the owners found out about it they banned me from ever renting from them again. I just happened to run into Tiffany yesterday, and she told me about this place and the party. She told me what you guys were doing. Figure I could do something to help. Anything you guys need."

"Okay," Harlan lit a cigarette. "Like what?"

Rod said, "I'm out there on the streets everyday, hearing what people say and think, getting things twisted in the wind, searching for wickedness... I can bring your word to the streets. You can call me a prophet if you want, spin it however you want."

"You still dealing?" Harlan asked.

Rod said, "I upgraded."

"Upgraded?"

"Move shit all over the country."

"You make more money?"

"A ton more."

"Really? I need to get into that."

Rod shook his head. "You don't want any part of that, trust me. You always have this thought of being busted. I can't do a drug rap again."

"That mean you're getting out?"

"I think that'd be the best thing. I can't afford to get busted again. I know lots who have drug charges."

"That's a hard ride. To make it worse they don't even give you your drugs back."

Rod laughed. "That'll be the day. What happens, they take it for themselves. Those pigs give you the charge and keep the goods."

"And they get away with it somehow."

"They have a racket going on, that's for sure," Rod nodded at the field. "It sure is silent out there...."

"Got it for a good price."

"You can't argue with that."

"Not these days... Prices, everything seems to be going up," Harlan continued smoking. "When you wanting to move in here?"

"Well, I'm living over at the Star Inn right now, so, as

soon as possible."

"Sure we can arrange that," Harlan nodded. "You still hang around those friends of yours I met?"

Rod looked into the night sky. "Sometimes. We all have our own things. Parties we used to have, hell, those days are long gone."

"It happens."

"You remember that guy Chuck?"

"What about him?"

"About four months after we got out he got arrested again. Got busted for running coke. Went in once and saw him, a couple days later his girl calls me up, tells me he caught another charge for knifing a guy to death. They gave him twenty more years."

"Damn," Harlan said. "That sucks for him."

"His girl said she always wondered what sort of stupid shit he was going to do to get in trouble. She didn't believe in him. She would say that they had a good time together, but she didn't see things last."

"I can see were that could be an issue."

"You can do that forever."

Harlan asked if Rod got with her.

Rod said, "Never thought about it, honestly. She's not for me."

"You don't need all of that for just one night."

Rod laughed. "That's a good one. Nah, heard she got with some rich dude."

"Well, good for her, I guess."

"Yeah, yeah," Rod said. "Anyway, about this thing, I think it's gonna be good. I have a feeling about it. You're gonna be famous, man. They're gonna write books on Church of Modo. it's a way of life, a mind-set."

"That's what we're hoping, that it lasts."

"Oh, trust me, it will. This is your time to shine, my friend. All those fucks who told you that you wouldn't amount to anything, you can just shove it in their stupid faces. Just tell them to go back home and jerk-off to their brother or sister, think they're the king of the world."

"Yeah."

Rod went on to further explain the good things he could do for Harlan. They talked more as people came and went.

People kept coming over to Harlan and thanking him for what he and his friends were doing. He'd just say he's doing God's work. He was pleasant to all of them. He knew if he was going to keep this ruse going for years he needed to do more homework. He would be the first to admit he had never read the Bible. He heard some stories here and there, read some sections of it, but didn't know much.

Harlan was eighteen when he was baptized, but then, after that he pretty much gave up on all of it. He couldn't understand why God would destroy the world he built, killed the men and women he made. At the time it didn't occur to him that Satan was also at the wheel, too.

The party continued until the sun came up the next day. A lot of them had been too drunk and high to drive, so they just stayed.

31

Harlan's vision was starting to take shape. The first compound was up and running. They had a total of one hundred people living at the location. There was a healthy mixer of men and women. Most of them had jobs outside the compound, but they would have to report back when their jobs were done for the day. Those who worked on-site did a variety of jobs; cooking for everyone, cleaning, doing laundry, and general upkeep on the compound. The people who worked at the compound worked in three shifts. Harlan wanted the place to be spotless at all times. He would tell them that they had to keep their place clean to welcome God into it.

They would always agree with him. They never wanted to get on his bad side.

One day, five of the guests got to witness Harlan scolding one of the cleaners for some dust left on an area of carpet. He hit the cleaner in the face and made him bleed.

"I had to do that," Harlan told the man. "Guys need to learn to do things my way. Fuck your way. Consider this a warning. Next time, I'll have to take you to the dungeon. Sorry, I had to hit you. In time you guys will thank me."

"Sorry, sir," the man said. "Anything you say. Won't let it happen again."

"That's good."

The man, William Hickson, was picked up from Florida in a little place called Swinafred. He had been with them for awhile now, but he still felt lost. William took the job cleaning because he didn't want the responsibility of anything meaningful. Of the others on the cleaning crew, no one seemed to include him in things. They weren't trying to be mean or anything, it was just that William acted as if he didn't want to be friends with anyone. He acted like he was better than all of them. They told him he needed to get off his high horse because he was no better than any of them. They were all in the same place.

Another day, about two weeks later, Harlan hit William again. William was moping, and Harlan noticed he was using too much water. After he hit William to the floor he picked him up and hit him again. When William was on the floor Harlan grabbed him by the hair and shoved his face into the water bucket.

"Just be glad it's not the dungeon," Harlan told him.

Bubbles exploded in the bucket.

Harlan lifted William's head. "That's it, that's it. How do you like that, buddy?"

Bubbles again, this time for a few seconds longer. Harlan repeated the act two more times. Each time got a little longer. Harlan took William's head out of the bucket.

"I'm going to give you one last chance, buddy," Harlan told him. "If I were you I wouldn't fuck up again."

"I promise I won't," William caught his breath.

"If you do anything anymore you won't have to worry about anything ever again."

"I'm sorry."

Harlan picked the bucket up and dumped it on William, and he told William to clean it all up. Later that day Denny and Ed went to William's room, trashed it, then took him to the basement, and locked him in one of the dirty mop closets for an hour. Denny wanted to do it for longer. Harlan told him maybe he could next time.

After the hour Harlan unlocked the closet.

William thanked him.

"Now, I don't want to be known as a mean guy," Harlan told him. "Sometimes you have to do things you don't want to. But things have to be done."

William shook his head. "I understand. It'll never happen again, Harlan."

Harlan continued. "I know. But we all have rules we have to follow. You wanna be the best you can, right?"

William just looked at him.

"I understand if you don't want to talk. Listen, I don't blame you for being mad at me. My hope is that you learn from this. Don't want to be a failure forever, do you?"

"I don't," William shook his head.

Harlan said, "You don't what?"

"I don't wanna be a failure my whole life. I won't let you down."

Harlan patted him on the shoulder. "Good to hear. We still need to shape you up, get you tough as nails."

"Yes, sir."

Harlan instructed him to get back to work.

A lot of times Harlan would write messages and manifestos and have them copied and given to everyone. If anyone had questions or wanted to talk to him about anything they had to make an appointment. He was always trying to get the best out of everyone. Most were willing, others weren't. The ones that weren't were punished. There wasn't just one way they'd hand down punishment, but a variety of ways. He would tell people he didn't like to punish people for things, but they weren't sure about that. If you asked some of them they'd tell you he loved it.

It was a Friday afternoon, and Denny, Mallory, Tiffany, and Laralyn were all sitting across from Harlan in his office. They were all smoking and drinking. They were talking about having a little carnival on the grounds of the compound.

Laralyn said, "It'll be fun. I've been thinking about everything we could do, all the games we could have people play. We could have one of those dunking booths outside. We could all take turns being the ones that get dunked. We could do the dart-throwing game. We'll have to get a ton of balloons and darts."

"That shouldn't be a problem," Mallory said. "You can find balloons everywhere."

"The best part is," Laralyn said, "we could invite the whole town. It'll be great."

Harlan stared at them behind his desk. "How many days were you thinking about having this?"

"Three," Laralyn told him. "And if things work out, next time we can have it for a week."

Harlan sat back in his chair and laced his fingers. "I like this. I just don't want people getting tired of us. Don't get me wrong, it's a swell idea. It's an opportunity to show people of the town we know how to have fun."

"We could get more members," Denny said. "More members equals more money."

Tiffany shook her head. "That's true."

"Yeah," Mallory agreed. "It's all about the big picture. A lot of positive things could come out of this. And I think everyone would see you in a different light."

"As opposed to what?" Harlan asked. "Do they think I'm a bad guy?"

"Not at all. I'm just saying it'll help with your public image. You want to get as many people as possible to like you. It'll come in handy."

"I see," Harlan said. "We have a lot of work to do, reach out to all sorts of people. It can carry a pretty hefty price tag."

"We should have enough," Denny told him. "If we need to we could always ask for donations—that's always better than just telling people they have to cough some dough up."

"Good point," Harlan said. "We don't wanna turn people off."

Tiffany said, "Do we want any rides?"

"I think we should," Laralyn said. "Now, I'm not sure how many. But I think we need to have some stuff."

Harlan shook his head. "We can make some calls, make it happen," he grabbed a pen from the desk and jotted something down on a sheet of paper. "If I don't write it down I'll most likely forget it."

They all laughed.

"It's all the grass you've smoked, hon," Tiffany stated.

Harlan laughed. "Could be. I could say that about all of you."

Tiffany continued. "I think you need to stop a minute and look at all you've done. Look at all of this. If it wasn't for you, and your insight, none of us would be here. This is an accomplishment like no other."

Mallory and Laralyn agreed with their friend.

"I do my best," Harlan told them. I kinda feel like a rockstar."

Denny asked if they wanted some beer and some grass. They did.

He went and came back a few minutes later with the supplies.

They got high and drunk.

"Thanks for your kind words," Harlan told them. "I don't think of myself as that big of a deal. I'm just a guy who thought it'd be a neat idea to bring people together."

"Don't be so modest," Laralyn said, pointing her finger at the door. "All of those people out there, they were all lost souls before you came along and showed them the path. They don't know how lucky they are. All those women, they should fuck you every day as thanks for what you've given them. I know some of the guys desperately wanna have their way with us girls. A bunch of those people are still lost. They were kicked to the curb by society and you built a place for them to go. They owe you everything."

"I've already told him that," Tiffany smiled at her.

"Oh, see, well, there ya go, Harlan," she looked at him

Denny said, "Okay, stop sucking his dick."

"Well, that's what's going to happen when you guys leave the room," Tiffany said. "Leave us girls to do what we do."

Denny laughed. "Okay, okay. Yeah, whatever you say. Let's get back to the business at hand."

"Yes, let's get back to it," Mallory said with a spark.

"So, anyway," Harlan said, "we'll get started on vendors, calling around to see who can help. We'll need permits for all this stuff, and for the rides if we're gonna have any."

They agreed they would. They thought they could at least get a merry-go-round, a tilt-a-whirl, a Ferris wheel, and maybe a little bumper car track. They figured that would be enough for everyone.

As they continued discussing the event a commotion started to brew outside the office door. Loud voices and knocking came to the door. Denny went and opened the door. David Hill was standing outside the door with another guy, Ryan Miley.

"Can I help you guys?" Denny asked.

David said, "S-s-sorry. Am I disturbing you guys? Are you talking about some wild and crazy stuff in there? You weren't talking about locking me away, were you?"

"Why would we be talking about that?" Denny asked.

David shrugged. "New people are always like that to me."

"Well, you have nothing to worry about," Denny looked at Ryan. "What was the noise out here?"

"Just messing around," Ryan told him.

"He called me a stupid motherfucker," David said.

Denny put his hand on David's shoulder. "Are you?"

"No, sir."

"Well, then, there you go. Why'd he call you that?"

"He said I was motherfuckin' brain dead."

Denny looked at Ryan again. "That true?"

Before Ryan could answer Harlan came over to see what was going on. They told him and the leader invited them to come in.

When the girls saw who it was they greeted both of them.

"I hope you guys are doing okay," Tiffany said.

They nodded.

"And how's your mother doing, David?" Laralyn asked.

"She's doin' okay, doin' okay," David said. "She's right up there in her room reading that Bible of hers. She knows that thing word-for-word."

"That's good."

"I know it okay, it's hard for me to concentrate sometimes. I try."

"That's okay."

"Hope we don't have any tests or anything. I'd probably flunk."

Laralyn shook her head. "No, nothing like that," she glanced at Ryan. "Have you been telling him that?"

"Not me," Ryan told her.

"We don't need to rattle him any more than he already is."

David asked him what she meant by that. She told him not to worry about a thing. Harlan told the girls to give them a few minutes alone. The guys had to talk about something.

Once the girls were out of the room Harlan told David and Ryan to take a seat.

"Guys," Harlan said. "Now, how are we today? I understand there's a problem?"

David nodded and pointed at Ryan. "He told me I was motherfucking brain dead."

Harlan sat back in his chair. "Well, are you?"

"No, sir, I'm as quick as a turtle, yes I am."

"A turtle?"

"That's what others told me."

"I think they were having some fun. By nature, turtles are known for their slow actions."

"Really? That means they were making fun of me?"

"Afraid so."

"That's not very nice to say."

"It's not."

David looked at Ryan. "You said I was the fucking retard, but you're the stupid one. Sir, you can eat my shit, little fucker. You even told my momma that she's a whore. You're stupid. She's a fine, up-standing woman."

"Is that true?" Harlan asked Ryan.

Ryan cleared his throat. "I was just messing around with him, trying to get a laugh. I didn't know he was gonna be a little pussy about it. Not my fault if the retard can't take a joke."

"I'll tell you this," David said, "you say that again and I'll kick your ass all over this world."

Ryan laughed. "You think? Who's gonna help you, your bitch mom? You couldn't even hurt a fly."

"I know how to use a gun. I'll shoot you between the eyes. Won't even know what hit ya!"

"Oh, yeah?" Ryan stood from his chair. "Wanna go right now, dude? When I'm done you can run to your mom. You're a fucking mongoloid. I'm surprised your mom didn't kill you when you became a fuck-tard."

That comment made Harlan get up from his desk and walk over to Ryan. "That's what you think, huh? What if I was to tell you I could take you out right now and no one would miss you?"

"That something you're libel to say?" he laughed.

"You're a funny guy, you know that?"

Ryan shrugged. "I know."

"Well, funny guy, what's going to happen now is my friend and I are gonna take you down to the basement."

"And then what?"

"You're gonna be sorry."

"I will? I'm not now. Why would you think it would change? I'm here for ya, buddy. What do ya get?"

While Harlan was keeping Ryan's attention he didn't notice Denny got a cattle prod from a drawer in the desk. Denny walked over to Ryan and zapped him with it, forcing him on the ground.

They took Ryan to the basement and strung him up by his arms. As he was hanging there he cried out, telling them to let him go.

"Shut up," Harlan hit him across the face, drawing a little blood. "I told you that you were going to be sorry."

"What are you going to do?" Ryan muttered.

Harlan hit him again. "You're going to apologize."

"To you?"

"No," Harlan shook his head. "To David."

"Fuck him."

"Sure you wanna say that?"

"And fuck you, too."

Harlan looked at his watch, then back at Ryan. "See, I'm big on respect. Everyone has to show respect for others. We have to work together, and if you have an individual who doesn't have respect for those he lives and works with, the whole thing starts to crumble. It's important to our mission. See, I need to get everyone on the same page. Look at it like this, it's not about you or anyone here, it's about all of those souls outside these walls, all of those who need guidance. I understand you don't have to like everyone, but you do need to show respect. Showing that sort of respect for those you don't like, shows character and growth. Now, you gonna be a good guy and apologize?"

"Fuck you!" Ryan blurted. "Better go somewhere else if you want that."

"You sure?" Harlan asked.

"Fuck you," Ryan looked into his eyes. "And fuck that retard."

Harlan threw up his arms. "Have it your way."

Denny, still carrying the cattle prod walked over to Harlan. They discussed something in hushed voices.

Denny turned to Ryan. "I think I can persuade you," he turned the rod on and zapped him again.

"Go fuck yourself," Ryan said.

Denny stepped back, turned the rod higher, then stepped forward and zapped the man longer.

"Fuck you," Ryan repeated. "I'm not giving you what you want."

Denny turned it higher and zapped for longer, making the man go limp. But he was able to repeat his statement from before.

"Damn," Harlan said. "I would've given up on the first one. You got balls, I'll give you that."

Denny zapped him again.

Still nothing.

The friends talked about it again.

"We could just fuckin' shoot him," Denny said.

Harlan took out his gun. "Guess that'll have to do," he fired three times in the heart.

"Maybe we should've done that from the beginning?

Denny said.

Harlan put the gun on a little table beside them. "We could've used that toughness when we were going the old jobs. What a waste."

"What do we do with the body?" Denny asked.

"We can't leave him here, can we?"

"I don't think so. People will find out. I don't think you'd want that."

"Shit, they'd get me for sure. They'd fucking kill me on the inside."

"That can't happen."

Harlan told David to go back to doing something else, and not to tell a single person what happened. After David left Harlan told his friend to get a couple of guys to help him get rid of the body. Harlan told him to drive out to the deep woods and bury the guy.

Over the next few days, they made all the preparations for the carnival. Everyone had a good time. A total of twenty people we recruited to live in the compound. When asked, Harlan told people Ryan decided to move out of the compound and move out of town. He told them that Ryan said how he didn't want to hear from them anymore, so don't bother trying; that seemed to put an end to that.

32

One of the guys who was there when Ryan got killed, a guy with orange hair from Texas named Travis James, burst into Harlan's office in protest. He told Harlan he'd go to the cops, telling them he knew what was going on. Travis was one of the guys who dug the hole that Ryan was in. Travis said he'd had enough of Harlan's mess, that he would tell everyone what happened to Ryan.

Harlan said, "You forget, you'd have to prove these things. If you go out there, say whatever about me, they are gonna ask for proof. Proof, my friend, is something you don't have. And I don't think you have the guts for it."

"Or why don't I just kill you right now?" Travis told him. "I'll save everyone some time. They won't miss you."

Harlan laughed. "You can try. If you think you can do it, do it. But I can tell you, you won't be able to. The only thing I can promise you is death."

"You think?"

"I know. Tell me this, how are you gonna do it? You don't even have a fuckin' gun on you. If you shot me you'd have a good chance of killing me. You don't have shit. Get the fuck outta here before you make me mad. Drop it. Do what you're fuckin' told or we'll be burying you next."

"I have a knife in my pocket."

"Planning on using that?"

"Maybe."

"I see."

"I tell you, Harlan, don't fuck with me. You don't know anything about me or what I'm capable of. I can be your worst nightmare."

"Sounds like you know your way around a fight?"

"I've been in a few."

"A real badass, right?"

"I get by."

"That's one of the best things you can hope for."

Travis took the knife out of his pocket.

Harlan looked at the knife. "You better know what you're doing with that thing. Boy, you're so fuckin' un-grateful! I can't believe it... I gave you a place to come to and this is what you do? You wanna kill me? Man, you're a real piece of trash. I should've left you there, you fuck. You need to be thanking me. Everyone here should be thanking me. Come on, buddy, you do this, it won't work in your favor."

"Don't have to worry about that."

Harlan came from behind his desk and grabbed the knife. Travis tried to hit Harlan's hand away. Harlan was able to get the knife away from him, slash his face, and kick him to the floor. Harlan stabbed him in the stomach a few times. Harlan dropped the knife to the floor and thought about what to do. He walked around his office for awhile then called Denny. He told his friend to get to his office as soon as he could. Denny showered a few minutes later.

"Thanks for coming over," Harlan said.

Denny looked at the body on the floor and sighed. "Shit... Man, I dunno... Another one? The fuck is going on here?"

"It's something that had to be done," Harlan said.

"What did he do?"

"Guy tried to take me on."

"Looks like things didn't work out for him, huh?"

"They didn't."

Denny said, "He should've run it by me before he went

to you. Whatever it was. He'd still be alive. What do you wanna do with him?"

"It's just one of those things that happened. I wasn't planning on killing anyone today. It's a nice day out. I didn't want any of this. He could've waited until later this week."

"Think that would've worked?"

"No."

Denny looked back down at the body. "Looks like a lot of people are trying to take you on these days, why do you think that is?"

"Jealousy? They all wanna be king until they're king."

Denny laughed. "I can see that, sure. Who said you were king? King shithead, that's what I'd say."

Both men laughed.

Denny knew he could get away with saying something like that because they'd been friends for so long. If you were to ask either man how many years they had been friends neither one could tell you. They were as close as brothers.

"We'll have to wait awhile, then bury him in the forest. Make sure no one is around."

"You got it. We're starting to make that our cemetery."

Harlan laughed. "Have to put the bodies somewhere. Can't just throw 'em out front."

"Guess so."

"That wouldn't be good for anyone."

"I would say not."

Harlan said, "The thing with this guy, he could've ended all this. He communicated to me that he was go-ing to bring us down. I couldn't let that happen. All the crimes, he was there for all of it. Guy said he was gonna kill me. It wasn't good. I had to. Guy only had a knife. Shit, at least have a gun if you wanna kill someone. Too many variables with a knife."

"That's understandable."

"In a perfect world, you don't wanna keep walking through life killing people. But if you have to, you better do it right, you know?"

"Yeah," Denny said. "Oh, hey, I don't think anyone would blame you. Sometimes you gotta be the rough shit when you're in charge."

Harlan said, "You just have to keep your eyes and ears open. You have to make rules. Being decisive is what it's all about."

"I can see that, sure."

Harlan said, "If I had to do it over I'd do the same thing. I can't afford anyone to ruin any of this," he went and sat behind his desk. "All the time and money we've invested into this thing would be for nothing if we let that go. I'm not saying it's good or anything, but that's what had to happen."

"And he could've told someone he was coming to see you. I dunno, maybe something would happen to him so he told someone, you think?"

Harlan lit a cigarette. "I got the feeling he didn't say anything. But who knows? I think if he did say anything no one would believe him."

"Maybe."

"It's a pretty wild claim when someone from the outside hears."

"You better hope, brother."

"Things go on. So, what were you doing?" Harlan asked.

Denny said, "Nothing much. Mallory and I were just listening to music."

"That's good. You two have made something together."

"I just hope it lasts."

"I have a feeling it will."

"There's no backup plan, so it'll have to work."

"If you want it bad enough you'll make it so."

"That's what I'm gonna do," Denny said. "I couldn't see myself with anyone else."

"For what it's worth, I can't see it."

"Thanks."

"I'm pretty good at these things."

Denny laughed. "You? Shit, man, don't make me start dyin' over here. I know you're full of shit."

"Hey, it's not my fault girls don't wanna stay with me."

"Yeah, yeah," Denny walked over to the window. "That's what ya say."

"Cross my heart."

Denny looked at him. "Don't have to convince me."

Later that afternoon, when nobody was around, Harlan and Denny carried the body to the trunk of Harlan's car. The two went out to the middle of the forest to bury the body. They didn't mark where the grave was. Harlan told his friend he didn't want to talk about it again, and said that the guy was a waste of time. Denny was loyal and had no problem doing what his friend asked.

When they got back to Harlan's office they tried to talk about other stuff to deflect the fact they buried another person. Harlan asked his friend if he wanted to get something to eat. Denny said he had to take a shower and get ready. When he got ready they headed out. They went to a burger place called Murphy's Grill.

"Tell me," Harlan asked, "you think I'm doing a good job?"

"Sure. I couldn't do this, my friend. You have a way with words. Tell people what they wanna hear... They're clay in your hands. You can tell them everything."

"They would, wouldn't they? There's a certain amount of power that gives you."

"But you need to be careful with it, Harlan. You're on top, the only place to go is down. Don't let it all go to your head. But, yeah, you're doing a good job. You keep this up, things will only get bigger."

Harlan said, "That's the plan. The more people join the more money rolls in. It'll be good for everyone. And I'm not ever going to forget what you guys have done for me. You all are forever in my debt."

"It's been my pleasure. I'm sure they all feel like that, everyone at the compound."

"Any way you slice it, that's the way it's gonna work. We can't have things falling apart on us."

"I agree."

"We do that, we might as well march down to the police station right now, and turn ourselves in."

"That won't happen."

"Glad to hear you say that. Just hope the others feel the same way."

Denny said, "We already got rid of some of the bad seeds. If we get more they'll be dealt with."

The two talked and laughed more. After they were done eating they went to the store to get some booze. They went back to the compound and got drunk, lost them-selves in stories of years past. They joked they needed to wake their girls and have a group romp. Denny men-tioned that Mallory always thought Harlan looked good. Harlan just laughed.

Denny said, "You can ask her yourself."

"Nah. I couldn't do that to you, man. Too much his-tory."

"That party we had the night you got out, if I wouldn't have been there she would've tried to fuck you. She's crazy in bed. If you want to test her out you have my blessing."

"Thanks for that. I'll pass. Not that Mallory is ugly or anything. Have a good thing going with Tiffany, wouldn't want to fuck that up. Now, I mean, if she was cool with it that'd be a different story."

Denny laughed. "You never know until you ask."

Harlan took a drink of beer. "That's a crazy one there, buddy."

33

The next day Harlan stood in front of the congregation, a little hungover. He looked out at everyone. They were waiting for him to speak. He didn't have anything planned. He was going to outline some sort of sermon, but that was before he killed Travis and drank the night away. Everyone was used to Harlan's unpredictable nature. They never knew what he was going to do or say. His temper could turn in an instant.

 Harlan cleared his throat. "I'm sorry. You have to forgive me. Been a little slow this morning. Last night, it was sort of a rough one."

A few people laughed.

"I was thinking about what I was gonna talk to you guys about," Harlan continued. "Many of you guys have heard me talk about how God told me to bring you all here, that it's all for a purpose. Some of you have asked about Jesus, have we ever had conversations? Yeah, he's not ready right now to come back. He told me that day is coming, though. The best thing for all of you is to be prepared. He said more of you need to go out and spread the word."

A few spectators looked at each other. They asked what could they do to help.

"The only thing you can do is tell others. Spread the word. Not everyone is ready to hear what we have to say. Hell, many of those people don't even believe in God and Jesus. You all know the game, when you start talking about either one they start trying to debunk you. They don't want to see the light. They're too afraid. They don't know any better. And honestly, I don't really blame them. Especially, if you're trying to convince someone who has trust issues—for those souls, all you can do is be persistent. They need to gain your trust," he held the Bible out in front of him. "This book, it's all you need. People always talk about how it's too long, too many stories, whatever story they come up with—for those people, I just think it all comes down to being lazy. Just an excuse. They say these things because deep down they're ashamed that they're not believers," he continued looking out at everyone as he walked around the stage. "Not sure about you guys, but if I'm gonna be here when Jesus walks the Earth. I'd want to do everything in my power to get into his good graces. As the book says, when Jesus returns it would really be in your best interest to be a believer. I understand that if you're not a believer you'll be cast down to Hell. I don't wanna be sent to Hell. From what I understand it's not that great of a place. I hope you guys won't wanna go there."

People in the crowd said they didn't.

Harlan continued. "All that smoke and fire just doesn't sound like my type of fun. To be in a place like that for eternity, I'm sure a proposition like that would turn people away. But a lot of people are in Hell. Guess it seemed like a good deal to them. Guess someone had to be there, right? Bet they thought they were clever. Just imagine shoveling dirt and ash every day in the heat could you do that? You can't think because too many people are screaming out in pain. The way to prevent that, you need to know the word of God. I know, there might be those that are still on the fence. I understand if you are. It's a big thing to believe in. That's why we have to help each other out. We have to love one another and make sure everyone knows the truth. Now, given I have certain rules about you guys leaving here, that's why I chose to broadcast sermons. My hope is people will join. And if we can't get them to join hopefully they'll still donate something. I understand asking people to come here and live isn't appealing to all," he pointed his finger into the crowd. "You guys know how hard it is convincing people of something. I'm sure all of you have done something like that in some capacity in your lives."

 As he continued, some of the people looked at one another. They whispered among themselves about concerns with the whole deal. There were some snickers as Harlan went on. As they hung on every word he said they smiled at each other. If they only knew! If they really knew what was in the mind of Harlan Reeves and his friends. Harlan knew that to keep things a secret he couldn't have anything leak out. When he killed someone he justified it by telling himself they wouldn't keep the secret. Everyone on the council understood why he wanted things the way he did. None of them were religious by any stretch. They all just wanted in on the con. Harlan's thought was that if he told everyone God talked through him they would let him do anything. He was right. He couldn't believe it. They would follow him to the end of the world if he asked. And if things kept going well he'd probably ask that.

 Along with the generous donations from those who lived at the compound, they also had telethons. They raised a lot of money. It was easy. Harlan would talk his talk, and for entertainment, they had a band. One of the guys, Chuck Ashlin, who prided himself as a comedian, came out and made some jokes. Once, someone called just to tell Chuck he wasn't a funny man, and that he didn't need to pursue a life in comedy.

 every now and then they'd have a movie night. Everyone seemed to like the movies. Before each showing Harlan would stand in front of everyone and tell them what the movie meant to him, and why he picked it. He told them how cool he thought it would be to go into acting.

"Why didn't you do it?" someone in the back row asked.

Harlan just shrugged and said he wouldn't want to spend all that time on a movie set. They all seemed to understand. He would tell them his true calling was to be there at the compound, to help them have a better understanding of what God and Jesus were really about.

Someone asked him once why God let his son, Jesus, die.

Harlan said, "God wanted to prove to all of us that he cared. Now, you may look at something like that and say you'd never do anything like that, that you'd never do that to a family member, your blood. Jesus asked his father why he was doing this to him. It's all about sacrifice, boys and girls, and the lengths one will go to prove to everyone they're all about love. It was done for you and me."

Some of the people had stunned looks on their faces. They said they never asked anyone to die for them.

Harlan said, "I've heard that a lot. You know, people ask that, but, no one can answer that. Listen, I'd rather nobody hurt themselves for my sake. But it's how things go. No need to get pissed over something you can't do anything about. I mean, fuck, you'll drive yourself insane doing that. Of course, if you wanna be insane then you'll already be there."

Some laughter came to the room.

"It boils down to this," Harlan told them. "Those who don't fully believe or understand will always try to justify things to suit themselves. It's just human nature, the way things are. We can't change it."

The service went on for a bit longer, and more had questions for him.

After he dismissed everyone Mallory and Denny came over, and asked if he and Tiffany wanted to join them for a beer in their apartment.

"I never shy away from an invite like that," Harlan told them.

The four of them went and drank some beer and smoked dope. It was a good time to be alive, they thought. They were young, nothing was going to stop them.

Mallory said, "Tell me, Harlan, what's next?"

"What do you mean?" Harlan asked.

"Just after all this is over... Don't get me wrong, we all think you should get a reward for the acting job you've done here. What's next? How long is this gonna last? What's the next con?"

Harlan stared at her for a bit, not knowing what to say, then. "What? Exactly how fuckin' high are you right now?"

"What?"

"How many fucking times have we been over this? Do you ever listen to what I say? Do I have to spell it out for you?"

"What do you mean?"

"This is it," Harlan told her. "I think I've told you more than a few times. I plan on ridding this one out until the grave. Man, have you seen the money we're making with this damn place? Oh, shit, days of robbing banks are over."

"Really? I liked doing that."

"I don't mean to tell you what to do or anything. Do what the fuck you want. I'm just saying with the revenue from the church we don't need to do that to support ourselves. See, before it was more of a necessity."

She shook her head. "I still like doing it."

"Suit yourself," Harlan said. "Who would join you?"

"Denny," she said.

Denny laughed. "You gonna drag me into this now?"

Why not?" Mallory smiled at him.

"If we get busted I'm tell 'em you put me up to it."

"Hey, we won't get caught. I took notes the whole time we were doing it."

Denny shook his head. "You wouldn't make it in prison."

"How do you know?"

"You don't have the gut for it."

Mallory stood from her chair. "Yeah, yeah, yeah... If you say so, buddy."

Everyone laughed.

Harlan told them if they wanted to go out and take down banks that they had his blessing. He pointed out, though, that if they get caught not bring him down with them. He said that he didn't need that.

Denny said, "Nah, she's all talk. She's not gonna do any of that. She's just my crazy little girl."

"Crazy like a foxy!" Mallory snapped. "And you better not forget it, buddy. I can do whatever I want and no-body's gonna say a damn thing about it. You think you can but you can't. I have the power over you. Come take a walk with me, babe, and I'll show you an insane life."

"I think we're already there."

"Sir, I'd say you're right about that one. Sometimes I just think 'Jesus, this is some fucked up shit here'"

Denny took her hand. "You're an insane bitch."

"I know."

They continued talking.

Mallory went and got more beers.

Another joint was rolled and smoked. At some point, Harlan looked at the time and told Tiffany they needed to leave. The two wished everyone a good night and left.

Harlan and Tiffany went to their apartment. The two

made mad passionate love. When they finished they smoked some dope. Tiffany started to talk to Harlan about how they still needed to talk with Laralyn. Harlan agreed, telling his girl they needed to get that out of the way. He told her that even though he wasn't for certain they'd tell her anyway. He told Tiffany that Laralyn wouldn't know anyway.

 "For all I know we could be right. Things like that happen all the time. Just look at some of the stuff those killers did."

 Tiffany agreed with him.

34

The next day Tiffany called Laralyn and said they
needed to talk to her. About twenty minutes later Laralyn
was knocking on their door. Harlan opened and invited
her in.

"How are things?" Laralyn asked.

"Pretty good," Harlan said. "The same old stuff. Went
to Denny's. Got a little stoned last night. It was a blast."

"Nothing wrong with that. Sounds like a good time to
me."

"It was."

"You have to enjoy life."

"Exactly."

Tiffany came over and hugged Laralyn. They went over
to the living room and started chatting about everything
in the world. They jabbered on like girls do. Tiffany
liked Laralyn. With her, she felt like she could tell her
anything. And Laralyn loved both of them a lot. Before
they came along Laralyn did feel like an outcast in her
hometown. She had a few friends here and there, but she
always felt that they were just hanging around her because they wanted something—but she never really had
much to give, so it was always a little strange to her that
people were even around. For the most part, she was a
loner. After her parents had died and she was left with
the family farm, she lost interest and let it go. After she
joined Harlan and the crew she told herself she'd never
go back to that place. The only thing she took with her
were some personal things and the bus they used.

Harlan asked if she needed a beer or anything.

'Of course," Laralyn told him. "Do you know me at
all?"

They laughed.

Laralyn looked down at her hands, studied them for a

minute then looked back at the two. "I'll take a beer."

"You got it," Harlan told her.

Tiffany said she'd take another. She told her friend they were just enjoying themselves. The couple brought out more dope.

"Well, fuck me sideways," Laralyn exclaimed. "That's what I need. Let's get this party started, right?"

After they got their drinks they sat around the living room.

Harlan rolled a fat joint and lit it.

"I hope you guys are doing good tonight?" Laralyn said.

Tiffany said, "Everything is going well. No com-plaints."

They passed the weed around.

"This is what it's all about," Laralyn told them. "Nothing like good friends having a good time."

"Got that right," Harlan said. "We aren't gonna be here forever, man. Might as well enjoy this world while we can."

Tiffany said, "Not if we live forever... Good times."

"But would you really wanna live forever?" Laralyn asked.

"Not really. I mean, in theory, it seems like a groovy idea, but at some point, it would just be a bummer."

"We would all be dead."

"Got that right."

Harlan took a drink of beer. "Hey, babe, want some acid?"

"Like tonight?" Tiffany asked.

"In a few days. Rod said he could get us a bunch at a good price."

"Oh, really? That'll be great. Yeah, tell him we'll take all he can give us."

"Okay, then."

"I just hope he doesn't get busted."

"He'll be fine."

After some more small talk, Laralyn asked why they called her over.

"We have something to tell you," Tiffany told her. "We were racking our heads, trying to figure out a way to tell you this. It's not gonna be easy for you to hear."

"What is it?" Laralyn asked.

Harlan said, "I hope you're not too shocked by this. If it makes you crazy, I'm sorry about that. We didn't know how else to tell you."

"What?"

Harlan continued. "The guys Denny and I killed in New Orleans, they were serial killers, you know?"

"Yeah. It was a little odd they were hanging around there, don't you think?"

"We discovered one of them was responsible for killing your family."

Laralyn gave them a blank stare. "What?"

"It's true," Tiffany said. "I know it's a shock. We didn't want to believe it ourselves."

"How do you guys know?" Laralyn asked. "That's heavy stuff."

"We figured it out. They didn't come out and say anything, but we know one of them did it. Based on what you told us and what we learned after we found out who they were."

Laralyn asked Harlan. "You didn't know who they were before you killed them?"

"We didn't have a clue. When we found out who they were we were glad we killed them. They had to be stopped sometime."

She looked at Tiffany. "But wasn't one of them your dad?"

"The guy, Mort, yes. I knew they were up to something but I didn't know what. We hung out, and when he told me he was my dad I really didn't know how to react. I mean, you know, he was never really there. Why waste love on something that doesn't love you back? He was too busy with other women to concern himself with my mom and I."

Laralyn's face grew sad.

Tiffany put her hand on Laralyn's knee. "You gonna be okay?"

"Yeah," a tear ran down her face. "It's just... It's just not something you expect to hear. It's just hard to believe."

Harlan said, "We dug around all we could. Yes, they were the only killers at the time. Provided it was them and they didn't get it from some random guy."

Laralyn started to cry.

Harlan handed her a tissue box.

"Thanks," she pulled a few out and wiped away the tears.

Harlan said, "Sorry we had to be the ones to tell you. We just thought you should know."

"Thanks for that."

"It's what family does," Tiffany told her. "We both love you a lot. You've been a huge benefit to us. We owe you a lot, and in due time we'd love to make it up to you."

"Really?" Laralyn crumpled the tissue in her hand. "You guys really think that much of me?"

"We do," Harlan told her. "You've been good for our team. We like the energy you bring. You're the breath of fresh air we needed."

"I do what I can."

"When we started this thing we didn't know how it would be received. I have to say, when you came along you helped people get the picture, get what we were about. And you brought the bus along. Before we met you we didn't have a bus."

Laralyn smiled.

"You're doing a good job," Tiffany told her. "I'm sure you'd do more if you could. We were blessed to find you, that you stumbled into our lives."

As it turned out Harlan and Tiffany just told her that to her to get her closer to them, to make their bond stronger. They didn't know who killed Laralyn's parents. But it was a possibility. Honestly, they really didn't give a damn. Harlan was just looking out for himself.

After Laralyn left the apartment, Tiffany and Harlan knew they had her in their hand. Tiffany felt a little bad about what they did, but she had to go with Harlan on what he wanted to do. The two got high again and made love. Laralyn, she went back to her apartment and cried herself to sleep. Just talking about her parents brought up a bunch of memories. Someone ripped a piece of her heart that day she'd never get back. She could travel the world looking for something to compensate, but nothing ever would. She'd have to live with the emptiness forever.

The next day after church, Laralyn approached Tiffany. They went to the dining room for lunch. There were always a variety of foods and drinks. Both of them got some pasta and a soda. They took a small table in the back of the dining room. The tables around them were all empty. Sometimes it was nice having a quiet lunch with a friend without loud talking from everyone.

Both ladies looked so beautiful.

They started talking about what a magical day it was, and about how they wished every day was just as fantastic.

Tiffany said, "About last night, I hope we didn't upset too much. I can only imagine what was going through your mind."

"It was okay," Laralyn said. "You know, I'd already come to terms I was never going to see them again, the reason doesn't matter. I think you just have to accept the fact we live in a world full of horrible things. But the thing we have to remember is to be positive and spread as much love as you can."

"That's a good way to look at things."

"It's better than the alternative."

"How do you mean?"

"You always have a choice how to handle stuff. You can let it defeat you, or, you can always rise above it."

"That's good. I like what I hear," Tiffany told her. "I hope you stay in our lives forever."

"I hope, too."

"Only you can make the dream happen."

"I'll have to remember that one."

Tiffany went on to tell her how Harlan appreciated what she was doing.

Laralyn shook her head slowly. "Yeah... Can I ask you something about him?"

"Shoot."

"It's something I've been wondering about."

"You can ask, what is it?"

Laralyn looked down at her food for a second, then back at Tiffany. "All of this, this place, us, this message he preaches, when's it all going to end? Is it going to end?"

Tiffany cocked her head at her. "I see."

"Don't get me wrong," Laralyn continued, "I love you guys more than you'll ever know and I love it here. I was just wondering if you had an idea?"

"We've talked about that before, a few times. To be honest with you, I don't think he wants things to end. There was a time he said he wanted to see things come to an end, but he changed his mind. I don't think he expected all of this."

"What was his real reason for starting this? I mean, I know what he tells people, and it all sounds good. But I know better. I can see through things."

"Yeah, I think the ruse has gone on for a little too long. He doesn't— Well, I shouldn't say that, because I don't know what he thinks. At first, he didn't believe anything he was talking about."

"And now?"

Tiffany tapped her fingers on the table and smiled. "He doesn't believe any of that. The plan all along was to get easy money. He first thought of this after he got out of prison. After he got out of prison he wanted to get married, but she didn't. It was this girl, Gretchen, he was seeing at the time. I don't think he wanted to get married. If I had to say, he was just wanting comfort after being locked up. It wasn't enough that they were boyfriend and girlfriend. He wanted something she didn't want. And that was about the time we started seeing each other. After they split he told Denny about his whole idea for this."

"Oh, I see. Does he ever worry about being caught?" Laralyn asked. "There's a lot of people at the compound."

"We've talked about it. But he said the way things are set up here cops will just think this is a legitimate thing. When anyone finds out the truth, what's going on here, he gets rid of them."

"Yeah, I know what he does. I feel sorry for them."

Tiffany laughed. "That's right. Yeah, he still does that."

"What have you guys been doing with the bodies?"

Tiffany nodded. "The woods across the field."

"Oh."

"And I'm not sure if they told you, but they had cells put in the basement."

"No, I didn't know. For what?"

"Nothing special. But as a form of punishment, he puts people in there."

"How many have gone in so far."

"None yet. It's just a matter of time, though. He was saying he'll only do it as a last resort."

"Damn."

"He's just using them for storage right now."

"I guess you have to put things somewhere."

"Between us, I hope that day never comes. I never wanted anyone to die."

"Why'd you go along with it?"

"You can say I'm weak if you want, but I didn't wanna get on his nerves."

"Oh, dear, I wasn't going to say that."

"I thought he might kill me. He assured me he wouldn't harm me."

"He ever threatened you?"

"Nothing like that. I just thought if he was willing to do it to others I'd probably be next."

"I'm glad he didn't kill you."

"Me, too. That wouldn't have been a good day for me." Laralyn smiled. "I gather that."

"I felt bad for those people," Tiffany took a drink of soda. "After thinking about it I was just glad it wasn't me."

"If it were you we wouldn't be having lunch today."

"Indeed."

"You have to be thankful for that."

"That's a little strange to think about," Tiffany told her. "Over my life, I've had to learn how to block things out."

"I hear that," Laralyn said. "When I was younger I couldn't understand why some things were the way they were. At some point, you just have to learn how to cope with things. Everything happens for a reason, right? That's what we tell ourselves, anyway."

"It makes you learn to be careful with things, not taking everything at face value."

"When you're right nothing can get in the way of that." Both women laughed.

After they finished eating one of the cooks came over to their table, a young girl they called Sally. She had long brown hair and blue eyes. She asked the two how their lunch was, and that if they wanted she could make them something special. They thanked her but told her they were fine.

"Well, if you change your minds," the girl said, "just let me know. I'll be happy to help."

35

Harlan ran into his old girlfriend, Gretchen, one day after one of his sermons. She was dressed all in black. She
had been sitting with everyone else. He was shocked, to
say the least. When he saw her all of that old stuff started
to stir around in his mind. They went back to his office
to talk. He looked her up and down and thought she
looked good. She told him that everyone had been nice
to her.

Harlan sat behind his desk, she took the chair across
from him.

Harlan said, "Can I get you something to drink or eat?"

"No, that's okay," Gretchen told him. "I'll keep that in
mind."

"Fair enough," Harlan took a pack of cigarettes and a
bottle of whiskey from the desk. He offered her the bottle.

She told him she didn't like the stuff anymore.

"What brought that on?" he asked.

"Oh, I dunno, I get too silly with it. It was fun while it
lasted but that's over."

"Never me," Harlan told her. "I know how to maintain
myself."

"You're so lucky."

Harlan smiled at her. "I'm blessed, what can I say? You
have to make your place in the world. What have you
been doing with yourself these days?"

"Oh, not much. Just living life. After we broke things
off I moved to Texas for a couple of years. I met a
lawyer there. We lived together for awhile but things
didn't work out. It's when I moved back here I met the
guy I married."

"You're married?"

"Not anymore. Caught him cheating. Long story I'd

rather not get into right now."

"Okay."

She went on. "Anyway, I heard about this place, about what you guys were doing, and thought I'd check it out."

"What do you think?" Harlan asked.

"I like it. I like what you've done with the place," she told him.

"It's getting there."

"It must've taken a lot of people to build?"

"It took a few years. If things go the way I want we will have more across the country."

"I like the sound of that."

"And then we'll go to other countries."

She laughed. "Harlan, you never disappoint, that's for sure. You always give it everything you have. I've always loved that about you."

"I do my best."

"Tell me, what's going on here?"

"We're just bringing the word of God to people."

"That all?"

"Of course."

She said, "I find that hard to believe. What, people live here?"

"Everyone here is here because they want to be. They want to live in this place. They can leave whenever they want. We don't have any contracts or anything. You have nothing to worry about. It's all on the up-and-up."

She frowned a little. "How long are you going to have this place?"

"Forever."

"Really?"

"It's my new job. There's a lot to do around here. It's the most work I've ever done."

A smile crossed her face. "Come, on, I bet you don't do much of anything. I know you, there's a con somewhere."

"You should stay and check things out. You'll see what it's all about. We're here to spread peace and love. I know you can get behind that."

"And these donations, where are all of those going? I hope to good use?"

"Donations are a big factor in it. We ask people to give what they feel comfortable with. They can come live here if they want. It's all legal."

"I'm not buying it."

Harlan shrugged. "That's okay, you think that way if you want. You're wrong. But if you stay I'll change your mind. I think you'll see how much I've changed."

"Stay? Like, live here?"

"Sure," Harlan told her. "I'll put you on the council."

"Sounds important."

"It is."

"Does it mean I get to make rules?"

"Yes, it does," he told her.

"That's good enough for me. Where do I sign?"

Harlan laughed. "It's nothing like that."

"Well, do we get paid?"

Harlan nodded. "That's what the donations are for. Well, a percentage, anyway. The rest is put towards things that are needed around here."

"I knew it. I knew there was a catch somewhere."

"Oh, nothing like that. Trust me. I understand your faith in me went out the window long ago."

"Whatever gave you an idea like that?"

He laughed.

She still wasn't sure about him. He told her they could get into more detail over lunch.

They went to lunch and he told her more about it.

He went around and had her meet everyone. He gave her a grand tour of the building and land. She liked everything she saw. She thought she could try it out and see how things went. Worst case scenario, she could always leave. She didn't have to do anything she didn't want. They talked it over and she agreed to stay. She didn't have anything else going on at the time.

Soon after she arrived, Gretchen became one of the heads of the community. At first, everyone thought it was a little strange a new girl would get that ranking so fast. There were whispers everywhere she went. There was this one time she slammed a girl's face into a mirror for calling her a nasty name. She wanted people to know she wasn't going to take shit from anyone. People got the message.

It got out here and Harlan used to be an item. Harlan had to hold some meetings to assure people everything would be fine, and that no one was showing anyone favoritism of any kind. Behind closed doors Denny questioned Harlan.

"You don't owe her anything. Why'd you say she could join us?"

Harlan thought about it. "Just trying to make peace with the whole thing."

"But she dumped you, man."

"I know it may sound crazy. I just think I should be the bigger person here. I want her to know everything is co-pacetic."

Denny said. "Tell me this, do you still have a thing for her?"

"Not at all. I have a girl. Nothing is gonna get in the way of that."

"Let's keep it that way. If things get fucked around here don't come crying to me. I won't be able to help with that."

"You have nothing to worry about."

"I hope that's the case."

"Okay, you won't hear me say anything else about it."

"Good."

36

Some of the others still had mixed emotions about Gretchen being there. They couldn't figure out why Harlan let her join them. As far as they knew she hurt him by rejection. Some thought she and Harlan would've made a great married couple. But they had their doubts when he made her part of the council. She didn't put in the time, that was the main thing they didn't like about it. He addressed everyone's concerns about it in one of their meetings when Gretchen wasn't there. He didn't want her to know that they talked about it.

 "Listen," Harlan said to them, "I know what you must be thinking, wondering why I'd let her join us, right? Well, the truth of the matter is this: She is still a big part of my life, and that's something that'll never go away. She and I, we've talked about it and we can go on being friends. I was glad for that. She stuck by me through a lot of shit. When I went to prison she stuck with me through all of that, and I can never forget that. You know, she could've cheated on me many times, screwed the whole town, she didn't do that. And the whole thing about her turning down the marriage thing, it was just one of those things, I'm sure it's happened to you before. We were just at different stages, and just thought about things on other levels. Yeah, I was hurt at first. Then, I didn't understand why she didn't wanna marry me. After some time apart I realized why she didn't want to. It was a harsh thing to face. I dealt with it the best I could. And, sure, demons show their heads before too long."

Everyone shook their heads.

"But," Harlan continued, "if any of you have any issues with it I'd appreciate it if you said something right now. If you have something best get it out now. This'll be the last time we ever talk about this matter. If I were you I'd just be thinking it was none of my fuckin' business and just move on. Next topic. But I'm not you, am I? I don't think so. I think you guys would have better things to talk about. Are you guys not bored with any of that? I never understood starting rumors about anyone. And think about this, if someone finds out they may beat your ass. You're lucky I don't beat any of you. Yeah, I wouldn't do that to any of you."

Mallory said, "Something I guess I never knew, did she know about Tiffany at the time?"

"She didn't," Harlan said.

"So, it was okay for you to cheat, right?"

"Where is this going, Mal?"

"Nothing. I was just wondering, you know? Just need to get the full picture of everything. I like to know all about my friends."

"I see."

"Both happened about the same time. But Tiff knew about her, right?"

Harlan shrugged. "She knew. It didn't seem to bother her. Looking back, that may have been a mistake having both going on at the same time. But I wanted both, and those things just happen. I guess I felt a little guilty. I was mad at Gretchen for making me get that janitor job, but now, I thank her every day she made me get it. If it wasn't for her Tiffany and I most likely would've never met."

Mallory said, "Glad you made it out alive. If Denny ever found out I cheated he'd kill me."

"I would," Denny said.

"That's not very nice," Mallory gave him an ugly look.

"Hey, man, no one's gonna get my baby."

Harlan chuckled. "I'd agree with Denny."

A few questioned whether or not they could trust her. Harlan told them they could.

They continued talking about business. Everything was becoming a business with the place. Harlan didn't realize how much work it was going to be when he first set all of it up. Along with the telethons they also had people calling, wanting to donate money. It got pretty unorganized in the room a lot of times, keeping up with who was donating what, what they were wanting to tell people, and keeping everything running. It didn't help matters that they were all on drugs—weed, coke, acid, meth, whatever they could get their hands on. For more revenue they had some of their people go on the streets selling drugs. Their friend Rod, he started making big drug deals all over the world. He always swore that he wouldn't get caught again, that he wouldn't be able to make it in prison.

On a Tuesday afternoon in October of 1984 Rod was pulled over for going a little too fast down the highway. They found ten kilos of coke. He was arrested. Since he was still on probation he was facing a few years in prison. Rod told everyone he couldn't do that kind of time. A week later he was found dead in a motel room. He had stabbed himself in the heart with a knife. It was a mess. The whole situation had cast a dark cloud over the compound. No one from the compound went to the funeral his family had for him. They had their ceremony for their fallen brother.

They all gathered in the main room. A few candles were lit and Rod's picture was hung on the wall. They wanted his body to pay their last respects, but they had to make do with what they had. Most of them were glad they had something. It was more than they had for some of the others.

One of the guys, Foxx King, whose real name was

Chris Jones nodded at Harlan. "Why are we doing this?"

"What?" Harlan said. "We're paying our respects."

"Waste of time if you as me."

"I don't recall anyone asking you. This was a good friend of mine," Harlan walked closer to the man. "See, Foxx, I'm not sure if anyone taught you about respect. Have you ever thought about being a teacher?"

"Teacher?"

"Yes."

"Like school?"

"Something like that."

"Nah. You have to go to school to be a teacher, and I'm not in school."

Harlan chuckled at the man. "See, already teaching...."

Foxx cocked his head at the man in charge.

Harlan walked over to one of the candles, picked it up, and brought it over to where Foxx was.

"What are you going to do with that?" Foxx asked.

Harlan looked down at the candle, then back at Foxx. "Today's important for you."

"Oh, why's that?"

"Because you don't have to worry about going to school to be a teacher."

"Huh?"

Harlan threw the candle in the guy's face. "You're gonna teach these people today. Teach them all to have respect, to have respect for everyone around you. Your life isn't the only one that's important."

Foxx fell to the floor screaming and holding his face.

Harlan looked at the others. "Pardon me, that'll only take a few minutes."

Everyone had a shocked expression on their face as Harlan dragged Foxx in front of everyone.

Harlan said to everyone. "Hopefully none of you do what this piece of shit just did. All of us here need to respect one another—it's not that difficult to do. All it requires, good manners. Now, I understand if you guys don't have these good manners. Most of you come from broken homes. Most of your parents never taught you any different. I understand. Some of you, your parents didn't even like you. That's a real bummer if you ask me. I could never relate," Harlan looked down at the man on the floor. "This guy, he knows not what he does. It's true, God's about forgiveness but he's also about vengeance for those that deserve it," he kicked Foxx. "Piece of shit. If he was on fire I wouldn't even piss on him to put it out. Motherfucker comes in here and says that shit about my friend? I should blow his head off, paint the walls red with him."

Everyone got quiet. Nobody wanted to say anything for fear they could be next.

"Could I have some help over here, please?" Harlan asked.

Denny and some other guys came over. They started to beat Foxx. Even though Harlan told everyone to look at the beating, most looked away. They couldn't take it. Some yelled for him to stop. After they finished they sent Foxx to the doctor. He was under medical care for about a week. After he was out Harlan told him that he'd better not tell anyone, that if he ever did something worse would happen to him.

37

Four times a week they had to attend church—which was held by Harlan in the main building. He would preach for a few hours at a time. He would talk about how good God was, and if you didn't believe like he did or in anything else that it was a sin. Everyone had to address him as "Lord." There were a set of rules and if you broke any you'd be punished; either a few hours in isolation in a closet, or, you would be remanded to some sort of hard labor, given the severity of the offense. For the most part, everyone followed the rules.

The ones who got to leave and go to their jobs on the outside, someone was always keeping tabs on them. There were a few instances where people fled, but they were caught, brought back to the compound, and punished. Soon they had the cops showing up at the compound asking about the missing. Harlan would tell them that everyone agreed to live on the grounds and no one was forced to do so. The police, not being able to do much about it at would leave it alone.

Every day of church he had a camera crew there. He wanted to capture every minute he could. He waited until everyone settled and then began to speak.

"I'd like to start by welcoming everyone today," Harlan said. "And people viewing this from your homes, I'd like to thank you for tuning in," he placed both hands on the podium. "For those of you who don't know, my name is Harlan Reeves. Some friends and I started the Church of Modo some time ago, and we spent the past few years traveling around this great country recruiting people for our cause. Our collective goal was to bring the word of God to those who needed it. We welcomed souls from all around, those who were left to fend for themselves, left abandoned without a home. And these are young kids. Young adults just starting to get their own identity."

Some of the people started to talk but Denny told them they'd have to wait until the end.

Harlan said, "I dunno about you, but if I had to walk this life alone I may have ended it for myself. I mean, with no friends, or loved ones, what's the point of it all?"

A few people started to clap.

Harlan pressed on. "We all have our paths we walk down. It's our choice what we're going to do with the time given to us. I know, I know, some of you may say that everything is part of God's divine plan, that he knows what he's doing. Some ask if he knows all and how everyone thinks, then he must know what murderers think about—after all, he created us in his image. If you take those words to heart then God must be evil or have evil tenancies. But if God is so evil then why create us to begin with? People have been turning that over in their heads for years. See, guys, Satan, he's a sneaky character. The Devil, whatever you wanna call him, is a very clever being. He'll have you believe all of it is God's work—it's not true at all. Long before you or I were created the two forces were in Heaven. There was a power struggle, and one thought the other was in the wrong. The Devil wanted to take the throne for himself. God created Hell and threw him into it forever. The Devil tried, and is still trying, to capture what he thinks should be his, to have ultimate power. So, this war rages constantly. With all the good that's in this world there are a lot of bad things in it—and surprise, that's Satan! He, like God, is gathering troops as we speak. Both think they're in the *right* and the other is in the *wrong*. I ask you, do you want to live in a place of peace and love, or, would you rather live in a dark place?"

People shifted in the crowd.

"The dark one always wants to keep you down, every-one must know this. He has ways of manipulating people into thinking what he wants them to think. You can say the same thing about God, too, but God has given you so much. All he asks in return is that people just believe him and his message. He even went so far as to have his only son, Jesus, die for you and me to prove himself to us. And yet some of, you don't believe in any of it. Well, I know Jesus is up in Heaven looking upon us with a smile on his face, saying to everyone up there how he can't wait to come back and get us all. I don't think it's gonna come as a shock to you but we're all gonna die one day."

Harlan went on to tell them about his past life of sin, and he apologized to those who had heard it before—which, for those who were on the road with the crew, they heard it too many times to count. To the followers, they just took it as a good method for Harlan to put things in perspective for people, to know they can change their lives through the power of God.

The thing he always wanted to get across to make the con work was that they had to believe what he was telling them. He told himself that younger people were more impressionable than any other group. When he was thinking all of this up he told himself that he didn't want to come off as too preachy and boring. He figured if it was boring they'd just ignore him. He didn't want to tell too many stories from the Bible. Some of that was due to the fact he couldn't really figure out the morals in some of the stories, and in others, he didn't even care what it was trying to say.

Harlan said, "Now like I was telling the new people we have here, we've been all around this country and have seen a lot of things. Some places I wouldn't mind going back to, others I hope I never see again. I saw a lot of Satan out there and not enough God. I heard someone say that they wished Jesus would come back again so they could kill him. God welcomes all colors. Everyone should welcome all types of people. Part of the reason I started this was to have people join together in love and understanding."

He looked at the time and saw he only had two minutes. He made his final remarks and told everyone to love one another and to have a good day.

After the sermon, when everyone was leaving, Harlan met some new people who were curious about what was going on. He got good feedback from people who said they loved what he and his friends were doing. They got a few new people that day. Harlan liked seeing the joy in their eyes.

In the next sermon, he talked the whole hour about God's love and how important it was to accept him into your heart. And you couldn't accept him if you were still living a life of sin. He told them if they were sinning and they lied about it that God would punish them. He said when you got punished by God it was just his way of showing that love has to be tough at times, and that wasn't the dark one at work.

The next few weeks went off without incident. At the end of each sermon, he asked visitors and viewers at home for donations. Some questioned where the money was going. People asked Harlan and he would just tell them that it's part of the machine that makes the beast run, that it was necessary to do what needed to be done. The subject of money would get swept under the rug and it wouldn't be questioned for another month or so.

Harlan and the company were very happy with the reception from everyone. They thought he was a prophet. The only people who knew it was all a con were Tiffany, Laralyn, Denny, Mallory, Clint, Zed, and a few others. A lot of the people had questions, but they were soon defused when Harlan heard about it. He would tell them it was okay to question things now and then but they just needed to trust him. And he told everyone that if they didn't like his answers they could leave. He told them he was no one's father.

38

At least twice a week he would call for everyone living
in the compound to come to the big recreation room.
He'd tell all the women to get naked and dance for all
the men, then, he would tell them to take a man and have
sex with him in front of everyone.

"The thing is," Harlan said, "don't think of it as being
obscene. Women, God gave you this fine body to serve
men, and men serve women. If he didn't want it like this
he wouldn't have made you as he did. He gave all of you
a gift, the gift of your bodies. There's no shame in it. It's
a practice that's older than time itself. No need to be
afraid by any of it. It'll become normal for you."

A few people objected at first, but then after Harlan
spun his web of lies they agreed. When they were done
with their dance they had to find another guy or girl to
have sex with—this would go on for a few hours. He
would select a different woman every night to be with.
Everyone seemed to be fine with it. Tiffany, she never
seemed to care. Just as long as they both knew where the
other's heart lay.

The same things would go on week after week. It got to
where they looked forward to it. Everything became routine. It was just the way things were. Now and then people would ask Harlan about the way things were. He
would just tell them sometimes it's best not to ask too
many questions. They didn't like it but had no choice.

One day after Harlan and Tiffany finished making love
they shared a joint in their big bed. He loved everything
about her, the way she moved, the way she talked, the
way she thought, everything.

"There's something I need to tell you," she told him.

Harlan looked at her. "What?"

"I need you to promise me something first, though."

"What is it, babe?"

"I need you to promise you won't get mad."

"What would I get mad about?"

Tiffany sat up in the bed. "When I tell you this I don't want you to think any less of me. I need your support."

"Why would I think less of you? You know how I feel about you."

She stared into his eyes for a few minutes. "I'm pregnant."

"Really?" he kept his eyes trained on her. "You sure?"

"I'm sure."

"That's some big news."

"It is."

"Why did you think I'd think any less of you?"

"I don't know," she said. "Just didn't know how you'd react to the news. I've never had to tell a guy anything like that before."

"Oh, babe, you don't have to worry about that. It's fantastic. That's the best thing I've heard in awhile. I needed that news today."

"I'm glad."

He crawled out of bed. "I'm going to be a father. That's wild, man! Just think about everything we can do. We'll be a nice little family. I couldn't think of anything better. When did you find out?"

"Went to the doctor yesterday."

"Why didn't you say anything? I would've gone with you."

Tiffany said, "I wasn't for sure, and I didn't want to get your hopes up. I didn't want you disappointed if I wasn't. I'd hate to see that happen."

He drew a big smile. "Well, baby, this calls for a celebration. I know, I know, you can't get too wild now that you're about to have a kid—don't want it deformed the kid or anything, that wouldn't be good for us. But I'm sure a little couldn't hurt. I'm not a doctor or anything but it'll be fine."

"I suppose not."

"Unless you—"

"Unless what?"

"Unless you decide not to have it."

"Of course I want to have it," she told him. "What were you thinking? You say you don't want the kid?"

Harlan shrugged. "Not at all. I didn't know what you wanted, dear. In no way was I trying to put words in your mouth, thoughts in your head."

She got out of bed and stood in front of him. "I'm telling you I want to be a mother. I've wanted it for a long time. I wanna be the best mom ever."

"That's good. I'm glad for you. That's a good thing to want to be."

"And you'll be a good father," she told him.

"Should be fun. Do you want it to be a boy or girl?"

"Doesn't matter to me. I just want the baby to be healthy."

"Me, too."

"And we need to make sure we bring the kid up in a safe place."

"Yeah."

"If we're gonna have the baby around here we need to make sure to keep things clean."

"Clean?"

"All the stuff that goes on here," she said. "I know all. I know things that go on around here that no one talks about. I know you."

"Baby, you know we keep nothing from one another. I'm an open book. This place, the kid, when they come along, they won't be exposed to any of this. I promise."

"How can you promise something like that if we're still living here?"

"Then, we'll move."

"Really?"

"We'll build a separate house on the property."

"You sure?"

"We'll figure it out."

"Thanks."

Harlan said, "I could get a little house built on the grounds."

"Really?"

"Sure."

They talked more about how they wanted the kid to be and what they wanted for the future. They told their friends about the pregnancy. There were lots of hugs. They had a big party and most people got sloppy drunk.

October, 3rd 1987, Luke William Reeves was born. Both parents were out of their minds, getting high and drunk every day. Some people asked Harlan why he'd bring a child into this place. He would tell them he had to make sure his legacy was going to last.

Tiffany told everyone she had to make up for lost time by staying drunk and high. The couple would spend most of the day locked in their room enjoying one an-other.

39

Luther Frost was only sixteen when he joined Harlan Reeves and his Church of Modo insanity. Luther came from a broken home, as many of the younger members did. Luther was one of these young kids who felt lost in the world, misunderstood, someone who felt everyone forgot about him. Even though his parents told him he was their pride and joy he had his doubts. He didn't think he had a place in the world. He packed a few things in a bag and hit the road. He didn't have a plan. He just wanted to get out, wanted something new. After walking for a few hours he found himself on a crowded street. Luther noticed a group of people around a man giving a speech. It was this guy, Harlan Reeves, talking about joining him in something he called Church of Modo. He became interested in what he was hearing. He liked all the people he talked with. They were all folks around his age. They joked and laughed as they listened. At the end of it, Harlan asked for a show of hands of those who wanted to join. Luther was surprised to see how many people were buying what he was selling.

 At first, when Luther got to the compound he wasn't sure if that was where he was supposed to be. He didn't know quite how to act in the situation. As he got around to talking with the others he understood a lot of people felt the way he did. A sense of relief washed over him, knowing that he wasn't alone, knowing there were others like him. For the first time in his life, he felt like he connected with people. All the years he was in school he felt out of place. He wasn't a very popular kid. Anytime he'd find a girl who showed interest in him, at first, things seemed okay but before things got too deep the girl would always tell him she just wanted to be friends. He felt rejected. He told himself after that happened that no one could hurt him if he didn't let them get too close. But deep down he held out hope. He saw people in happy, healthy relationships and wanted that for himself.

He started to get along pretty well inside the compound. He took a job in the kitchen. He liked the job and those he worked with. He liked the fact he was helping people. He took pride that people would eat the food he made, that would use it to power their bodies so they could do good things.

He met a girl, Brenda, while staying at the compound. He liked her and imagined a future with her in it. They dated for five months before they broke things off. It was a little awkward for the both of them because they still saw each other all the time. In hindsight one of them could've just left, but they didn't want to do that. Both of them wanted to be a part of the place.

A few weeks after they called things off Brenda started seeing another guy, Ross. Luther didn't like Ross. When Ross got a job in the kitchen he and Luther got into a fistfight over her. Some of the others who were there broke it up before things got too out of hand before Harlan found out about it. There was always a chance someone would tell him but no one ever did. That was one of the rules, Harlan didn't like anyone fighting. He didn't like the attention something like that would bring.

One day Luther crossed Harlan's path as they both walked down the main hall. Harlan was on his way to his office, Luther on the way to his apartment. They nodded when they saw each other.

"Hey, Harlan," Luther said, "I hope you're having a good day."

"It's pretty good. Just doing what I do."

"I know what you mean. I'm just going back to the

apartment. Need to get some rest."

"I see."

"Hey, I'm glad I ran into you. I wanted to tell you if you needed anything I'm here for whatever you want. I think it's a good thing what you're doing here."

"Thanks."

Luther smiled. "Everyone has to earn their keep, am I right?"

"It's true," Harlan looked at him. "Glad to hear you say that. Say, what are you doing right now?"

"I'm a team player."

Harlan told him when he woke up from his nap to come to his office, that there was something he wanted to run by him. After Luther woke from the nap he walked over to where Harlan's office was. He knocked on the door and was told to come in. When he walked into the office Harlan was behind his desk looking over some paper-work.

Harlan looked up. "How's it going, kid?"

"Better now that I got some rest."

"That's an important thing. Not enough rest, it'll kill ya if you aren't careful."

"It does."

"I was about to go to the cafeteria and get something to eat. Wanna join me?"

"Sure. I can always eat."

Harlan laughed. "That's the other thing that keeps you going. If drugs aren't your thing you have to get some-thing."

"I know."

Harlan walked over to him. "You do drugs?"

"I don't do any of that stuff."

"We're gonna have to change that."

"Nah, that's okay. I'm fine."

The leader shook his head. "Nah, nah, nah, that's not gonna work. You need to be introduced to the sweet stuff sometime."

"Is it gonna kill me?"

"You should be fine."

"Any trick to it?"

"Yeah, don't die from it," Harlan laughed. "Oh, man, we're gonna have good times."

"Yeah?"

"Why wouldn't we?"

"I dunno."

The two went to get something to eat. As they ate lunch Harlan asked Luther if he wanted to go undercover for him, to help spy on people. Harlan wanted to make sure everyone was following the rules of the compound, rules Harlan and his friends made. He didn't want to leave any stone unturned. Harlan needed to make sure he could trust the people he was living with.

"I can do that," Luther told Harlan. "Yes, sir, sounds like fun."

"And it pays."

"That's good. Everyone needs money."

"This thing, it's turning into a big operation. Sad to say I can't look into everything. When I first started this I had no idea it was going to grow like this. But now that it has we need more help. This could be a big thing for you."

"I can see that."

"Let me ask you, do you ever think about your parents since you've been here?"

"Sometimes. Sometimes I wake up at night, thinking about the two of them. I'll be doing some everyday thing and it'll just hit me. I don't know if they ever think of me or not. I think if they cared I wouldn't be here with you today. Nah, fuck them.”

 “Well, that’s normal. I’m sure they’re okay. Here’s the thing, they probably got to a point where they said you’d have to make your way. Everyone has to grow up some-time, you know?”

 “It would’ve been nice for them to contact me.”

 “So, you always gonna cry about it?”

 “No.”

 “We are your family now. We’re all in this together. Ev-eryone treating you well?”

 “They’ve all been nice. No problems from anyone.”

 “Good, that’s good. You can’t always be at odds with those you live with. If you do then you have a problem. You can’t live like that, you know? It can get tough sometimes, believe me. You just have to push that stuff out sometimes. I invited the crazy world to live in these walls. We all just have to stay focused on what we’re do-ing here.”

 “Yeah.”

 “Now, believe it or not, I’ve been watching you for some time. Had to make sure I was making the right de-cision. See, in the past, I’ve been known to not make the most sound choices.”

 “You mean when you went to prison?”

 “That among other things.”

 “No, yeah, I understand what you’re saying. It’s about evolving. We’re always evolving.”

 “That’s some of it, sure. I just wanna leave something people will remember me for.”

 “It’s going good so far.”

 “It needs to stay that way. The sky’s the limit.”

 “Yes, sir,” Luther nodded. “So, this job you want me to do, spying on people, what do you want done when I see something?”

 “Just tell me. I’ll handle it.”

"Violence?"

Harlan sighed. "We need to make sure everyone is on the same page. We don't need to get our goals compromised."

"Yeah, I can see where that can be a problem."

"And I'd hate to see anyone get hurt around here. Sometimes people don't know what's best for them. It's up to God to tell them. It's up to those who work through God to tell them, and make sure they do the right thing."

"The right thing, huh?"

"Someone has to do it."

"A lot of times they don't listen."

"It comes with the territory. You can only do your best. Try to influence the best you can."

Luther laughed. "They wouldn't listen to me. I've never been the type to take charge like that."

"It takes time."

Luther said, "Who knows? With this spy stuff, you know, it's like I'm gonna be a secret agent or something, you know?"

"However you wanna look at it, sure," Harlan said. "And you know, if this goes well, there will be bigger things to come. The future is yours. It just depends on how willing you are to do what needs to be done. You'll find it won't be easy all the time, but what is? This is the thing you might have been born to do. Some people have it, some don't."

"Hey, I'm all about it," Luther told him. "You can count on me."

"I know you won't let me down."

"I'll try not to."

"You'll get used to it."

The two continued talking as they ate. Luther felt good

about himself like he was part of something. As they talked Luther started looking at Harlan as somewhat of a father figure. He wanted to please him. At that instant, all the troubles he had with people faded away. He asked Harlan about being part of the council. All the man told him was that they'd have to wait and see what happened. He went on to ask Harlan about the single girls on the council.

"We have a few," Harlan told him.

"I bet you could have a good time with them."

"That's the idea."

The next day Luther started his job spying on people. He was told not to discuss the job with anyone except those on the council. He would go where groups would be. It wasn't out of character for him to be seen around people. He was liked by many. At first, he felt a little guilty about doing what he was doing. But then he figured out the great things that could come. If he played his cards right things would work out well for him. Someday he could take his place on the council. The only thing, he didn't like Denny. He figured when he got on the council he would have to beat Denny up and show him he wasn't anyone to mess with. Harlan told him that you had to stand your ground and let them know you aren't one to be messed with.

Luther would report to the council at least once a week, sometimes twice. He'd go up to Harlan's office when he knew no one was watching. He knocked.

Denny answered. "Come on in, kid."

Luther walked in and nodded to all of them.

Harlan said, "Well, well, well, look who it is! It's my spy," he laughed. "How are you doing, kid?"

"I'm good," Luther said. "Just been hanging around," he looked around at the people in the office. "You guys doing okay?"

Everyone nodded or shrugged.

"Well, look at ya now," Harlan told him. "It takes a lot to do what you're doing. Don't think of it as doing a bad thing. You're performing an outstanding service for your fellow man. We're all proud. Can we get ya a drink or anything?"

"Thanks," Luther said. "That means a lot. No, I don't need a drink."

"More for us. Come, boy, take a seat," Harlan pointed to a chair.

Luther sat. "It's been a pretty nice day around here."

Denny nodded at him. "You gettin' along okay?"

"I guess."

"Nobody makin' problems for you?"

"Not at all."

"'Cause you know, if there is, tell us, we'll figure it out for ya. You're gettin' closer to being one of us. You say the word we'll kick someone's ass. We know our way around a fight."

Luther smiled. "No, no, I'm okay. There won't be any need for that."

"Just making sure. You never know."

"If something comes up I can handle myself."

"Good, good," Denny told him. "But if things do turn sideways you know where to turn, right?"

After some small talk, Luther handed them a notebook.

"Let's see what we have here," Denny opened the notebook.

Luther said, "Something I forgot to put in there, I was at lunch yesterday and Drew was talking about how he thinks something is going on here with this. He said, well hinted, that he might get the cops involved. He said things don't seem on the up-and-up around her, that's something stinks. He didn't say what, though. He was saying how he thinks something isn't right with all the people who have left. I guess the guy thinks there's more behind it. He was saying how he thinks things should change. I dunno, I guess he thinks he could do a better job. He might just be talking out of his ass. I didn't hear him say anything about taking anyone on or anything, but you have to wonder. I didn't say anything to him. I just let it go. Figured he was pissed about something and just took it out on this place."

Zed told them. "Guy thinks he can do better? Hey, you can give him a shot, and see if he has the balls for it. You might get an answer before you know it. I mean, what the hell is going on with these people? Why the fuck do they wanna turn on you?"

Clint said, "Might need to bring him in, tell him how things are. We can't let this stuff go. He might pull something?"

Harlan glanced around the room. "We'll keep an eye on him. Make sure he doesn't try anything. Can't afford to have this guy going around, telling people about conspiracy theories or whatever."

"That's the thing," Laralyn said. "You get these imitators that want to be you, Harlan. But there can only be one Harlan Reeves. They all want to be king."

"Thanks for that one," Harlan smiled.

"They see the good you're doing and they want to do the same. You inspire people, Harlan. They wanna taste the sky where you are."

Mallory said, "I've heard girls talk, word around is they wanna fuck you."

Tiffany said, "Can you blame them?"

Zed shifted in his seat. "I've heard people say it, too. They all wanna fuck the king. They know where you live if they want more. I know my girl, if she ever said that shit to me I think I'd go the-fuck-crazy. I'd tell her if that's what she wanted you better fuck-fuck twenty-four hours a day, and don't call me back. Fuck that shit. I can't go there."

The girls laughed.

Harlan thanked them.

Zed told Harlan. "Something tells me your girl would kick their ass if they tried to get with you. I've never seen her do it, but I think Tiff could rip someone up. I dunno, something like that I'd watch. I need to get my popcorn ready. That'd be better than going to the movies."

Tiffany smiled at Zed. "Who me? Oh, I'd never do anything like that. I wouldn't dream of it. I'd just shoot the bitch."

"I could see that."

Tiffany made her fingers into the shape of a gun and shot.

"You need to put that on a memo," Zed told her.

"It's the power," Luther said. "They wanna be with someone who has the power."

Denny continued with the notebook. "This Chester Rowe, this says you thought he was acting strange?"

"That's right," Luther said.

"In what way?"

"The other day I was roaming around, all hush-hush-hush, he was talking to everyone and saying he had a big secret he wanted to share with everyone. I was gonna snoop around some more, and see if I can get something more. But that could be nothing. That guy, he's a crazy one."

"Yeah, I've talked to him a few times. Seems like a good guy. But things always have ways of unraveling. That's just the sad truth of things. If I told you all of my experiences with that we'd be here all day."

"I can see that. Yeah, I dunno, things just seemed a little off, a little odd. On the other hand, it could be nothing.

The thing I had to tell myself, I had to tell myself while I was spying was that I was seeing things differently. Everyone else was acting like they always did."

"That's a good point," Denny told him.

Harlan added. "Just don't let on what you're doing. That wouldn't be good. It would be pure anarchy."

"I get that," Luther told him.

Tiffany said, "We want you to know you're an instrumental part of the team. We couldn't trust this with just anyone."

"Don't think of it as a bad thing," Laralyn said. "If the others found out, sure, they wouldn't trust you. We want everyone to get along the best they can. We all, all of us, are here for one reason, because one man brought us together. Think about this, where would you be if Harlan hadn't come along?"

"I'm not sure," Luther said. "I know I would've moved away from where I was. I just knew I needed to get away from there. Sure as hell didn't wanna become one of those cats you see who worked himself to death, not having anything to show for it, just doing whatever to get by every day."

"What would you like to do?" Laralyn asked him.

"I dunno. I like to write and the movies. I was thinking I could get into that business one day."

"Sounds groovy," she said. "I dig that stuff, too."

"It's fun to make things up."

Laralyn smiled. "It is. When I was a little girl I loved playing dress-up, pretending I was someone else."

Luther nodded. "I can see that. I think you'd be good with something like that."

"You think?"

"You better believe it. When I get something going I'll have to give you a call."

"Sounds fun."

"I bet it will be. You'll be a star. You have the look for it."

"Well, thank you. That means a lot."

Denny said, "You two should get a room."

Everyone laughed.

Denny continued talking to Luther about his report. In the end, they told him to let them know if there was anything they needed to know about. After some more talk, Luther was dismissed.

40

When he left the office he went over and got something to eat, a burger and fries. He was hungry and hadn't eaten anything all day. He met up with some people and had a few laughs. In a lot of ways, he was very thankful for everyone he met at the compound. When he got back to his apartment Laralyn was waiting by his door. She was dressed in a short red skirt and smelled amazing. Her lipstick complemented her skirt quite well.

"Hi," Luther said.

"Where were you at?"

"Had to get something to eat."

"Oh, I see. Hope it was good."

"It was."

"What did you have?"

"A burger and fries."

"Oh, those are some of my favorites. Next time we'll have to go together."

Luther walked closer to her. "Sure. We'll have to do that sometime. I'd love that."

"What are you doing?" she asked.

"Not much. I was just going to go in and relax."

"You want some company?"

"I can always use some of that. I don't have any plans."

"Great," she said. "I bet we can figure something out. Got any dope inside?"

"You know I do."

"Perfect."

"You always have to have some dope around."

"Got that right."

They went into the apartment and enjoyed one another, drank, and had mad sex all night. The next morning, by the time Luther woke Laralyn had already left. Later that day he tracked her down when she was eating lunch. She was sitting at a table alone. He sat across from her.

"Why didn't you stick around? I could've made you something to eat," Luther asked her.

Laralyn looked at him and brushed the hair from her face. "I needed to leave early."

"Why?"

"I couldn't afford to be caught. If someone saw me that could be bad."

"How come? I mean, we're two humans who like each other. Shouldn't matter what anyone else thinks. I think when that happens it just means that they're jealous of what they don't have."

"Maybe."

"Well?"

"It's against the rules. Harlan has a few rules we in the council have to follow. I know it may sound stupid or whatever, but that's just how he is."

"You're joking, right?"

"No," she said. "It's all pretty stupid. But he told us if we violated any rule he'd punish us."

"In what way?"

"We will be locked away in the basement, if not dead. All the rules center around fraternizing."

"What's wrong with that?"

"He told us separation is important to what the mission is, that classes are important, and that we all have a role to play in all of this. One of the things he'd say, he'd tell us you have to push people down, hold them there to inspire them to rise above."

"Something about that doesn't sound right."

"He said making that distinction is paramount."

Luther said, "That just sounds stupid. Who's he to say who you can spend time with? Where do I fit in? We aren't little kids or anything."

"I can tell you you're pretty high on my list, babe. I have to say you sure know how to please a lady. I see good things in your future. The both of us can go far if we keep this up. Harlan, something might happen to him one day. Someone's gotta be there to fill those shoes. I like you. When he gave you the assignment I knew you'd do great."

"Is something going to happen to him?"

"Of course not. I'm just saying you have to prepare for anything."

"That's true. But what about Tiffany? Wouldn't she pick up the reins?"

"I'm sure she would, but everyone needs help. And you're talking about a big project."

Luther shook his head. "I can see that, sure. It never hurts to get help from others. People say that might be a sign of weakness, but they aren't in your shoes. They don't know what it's like to be you. I mean, that can say they do all they want but they don't know. You have all these guys running their mouths, trying to get their two cents even though it doesn't amount to anything."

"Exactly. I tell people that all the time. Well, not all the time, but you know what I mean. It's all just a bunch of chatter. Everyone wants something."

"Sure, sure. Yeah, they gotta understand. You're right, you're fuckin' right. If you wanna teach you have to get on their level."

"That makes sense."

"Don't get me wrong, I'm not saying I'm smarter than the next guy or anything, it's just that they might not fully understand what you're trying to tell them. Let's face it, with some people you can try and try and still not get anywhere. I don't know much but I know that."

Laralyn took a drink of her water. "It's anyone's guess. Who knows anymore what goes on in people's heads?

You can try all you want and still get nothing.”

“Yeah.”

“So tell me,” Laralyn said, “what do you want for your future?”

Luther thought about it. “I wanted to go to college and get a degree in English.”

“Is that so.”

“With all of this, I’m not sure exactly when I’m gonna go. I need to get it over with as soon as I can. You can make a pretty good living teaching.”

“Why English?”

“I’ve always been good at it. In high school, one of my teachers told me I should get into writing and get something published.”

“That’s pretty cool.”

“Thanks. Yeah, I do write. I’m working on a novel. My hopes are I can get it published.”

“How long have you been working on it?”

“A few months.”

Laralyn said, “What’s it about?”

“Can’t tell you that.”

“I won’t tell.”

“It’s not that or anything. It’s just that it’s too early to explain. It’s a process. That may sound dumb, I know.”

“Not even. I understand.”

“Thanks. Some people don’t get it.”

“It’s okay. Just show it to me when you want. I can wait. I’ve always loved surprises.”

“And believe me, you’ll love this one.”

“Can’t wait, babe.”

Luther looked at her. “What about you?”

“I never really thought about college. I had to stop going to high school when I was sixteen. I had to help my parents with the farm. Even if they never needed me I think I would’ve quit anyway. I didn’t like that place. I thought I'd get back to it someday."

"What would you want to do?"

"I would like to get into fashion, like making a line of clothes."

"That'd be good. Well, you already have that."

"Have what?"

"Fashion," he told her.

"You think so?"

"I know so."

She smiled. "I wouldn't know how to get into that world. I'm sure I'd have to go to school for it."

"Well, maybe now that you're out on your own it'll give you more drive to do what you want."

"I'm pretty hard-headed."

Luther got some food and they talked more.

41

As time went on Luther would tell Harlan about little infractions. He let the big ones slip his mind. He knew telling Harlan about some of the big infractions could very well result in the person getting hurt.

Luther and some of the others never wanted to say anything for fear of what would happen. Something had to be done but they didn't know what. As the meetings and spying continued Luther started feeling bad about what he was doing. There was a part of him that wanted it all to be over. He didn't know if he could tell Harlan or not. He didn't want anything to happen.

One day while eating lunch with some people the subject of what they were doing at the compound came up.

One of the guys, Dustin, said. "I don't know about this anymore."

"What do you mean?" Luther asked.

"This church," Dustin said. "It seems to me if this was so important that he'd want to take this outside the walls. Wouldn't he want his word to get to as many people as he could? Maybe I'm wrong in saying this?"

"I think you are wrong," Luther told him. "I think it would be best if you just went with what he wants."

"Why?"

"It's not your job to question him."

"I don't get it."

"It's not your job to do so."

Dustin said, "Who the fuck are you to tell me what my business is?"

"You don't wanna go there with me, man."

Another guy at the table, Josh, said, "You just need to forget about it, Dustin. Don't worry about it. Don't wanna get busted up do you, Dustin?"

Dustin looked at Josh. "You sayin' you wanna fight me? Well, bring it on, boy. I'm always up for a good fight. Give it your best shot."

Josh started to get out of his seat, but Luther told him not to move. Josh mumbled something to himself but did what he was asked.

Dustin laughed. "You didn't have to do that for my sake. Come on, I'll put the little fuck to sleep."

"No you won't," Luther told the man.

"Why?"

"Because I said so."

"And I should listen to you?"

"You will if you don't wanna get hurt."

"The balls on you! You're all grown. Look at you. Yeah, yeah, yeah, give me what you got."

Luther said, "Want me to tell Harlan?"

Dustin looked at him. "You tell him and I'll let him know about that piece of pussy you've been fuckin', man! Yeah, I know all about it. I've seen the two of you around. Tell me, how was that pussy taste? I bet she fucked and sucked good?"

Luther told Dustin to shut his mouth.

Dustin continued. "You think if I asked she'd wanna fuck me? Yeah, I think that's what I'll do. I'll go over there, fuck her, then eat that sweet pussy until she's dry."

Luther stood and walked over to Dustin. Luther gave a nod to Josh across the table. Luther put his hand on top of Dustin's head. He grabbed a chunk of hair and slammed Dustin's head on the table. He repeated it another time. Everyone else sitting around got out of the way. Luther picked up one of the metal trays and slapped the guy in the face with it, knocking two teeth on the floor. Some guys rushed over to Luther and tackled him to the ground.

Luther was brought to Harlan's office.

When Harlan saw the kid he asked the guys what happened. They filled him in and Harlan told them to leave
and get Denny. When Denny came in Luther thought he
was going to get it for sure. He just wanted it to get back
to his family and how he died. Someone had to hear the
truth about what happened.

Harlan looked at him. "So, you get all of that anger out
of you? You fucked Dustin up good, huh? Oh, yeah, you
put it to him."

"Yeah, I guess," Luther told the man.

Harlan laughed. "I didn't know you had it in you. When
they told me I couldn't believe my ears. What the fuck
happened over there?"

"We were having lunch," Luther said. "We were just
talking about stuff, about how we were doing, then, the
subject of you came up. And we talked about that stuff."

"What about me?"

Luther looked down for a minute, then back at Harlan.
"We started talking about you and what we were doing
at this place, the reason we're here. He started talking a
bunch of shit, saying how evil you are for keeping us
here, that you were a monster. I told him if he didn't like
this place he could leave. He said I was a stupid fuck-
face."

"Are you a fuck-face?" Harlan asked.

"Huh?"

"Are you a fuck-face?"

"No."

"Why did you let that bother you? Don't let that get under your skin."

Luther shrugged at the question. "I don't know. But the
thing that got me was when he was talking about you."

"That so?"

"Felt bad. Told him he didn't know what the fuck he
was talking about. The way I told him was like this, Har-

lan gave us so much, gave us the world and we can never repay him. We can never thank you enough, Harlan. If it wasn't for you I don't know where I'd be. You've been like a father to me. You've taught me a lot."

"I thank you for saying that. I didn't intend on being anyone's anything when I started this. I'm glad to hear you say something like that. I never wanted kids. But, hey, now I have a kid. And then I have all of you. You guys make me proud."

"I think that'd be a hard thing, having a kid. I couldn't do it. I guess if it was something that came up I'd have to deal with it, you know?"

"This life and kids, you have to find that balance."

"Yeah, I can see that."

Harlan laughed. "It was a little crazy for me at first, but I found my way. It was about asking what was important to me," he looked at Denny. "Would you have kids?"

Denny said, "Not on your fuckin' life. That kid, he would be one fucked person to have us as parents. I'd feel sorry for him, for sure. On the other hand, your kid, he's a pretty cool guy."

"Thanks," Harlan said. "I'm sure he feels the same about you."

Denny said, "I just hope the very best for him."

Harlan continued with Luther. "With all of that being said, along with thanking you for your kind words, I also have to warn you. I can't have you guys in here beating one another. I don't need someone dropping a dime to the cops, have them come in here, throwing me in a cage. I don't need any of that shit."

Luther said, "I understand where you're coming from. But I thought it was the best thing to do at the time. I dunno, he just pissed me off. I just lost it."

"It happens," Denny interjected.

Harlan looked at Denny. "We know all about that, don't

we?"

Denny shook his head. "Too many times, too many days."

Luther said, "I need to learn to control my temper."

"Yes, you do," Harlan told him. "That could get you in trouble in the future. You're fuckin' lucky you didn't kill him."

"Did they tell you how he was?" Luther asked.

"He was hurt pretty good. After a few days, he should be good. He has to get dental work done."

Luther frowned a little. "I didn't mean to go to that extreme. I guess I'm gonna get punished. I'll do whatever you want me to do. I need to prove myself to you again."

Harlan let out a deep sigh and patted his desk. "Just don't do it again. Next time, I might not be as nice. See, if you were anyone else I'd shoot you right here. I don't give a fuck. If I get pinched for murder, they'll send me to prison. Killing me would be too easy. I wouldn't wanna have to kill you, someone I like. I don't like doing things like that unless I have to. I have my good side, we all do. Hell, the first time I ever killed someone I got sick. Didn't think I could live with myself."

"But you're still here," Luther told him.

Harlan smiled. "Indeed, I am. And I'm not going anywhere. I'm here to stay. You guys are gonna have to put up with me a little while more."

Denny told his friend that they couldn't live without him. He told Harlan only he could do what he did. Luther agreed.

Harlan said, "Tell me something, Luther."

"What's that?" the kid asked.

"Do you have eyes for anyone here?"

Luther thought it wouldn't be best to tell them he already had a thing going with Laralyn. He wasn't sure what the reaction would be, so he didn't tell them. He just looked at the two men and said he didn't. He knew what Laralyn told him, and he didn't want to end up dead somewhere.

Even though they had an orgy a few times a week, none of the council members were allowed to take part in those—even though some of them wanted to. At some point, Harlan changed the rules about the orgies, and even council members had to participate.

As the three talked Luther started to think about the possibility he could be Harlan's number one guy one day and Denny would be out. Denny would be dead or he would just step down because Harlan would ask him to, because Harlan finally saw Denny wasn't worthy of the title. Luther could finally start doing something that mattered to the world. Luther didn't have anything against Denny or anything, he just thought that everyone should have their time to shine.

About two weeks later the thing Luther and Laralyn had was over. She had to make it clear to him that he wasn't supposed to talk about it with anyone. Even though they were done they still had to have sex because of the orgies.

After Laralyn there was a string of other women. He was surprised that he'd been with so many girls and they wanted to be with him. He could never understand what they saw in him. Harlan told him that it might be because the girls were trying to get a father figure.

42

As weeks went on Luther continued spying on everyone. He was still reporting back to the council every day.
After a few people started to take notice of what he was
up to, he would hear whispers around the compound.
When he was confronted by a few people one day he de-
nied it, telling them they must be crazy and didn't know
what they were talking about. He told them they must
feel guilty about something. But he was the one who felt
guilty. He felt bad that he was spying on all these people
who had been so nice to him, who took him as one of
their own. He tried to come to terms with it, but in the
end, he couldn't find a way to.

On a Sunday afternoon, he walked into Harlan's office
and told him he couldn't continue doing what he was doing. As he was telling the leader this he felt more than a
little nervous. He didn't know what the reaction would
be.

Harlan said, "If that's what you want, I guess that'll be
okay."

"Sorry about that."

"Don't be. After looking into all of this stuff I found
there was nothing to any of it. You can forget everything
you thought. Sorry to put you through all of that. These
people, they were all talking. I don't think any of them
have the guts to do anything."

Luther said, "That's a huge weight off my shoulders. I
didn't know what your reaction was going to be."

"Yeah, I know how you feel. Guess I never thought
about the spot that put you into."

"It's okay."

"Good," Harlan told him. "Let's move on."

Bradley Davenport

The two talked more.

Weeks passed and everything was normal—as normal as it could be. Some of the people got tired of being there and left. Harlan had no problem with seeing them go. He told them if they didn't want to be there then just leave and never come back. There were a few people around who went around saying they thought Harlan had lost his heart for all of it. Of course, no one would dare come out and ask him. They kept it to themselves.

At the end of one of his sermons, Harlan asked, as he always did, if anyone had anything they wanted to talk about.

This guy, Fred Moore, said, "If I could just say something here: I've had a few people ask me about moving in here. When I go to work I've been asked. What should I tell them?"

Harlan said, "Hey, tell them to come on down, brother. We can always use more people. They'll love it. There's plenty of room."

"I'll let them know?"

"Is it a guy or a girl?"

"One of each."

"Right on, man."

A little blonde, Sherry Yates said, "We'll always be there for you, Harlan, no matter what it is."

"Thanks for that," Harlan told her. "And anything any of you guys need just ask. If any of you guys need anything just ask. I'll do everything in my power to help."

"They all said you were a good man."

A few people asked if they could have a party. Harlan told them he'd think about it and get back to them. Later that afternoon in his office Harlan sat down with the council to discuss a few matters. They decided they were going to have the party. He enlisted Zed and Denny to get the booze and other party favors. Two nights later they had the party. Everyone had fun and got drunk. It was good for everyone to cut loose. At some point during the party, Harlan took Luther to his office to have a little chat. After about an hour of talking a knock came to the door. When Luther answered Sherry Yates was there to greet him.

"Welcome," Luther told her. "Come on in."

"Thanks," she walked into the office. "Good night, isn't it?"

"It's not bad."

Harlan told her to take a seat.

"Don't mind if I do," she said.

Harlan handed her a glass and poured whiskey into it. "You enjoying yourself?"

"Absolutely."

"I just want everyone to have a good time while they're here," Harlan said. "Don't want you guys thinking I'm just about preaching. I'm a man of the world. We're all just people of the world."

"Of course."

Luther said, "We're all about fun here. They'll look back on all of this and be amazed. Gotta leave your mark, know what I mean?"

Sherry took a drink. "This is good."

"I buy what I can," Harlan told her.

"I don't do the hard stuff all the time."

Harlan said, "Really?"

"Yeah, after seeing my brother have the problems he did with the stuff I knew I had to take it slow. I didn't want that life for myself."

"Did he die?" Luther asked.

"Nothing like that," she said. "He just got thrown in jail a lot; fights, drinking and driving, stuff like that. He's doing better now. The last time I saw him I flew over to Florida. We went to the beach."

"Sounds nice."

"It was. I always loved the water. I'd love to live there someday. It's so peaceful."

"We'll have to go some time."

Sherry said, "Where's Tiffany tonight?"

"I'm not sure," Harlan told her. "I think she's with Lara-lyn somewhere. They're most likely off drinking some-where."

"It's a shame you aren't with her."

"I guess so. We talked about it and agreed we could do our own thing tonight."

"Oh, I see."

"It's okay. Sometimes you just have to go off and do your own thing."

"I can see that. Sometimes you have to get time away. It'll make the relationship stronger."

"I guess so."

"And we told each other we couldn't ask what the other did," he laughed. "It'll be a free night."

After some more talk and more drinks, the two men talked her into getting into a sex romp. After a couple of hours, they kicked her out of the room.

One of the guys who was there when Ryan got killed, a guy with orange hair from Texas named Travis James, burst into Harlan's office in protest. He told Harlan he'd go to the cops, telling them he knew what was going on. Travis was one of the guys who dug the hole that Ryan was in. Travis said he'd had enough of Harlan's mess, that he would tell everyone what really happened to Ryan.

Harlan said, "You forget, you'd have to prove these things. If you go out there, say whatever about me, they are gonna ask for proof. Proof, my friend, is something you don't have. And I don't think you have the guts for it."

"Or why don't I just kill you right now?" Travis told him. "I'll save everyone some time. They won't miss you."

Harlan laughed. "You can try. If you think you can do it, do it. But I can tell you, you won't be able to. The only thing I can promise you is death."

"You think?"

"I know. Tell me this, how are you gonna do it? You don't even have a fuckin' gun on you. If you shot me you'd have a good chance of killing me. You don't have shit. Get the fuck outta here before you make me mad. Drop it. Do what you're fuckin' told or we'll be burying you next."

"I have a knife in my pocket."

"Planning on using that?"

"Maybe."

"I see."

"I tell you, Harlan, don't fuck with me. You don't know anything about me or what I'm capable of. I can be your worst nightmare."

"Sounds like you know your way around a fight?"

"I've been in a few."

"A real badass, right?"

"I get by."

"That's one of the best things you can hope for."

Travis took the knife out of his pocket.

Harlan looked at the knife. "You better know what you're doing with that thing. Boy, you're so fuckin' ungrateful! I can't believe it... I gave you a place to come to and this is what you do? You wanna kill me? Man, you're a real piece of trash. I should've left you there, you fuck. You need to be thanking me. Everyone here should be thanking me. Come on, buddy, you do this, it won't work in your favor."

"Don't have to worry about that."

Harlan came from behind his desk and grabbed the knife. Travis tried to hit Harlan's hand away. Harlan was able to get the knife away from him, slash his face, and kick him to the floor. Harlan stabbed him in the stomach a few times. Harlan dropped the knife to the floor and thought about what to do. He walked around his office for awhile then called Denny. He told his friend to get to his office as soon as he could. Denny showered a few minutes later.

"Thanks for coming over," Harlan said.

Denny looked at the body on the floor and sighed. "Shit... Man, I dunno... Another one? The fuck is going on here?"

"It's something that had to be done," Harlan said.

"What did he do?"

"Guy tried to take me on."

"Looks like things didn't work out for him, huh?"

"They didn't."

Denny said, "He should've run it by me before he went to you. Whatever it was. He'd still be alive. What do you wanna do with him?"

"It's just one of those things that happened. I wasn't planning on killing anyone today. It's a nice day out. I didn't want any of this. He could've waited until later this week."

"Think that would've worked?"

"No."

Denny looked back down at the body. "Looks like a lot of people are trying to take you on these days, why do you think that is?"

"Jealousy? They all wanna be king until they're king."

Denny laughed. "I can see that, sure. Who said you

were king? King shithead, that's what I'd say."

Both men laughed.

Denny knew he could get away with saying something like that because they'd been friends for so long. If you were to ask either man how many years they had been friends neither one could tell you. They were as close as brothers.

"We'll have to wait awhile, then bury him in the forest. Make sure no one is around."

"You got it. We're starting to make that our personal cemetery."

Harlan laughed. "Have to put the bodies somewhere. Can't just throw 'em out front."

"Guess so."

"That wouldn't be good for anyone."

"I would say not."

Harlan said, "The thing with this guy, he could've ended all this. He communicated to me that he was going to bring us down. I couldn't let that happen. All the crimes, he was there for all of it. Guy said he was gonna kill me. It wasn't good. I had to. Guy only had a knife. Shit, at least have a gun if you wanna kill someone. Too many variables with a knife."

"That's understandable."

"In a perfect world, you don't wanna keep walking through life killing people. But if you have to, you better do it right, you know?"

"Yeah," Denny said. "Oh, hey, I don't think anyone would blame you. Sometimes you gotta be the rough shit when you're in charge."

Harlan said, "You just have to keep your eyes and ears open. You have to make rules. Being decisive is what it's all about."

"I can see that, sure."

Harlan said, "If I had to do it over I'd do the same thing.

I can't afford anyone to ruin any of this," he went and sat behind his desk. "All the time and money we've invested into this thing would be for nothing if we let that go. I'm not saying it's good or anything, but that's what had to happen."

"And he could've told someone he was coming to see you. I dunno, maybe something would happen to him so he told someone, you think?"

Harlan lit a cigarette. "I got the feeling he didn't say anything. But who knows? I think if he did say anything no one would believe him."

"Maybe."

"It's a pretty wild claim when someone from the outside hears."

"You better hope, brother."

"Things go on. So, what were you doing?" Harlan asked.

Denny said, "Nothing much. Mallory and I were just listening to music."

"That's good. You two have made something together."

"I just hope it lasts."

"I have a feeling it will."

"There's no backup plan, so it'll have to work."

"If you want it bad enough you'll make it so."

"That's what I'm gonna do," Denny said. "I couldn't see myself with anyone else."

"For what it's worth, I can't see it."

"Thanks."

"I'm pretty good at these things."

Denny laughed. "You? Shit, man, don't make me start dyin' over here. I know you're full of shit."

"Hey, it's not my fault girls don't wanna stay with me."

"Yeah, yeah," Denny walked over to the window. "That's what ya say."

"Cross my heart."

Denny looked at him. "Don't have to convince me."

Later that afternoon, when nobody was around, Harlan and Denny carried the body to the trunk of Harlan's car. The two went out to the middle of the forest to bury the body. They didn't mark where the grave was. Harlan told his friend he didn't want to talk about it again, and said that the guy was a waste of time. Denny was loyal and had no problem doing what his friend asked.

When they got back to Harlan's office they tried to talk about other stuff to deflect the fact they buried another person. Harlan asked his friend if he wanted to get something to eat. Denny said he had to take a shower and get ready. When he got ready they headed out. They went to a burger place called Murphy's Grill.

"Tell me," Harlan asked, "you think I'm doing a good job?"

"Sure. I couldn't do this, my friend. You have a way with words. Tell people what they wanna hear... They're clay in your hands. You can tell them everything."

"They would, wouldn't they? There's a certain amount of power that gives you."

"But you need to be careful with it, Harlan. You're on top, the only place to go is down. Don't let it all go to your head. But, yeah, you're doing a good job. You keep this up, things will only get bigger."

Harlan said, "That's the plan. The more people join the more money rolls in. It'll be good for everyone. And I'm not ever going to forget what you guys have done for me. You all are forever in my debt."

"It's been my pleasure. I'm sure they all feel like that, everyone at the compound."

"Any way you slice it, that's the way it's gonna work. We can't have things falling apart on us."

"I agree."

"We do that, we might as well march down to the police

station right now, and turn ourselves in."

"That won't happen."

"Glad to hear you say that. Just hope the others feel the same way."

Denny said, "We already got rid of some of the bad seeds. If we get more they'll be dealt with."

The two talked and laughed more. After they were done eating they went to the store to get some booze. They went back to the compound and got drunk, lost themselves in stories of years past. They joked they needed to wake their girls and have a group romp. Denny mentioned that Mallory always thought Harlan looked good. Harlan just laughed.

Denny said, "You can ask her yourself."

"Nah. I couldn't do that to you, man. Too much history."

"That party we had the night you got out, if I wouldn't have been there she would've tried to fuck you. She's crazy in bed. If you want to test her out you have my blessing."

"Thanks for that. I'll pass. Not that Mallory is ugly or anything. Have a good thing going with Tiffany, wouldn't want to fuck that up. Now, I mean, if she was cool with it that'd be a different story."

Denny laughed. "You never know until you ask."

Harlan took a drink of beer. "That's a crazy one there, buddy."

43

When Luther had that little affair with Laralyn he thought that would've got him closer to the inside. But it didn't do anything for his career. Yes, she made a good bed partner, someone to have deep conversations with but that was about it. After all of that, he told himself he wouldn't mind spending more time with her. He liked her. She was a breath of fresh air. He thought she was very sexy. He loved the way she smelled. He thought he'd find her and try to win her over. They might be about to go out to a fancy restaurant or something. He knew he needed to get to know her better, her life story, her likes and dislikes. He already knew some of that stuff, but he wanted to know more. He didn't want to ask the guys he was talking to about her. He didn't really know if he should even let them know he liked her for fear of what they might say or do. He figured he'd keep that secret to himself.

When he left Harlan's office he walked around for a bit. He found himself in front of Laralyn's door. He knocked. After knocking a few more times he told himself she wasn't in. He wondered where she was. He walked the halls. He didn't feel like going back to his apartment, so he went to one of the open areas in the compound to see who was hanging around. People were still walking around drinking from bottles. When he got to one of the areas, a group of familiar faces were sitting around a table talking and playing cards. When they saw him they called him over. Luther walked over and took a seat. He played a few hands of cards with them. They were all drunk and slurring words. After more drinks and laughs he left the group.

He went to Laralyn's door and she was there. She invited him in. She wore a blue bathrobe with wet hair.

"You just take a shower?" he asked her.

"What gave it away?" she gave him a smile.

He loved that smile. He could stare at it all day long.

They walked over to the living room and sat on the couch.

"How's it going?" she asked.

"Okay, I guess. Not much here. I came by awhile ago but you weren't in."

"Yeah, I was still with Tiffany."

"What did you guys get into?"

"Not much. We just drank. She just needed some girl time. What were you doing?"

"Hung around. I went over to Harlan's office at some point. We just drank and hung around there."

"Sounds fun. We missed it."

"You would've love it."

"Next time, I promise."

He smiled at her. "You know it's not nice to break a promise."

"I won't."

Luther told her why he was there, that he wanted to talk to her about something. She got a little nervous. He told her that he wanted her to be in his life again. He explained to her how he wanted to be an item once again.

She thought about it for a minute. "Why?"

"What do you mean?"

"Why do you want to be with me?"

"I fell in love with you," he told her. "I can't help it."

"I like you, too."

After talking it through they decided to be an item. She told him she'd break the news to Harlan. She told Luther that Harlan liked him a lot and that it shouldn't be an issue. And if it was going to be an issue they'd just leave.

Harlan didn't have a problem with it. He loved the fact that they got together.

44

One day when Harlan was writing a letter in his office a knock came to the door. It was Zed.

"What can I do for you today?" Harlan asked.

"Hey, man, sorry to bother you at this time. I know seeing my face was the last thing you wanted to see today."

"Fuck you talking?" Harlan said. "Nonsense. I always like talking to you."

"I'm glad to hear you say that," Zed laughed.

Harlan offered him a glass of whiskey.

"Maybe later, man. Something we have to deal with first."

"What's that? Something wrong?"

"We have an issue with someone."

"Who is it?"

"It's a long story."

"Oh, boy."

"Yeah."

"It's gonna be one of those, huh?"

"Afraid so."

"Man, I hate those."

"I know you do."

"But it has to be done."

"That's the bitch of it."

"And that makes us the bad guys."

"That's about right."

"Someone always has to be, I guess."

Zed filled Harlan in on what was going on as they walked. A guy, Chester Maynard, was fighting with another dude, Bruce Taylor. It seemed the fight was over chores. As Zed was telling him all this, Harlan got a confused look on his face, asking what the deal was. Zed didn't know the heart of the problem. The fight started small, but then, it grew into something that was big. Apparently, Chester threatened to do something very bad to Bruce. They had to get four people to break the two up.

They were all gathered around a vending machine outside of a television area two hallways away from Harlan's office. Both Bruce and Chester looked as though they wanted to rip the other apart. The men around the angry two drifted away when they saw Harlan. They knew things would be sorted out, and it wouldn't end well for at least one of them.

"What the problem here?" Harlan asked.

Bruce scratched his arm, shrugged. "I was just about to get some cleaning done, and he comes over and starts talking trash to me."

"Why's that?" Harlan asked.

Bruce shrugged again. "Because I'm going out with this girl who left him. He's been an asshole to me about it."

"That true?" Harlan asked Chester.

"Man, he's just a simple fuck," Chester said. "I was just messing around. He should've known I didn't really mean anything by it. I don't really care who that fucks anymore. I already told her I thought she was a stupid whore."

Harlan held up his finger. "Tell me, what girl is it?"

Bruce said, "Julie."

"Julie who?"

"Hartner."

"Oh, really?" Harlan nodded. "I hadn't talked to her much."

"Well, they broke things off due to his temper. She told me she didn't want him to beat her."

"Can't say as I blame her. Don't know anyone who

wants that."

Chester raised his brow. "That's not true! If she told you that she was lying. I'd never do that."

"Would she say that if I asked her?" Harlan said.

"I don't know what she'd say. I can't read minds."

"Don't get smart with me, guy."

"I'm just letting you know how it is."

Harlan said, "I'm the one who is going to tell you how it is."

"That so?"

Harlan told him they were going to go to his office and sort out the matter. He told Zed to find Julie and have her go to his office. Chester laughed as they walked to the office. Soon after they got there Julie showed.

Harlan told the three to take a seat in front of the desk, and for Zed to stick around. Zed had an idea about what was going to happen. He'd seen Harlan hand down discipline before.

"This gonna take long?" Chester said. "I have a few things to take care of."

"I bet you do," Harlan smiled.

Julie shifted in her seat. "How are you, Harlan? What's this about?"

"I'm good," he told her. "Hopefully we won't be long. There's just something we need to clear-up."

"What would that be?"

Harlan nodded toward Bruce. "Seems Bruce and Chester, they got in a fight over you."

Julie's eyes darted to Chester. "What did me do?"

"Me?" Chester pointed at himself. "What makes you think it was me? Why don't you as him?"

Julie said, "Because I know you, Chester. I know how you act."

"Well, that's not saying much, dear."

"Take it or leave it."

Harlan interrupted. "Whatever the case, this fight happened because of you."

"Saying it's my fault?" Julie said.

"Not as such," Harlan said. "Thing is, I can't afford to have these things happening. Someone gets mad at someone else, goes outside and tells someone about the inner workings here, this place is fucked. Everything we've worked for is gone forever."

Bruce said, "He's the one that started the fight. I can't help he has a problem with me dating Julie. That's his deal. Who the hell does he think I am? I'll rise-up on him."

"I understand that," Harlan said. "I'm telling you guys how it is. I'm not a relationship counselor. I don't care. We can't have this. You guys are gonna have to figure things out on your own. But no fighting. I don't wanna have to tell you guys again."

"Or what?" Bruce asked."

Harlan walked closer to him. "Don't give me a hard time. There's a lot on my plate right now, and I don't have time for any of this shit. Now kiss and make friends again."

Chester said. "I'll bash his face open."

"Really?" Bruce said. "You think so?"

Chester looked at Harlan. "The one thing my daddy did teach me before he left my mom and I was how to fight. He likes to test me, but buddy, I'll beat his ass. I'll beat him so bad he'll have to get a new ass. Fuck that motherfucker!"

Julie jumped out of her chair. "Okay, I want you both to stop. Fighting over what? Fighting over me? If you guys don't start acting right I won't be with either of you. I'm not just some piece of meat. Come on, guys, don't act like kids."

After about an hour the three agreed to play nice with each other. After they left Harlan had his doubts about the whole thing. He didn't trust Chester, and he only trusted the others a little.

Later that night Harlan and Zed paid a visit to Chester's apartment. They brought some beer to let him know there were no hard feelings. After getting drunk they convinced Chester to go out into the woods behind the compound with them, telling him they had some women waiting for them and they were going to party. When they got into the woods Chester asked about the girls. When he discovered he had been setup Chester started to run. Harlan chased him down and stabbed him in the back a few times. Once Chester was down he stabbed him in the throat. They dug a hole in the ground and threw the body in.

The next night Harlan invited Bruce and Julie to double date with Tiffany and himself. They were going to Mo's; a steak house in town. They drove in separate cars. They were parked at a red light when a masked gunman rolled up on Bruce's car and sprayed bullets, killing Bruce and Julie. After the shots the masked man sped away somewhere in the night. The police shut down the street while they gathered evidence, sending the commuters to alternate routes.

Despite being a little shocked at what happened, Tiffany and Harlan enjoyed themselves. They talked at great length about what happened. When they got back to the compound Harlan went to visit Zed. The two got drunk and smoked grass into the early hours of the morning.

When news hit the papers about what happened to

Bruce and Julie people at the compound were devastated. For all anyone knew it was exactly what the papers said it was, just a random act of violence.

Some of the others, the ones who found their finally resting place in the woods, their families came by the compound and talked to Harlan about their missing loved one. Harlan would tell them that they just left without saying where they were going. He said that he just assumed they went back home, that they lost interest in the cause. At any rate, they were never going to find their loved ones. To further play along Harlan even helped when they formed search parties. As far as he was concerned the only people who knew the truth were going to be the only ones who ever knew. No one else needed to know a thing. It wasn't anyone's business, he told himself.

The next time he was doing a sermon he mentioned those whose fate were unclear.

"Over the past few years we've been asked by family members of people who used to live here, they've asked what happened to their loved ones. I just assumed they went back where they came from. But it became clear to me some of these families think their loved one died at some point. I don't have any proof of that. Truth is, they most likely left here in search of something else. Some people, it takes some time before they find their way in life. I hate to say this but a lot of those people were still lost. You just have a bunch of folks looking for their place in this crazy world. I did all I could to help. I wish nothing but the best for them. As I tell everyone, my door is always open if anyone ever needs to talk about anything. If anyone hears from any of these individuals just ask if they're doing okay."

People clapped.

Some of them couldn't hear what Harlan was saying

and left. He didn't say anything to them.

Harlan continued with the sermon. At the end he gave the number so people could call and donate. About two hours after the sermon he called everyone to attend the orgy. For the next few hours everyone indulged in their fantasies with one another.

"It's all about being one with each other. You guys, you guys are different but the same. It's about so much more than you know. It's about seeing how much you care for each other. I know all of you really care about your—there's nothing wrong with it. If more people cared about each other we wouldn't have so much violence in the world."

Since the early days of the compound he had been providing the people with LSD everyday. He would tell them it was to get more in touch with themselves, to go beyond the reality they knew.

"Do you know each other?" Harlan told them. "You need to grow together, be together, be everything and everyone. Just take the step, see where it takes you. You'll be surprised at what you find. Don't be afraid. This is how it has to be."

After everyone had their dose he told everyone they should be free to discover themselves. When the session was over he told everyone to return to what they were doing before. Some guys asked Harlan to join them for a game of billiards. With him playing it made four—an even number. After two games they decided to place money on it.

45

A few days later Harlan and Denny were standing in front of a man who was bleeding all over the floor of the basement. The victim, a man in only his underwear, Bobby Cooke, thought he could get the upper-hand on Harlan. They had been in an argument earlier about some of the rules of the compound. When Harlan told the man to shut-up he just kept on. Finally, it got to the point where Harlan told Bobby if he thought he could beat him to take his best shot. Bobby did and it didn't go well. Bobby actually took three hits. Harlan would later admit that it took his breath away.

"You done?" Harlan said to him. "Man, you can pack a punch, can't ya?"

"Yeah," Bobby barked. "You're lucky."

"How's that?"

"I could've killed you."

"Why didn't you."

"I was taking it easy on you."

Harlan laughed. "Don't do me any favors. I'll give you one more shot. You better make it good."

"Fuck you."

"Yeah, yeah, yeah."

Bobby threw his left fist at Harlan's face. Harlan kicked him in the testicles, making Bobby fall to the ground. Harlan kicked him in the testicles a few more times. Harlan hit him with a pipe. When Bobby came to, Denny and Harlan were standing in front of him taking turns beating him.

"You still a tough guy?" Harlan said to him.

"You piece of shit," Denny muttered.

Halan stomped on his head. "It'll teach you not to do

that. You should be ashamed. Fuck you! I don't know why I brought some of you guys here."

"He's just worthless. Yeah, sometimes all you need is a good beating," Denny walked away from the guy.

After they talked about it Denny ran over and gathered about thirty people to come see what they were doing to Bobby. He wanted it to be a reminder to never cross him.

"This man laying on the ground thinks he knows more than me," Harlan told them. "He decided he wanted to run things, to take the big seat. I want to make this clear to all, this is my fucking world. I'm the motherfucking boss. If any of you, like this guy, have a problem with that it'll have to be dealt with. Bobby here, he wanted to take my life. He said he'd kill me. He wanted to ruin me and all of this. I had to let him know who's still in charge."

They beat him more with the pipe, then, Harlan took a handgun and shot him in both knees. He let Bobby scream in pain for a couple minutes before he shot him in the face and heart.

A few people tried to tackle Harlan but he shot them, killing them. The others were silent. They didn't know what to do. Harlan told them he had to do what he did. He told them that if they told anyone he'd kill them.

46

At church the next day Harlan told everyone they had
to act as a family, he said, "All of my brothers and sisters, we've come a long way since this whole thing
started. I have to say I'm proud of all of you. I've seen
all of you grow in ways that might not have happened if
it wasn't for those that helped start this thing with me.
The thing is, you know, we have to stick together. The
world outside, they still don't understand us. They have
blinders on and don't want to hear the truth. They see me
out, they ask how I know all this stuff I preach. After I
tell them I'm a messenger of God they don't believe me.
They think I'm nuts, crazy, insane. When I see them they
turn and walk away. I'm here to tell you all, everything
I've been saying has been true. See, all those people who
say that, they don't have faith. People joke about things
they don't know. They don't have faith. In a life like this,
in these times. you need faith. Everyone needs something, to cling to, something that's pure. Point is, you
can't believe everything you hear. At first I couldn't explain it, God talking to me. I figured when I first started
telling people they'd send me away to a padded room
somewhere. Glad that never happened. Just by seeing all
of these new faces I can tell them that I was never crazy.
Calling me crazy, they might as well call all of you
crazy. People might say I act high and mighty... but those
people have no idea what it's like from the ground up, to
watch something grow, blossom, into greatness. God
told me you guys are doing a good job but you have to
do more. I bet you God would come down and party
with all of us, but he has things to do where he is. He's a
busy guy."

People told Harlan he wasn't crazy.

Later on, after church, Harlan was back in his office when a knock came to the door. He called for whoever it was to come in. David Hill stepped into the office. He was wearing a big floppy hat and a pair of thick glasses.

"David," Harlan said. "How's it going, my friend?"

"Good, good. Y-y-you called me your friend?" he said with a surprised look on his face.

"Of course I did," Harlan said. "You know I think of you as a friend."

"Thanks, Harlan."

"Sit down if you want."

David took the seat in front of Harlan's desk. "Hope I didn't bother you by knocking on your door."

"No, no, no," Harlan told him. "I was just about to take a break."

"Good."

"How've you been?"

"I've b-b-been fine, sir. Real fine. My momma, she's doing good. N-n-no problems. Everything's fine like peaches."

Harlan put a stack of papers on his desk in an envelope and placed it in a drawer. "We're just busy, busy, busy around here. What can I do ya for?"

David cleared his throat. "I just wanted to start by say-ing from my momma and I, well, how's your baby do-ing?"

"He's fine. Thanks for asking."

"Yes, sir."

"You want kids someday?"

"Maybe. It's always nice to have a little critter around. They bring a lot of joy to everything."

"They do, don't they?" Harlan said. "I'll pass the mes-sage along to Tiffany. I'm sure she'd appreciate that."

"Thanks."

Harlan said, "So, David, what can I do for you today?"

"I have a question."

"Shoot."

David took his floppy hat off.

"Gotta say, I dig the hat," Harlan told him.

David ran his hand over his hat. "Got it at the mall. Went to Shade, got it for twenty percent off."

"Looks good."

"That's what they tell me. They have more if you want one."

Harlan said, "I'll have to check it out. What can I do for you today?"

"Well," David said, "I was wanting to do something around here."

"What did you have in mind?"

"I was thinking I wanted—I wanted to start a band."

"A band?"

"Yeah."

"You like music?"

"I do."

"You play any instruments?"

"Guitar and drums."

"Oh, really? I didn't know that."

"I've always been into that stuff, ya know? I thought about a talent show."

"Talent show?"

"Wouldn't that be so much fun?" David said.

"I could see it."

"What we could do, we could have a sign-up sheet posted somewhere and people could sign their names if they wanna be in it."

Harlan shook his head slowly. "Yeah, that's sounds good."

"Really?"

"Yeah."

"Nice."

"I'll even put you in charge of it."

"That's cool. Thanks. I won't let you down, Harlan."

"I know you won't."

"I'll get to prove my mom wrong. She said that you wouldn't be interested."

"That right?"

"She said I was a damn fool for having an idea like that."

"Why'd she say that?"

David shrugged. "She's always doing that type of thing. She still thinks I'll never amount to anything, so she says stuff like that to keep me down."

"I know your mom. She doesn't seem like she'd be one to say something like that."

"In public, you know?" David said. "See, when she's in public she's nice to me, but, when she's not, she's not nice."

"How?"

"She's always putting me down, saying I'm a retard and stuff. Says that my daddy left her because of me, because I was an idiot. I think she blamed me for all of that."

"Sorry to hear."

"I'm okay with it."

"That's not right."

David put his hand up. "I don't blame her. She didn't know any better. She was just a kid when she had me. She was doing all sorts of bad thing, smoking those cancer sticks, smoking grass, doing all those drugs, and she was drinking all the time. When she had me, that didn't stop her from doing all that stuff. When the doctors told her and my dad what was wrong with me my dad became upset and my mom got sad. After a couple years he left, telling her I was why he was leaving."

"That's a sad story, David."

"It's okay."

"Is it?"

"Stuff happens to good people, some is bad. I get by okay, though. But I still don't understand why my mom blames me."

Harlan said, "I don't know. I'd think it has less to do with you and more to do with her feelings about him."

"If that's true she doesn't have to take it out on me. Behind closed doors she's always calls me an idiot and a retard. One time before we came here, she got so mad she beat me with a broom. She would lock me in a closet for a day or two. I-I-I don't know if you've ever been locked in a closet but it's dark in there."

"That's never happened to me, no."

A small tear started to roll down David's cheek. "It makes me very sad. I want it to end."

"I can imagine." Harlan said. "Wish I could help you," he stood. "Can I get you anything? Soda? Coffee?"

"Soda, if you're getting yourself one."

"I was."

"Okay."

"I'm buying."

David laughed. "That's the best soda, the kind you don't have to buy, Harlan."

"Think nothing of it."

"I'll pay you back."

"You don't have to do that."

"But I want to."

"Well, thanks."

"I don't mind."

"You're a pretty good guy, David."

"I try."

The two walked out of Harlan's office to the Soda machine in the hall. Harlan asked David more about the talent show idea. When he finished Harlan told him he'd take it to his people. They'd decided on a date, and then everything was up and moving forward. David got a few people together and started to play music. They weren't that good. There was a girl in the show who did some magic tricks, a few singers, someone who danced, and they had a few other acts. None of it was really that great, but everyone figured it was something to pass the time.

47

About three weeks later, on a Friday night, Harlan arranged to have David and a few others go downtown to the movies. They went to a pizza place and then to the theater for the movie. When they were gone Harlan paid a visit to David's mom. The two ended up having sex. After the sex he told her he had a gift for her. When she asked what it was he told her it was in the basement, in one of the closets down there. He told her it was a secret and to not tell anyone. She agreed. On their way to the basement they got Denny to join them. When they got to the basement Harlan told her to look in the closet. When she looked in he pushed her all the way and locked the door. After he locked the door he said he was going to destroy the key. It dawned on him, as she started to scream, that she would be screaming all the time. He unlocked the door, grabbed her, pressed his gun tightly against her and fired two times, leaving her limp. He threw her back in the closet and locked it.

"Now I can destroy the key."

Denny looked at his friend. "Fuck, Harlan! What did she do? We just killing everyone now? At that rate we'll run out of folks."

Harlan told Denny what David told him.

"He's going to ask," Denny said. "What are you going to do about that?"

"Leave that to me," Harlan told him. "I can handle David. You don't have to worry. Trust me, he won't be looking for her."

"Why wouldn't he?"

"Because of something he told me."

"What was that?"

"About how she treated him."

"I see. I think you should really think about this stuff. Eventually, I think people are gonna start to talk, word is gonna get out."

"People already talk. People, they don't need the truth. If they think something's going on then it is. They've already made their minds up."

"You don't wanna have to deal with cops."

"If it happens It'll be dealt with."

"Okay," Denny said. "Just so you know, I have your back no matter how things play out."

"That'll come in handy."

"If we go down they'll have to take both of us. I have a feeling that day is gonna be here soon."

"Don't say that."

"It's just that everything has to come to an end."

"You think too much."

"Aren't you worried at all?"

"Not really," Harlan said. "I have bigger things to worry about."

"Like what?"

"My kid and Tiffany."

"Yeah, you're right about that," Denny said. "When are you guys going to get married?"

"Not sure. I mean, we like the way things are going now. It hasn't been a problem so far."

"Let's hope that lasts."

Both of them laughed.

After they got back from the movie David went around asking if anyone had seen his mother. When he asked Harlan he was told that his dad came back, found where she was staying and they ran away together. The leader told David that his mother said to keep her son where he was, that she found her true love again and that David should not look for her. Harlan told David that his mother told him she never liked him, that she always thought he was nothing but a retard. After a week David was still out of sorts and didn't know what to do, where to go in life. He decided to leave the world, that there was nothing left for him. One day, in the kitchen, as he was washing dishes, he grabbed a sharp butcher knife and slit his throat, spilling his blood all over the kitchen floor.

48

When Tiffany found out what happened to David and his mom she got upset. They had just finished dinner.

"The thing that gets me," she said, "I don't fucking understand why you felt the need to do what you did. David was nothing but nice to you. He was a sweet man."

"Babe," Harlan said. "I did it to help him."

"To help him?"

"After he told me that sad story I knew I had to do something."

"It wasn't your place."

"Someone had to do something. I couldn't sit by and do nothing. Couldn't live with myself if I sat back and did nothing."

"So, you tell him a story so sad it makes him kill himself? How fucked up is that? And I'm not even gonna start on what you did to his mom."

"I didn't tell the guy to kill himself."

"You might as well have. What the fuck, Harlan? See, this is the kind of stuff I was talking about. We can't do this anymore."

"I'm sorry."

She sighed. "What are we doing? You told me things were going to change around here. Why are things getting so violent? This wasn't what we set out to do."

"I'm sorry, baby. I need to get these people behind me. I need to let everyone know I'm in charge. Sometimes drastic measures need to be taken. We need to make sure everything runs without a hitch."

"A hitch? I'd say you haven't done that good of a job of it. I didn't know we were going around killing the people we're trying to help. You keep this up no one will be left around here. Next thing I know you'll wanna kill me."

"I'd never kill you."

"Thanks for that. Our son will thank you one day. I'll tell him about the day his father promised he wouldn't kill me. Don't worry, Harlan, I'm never going to tell anyone outside these walls. I'm not gonna go to the cops, it's not my style. I could bury you if I wanted. I'm not going to do that to you and Luke. A son needs his father. I would never betray you like that—just know I can. And I'll hold it over your head forever."

"Okay."

"And don't think about killing me. I'll make sure my ghost will haunt you for the rest of your days. That'll drive you insane."

"That'd be foolish of me."

"Got that right, sir."

They talked about it more, and it was decided to stop talking about it. She went to see their son, he went to hang around some of the guys. That night they made up by making love.

The next few weeks went without any problems. The both of them knew where the other stood on certain matters, and neither wanted to disturb the flow of things. Soon after, Harlan was hearing whispers someone was talking about things that were going on in the compound—things that shouldn't be mentioned. The next time they gathered for church, after Harlan preached a little,, he told everyone how important it was for them to always obey him and never tell anyone what happens within their walls, that if he heard of anyone speaking about such things they would be punished. He reminded them he had ears and eyes everywhere. He went on to tell them it was crucial for them to listen to their master. He told them Jesus listened to his father and master, that he was so dedicated that he let himself die on the cross for people he didn't know.

"But he came back to life," someone in back yelled.

"True, brothers and sisters. But here's the thing, he didn't know he was going to rise. All he knew was that he was putting his life on the line for the greater good, that he was giving back the greatest gift of all. For years some have said that he wasn't dead, that he was just asleep or whatever. I guess you can believe what you want. The thing is, it doesn't matter what you believe but what really happened. You know, when God first introduced himself to me he said every man has his own quest. My quest, he told me was to start this church. He told me he didn't care what sin I did, that I could redeem myself. I guess, you could say, that's how we all got here. God told me to do this for as long as I'm alive and that's what I plan to do. I answer to the Lord above. We answer to him. He knows all. He tells us his word, sometimes we get the message and sometimes we don't. There isn't exactly a blueprint to this game. Just when we think we have everything figured out the story changes. I just ask you, believe in me and we can get through this together."

Someone said, "Hell yeah! Everyone needs you in their lives. We could just pick your mind all day long."

"Thanks for that," Harlan said. "I'll amaze all of you."

As Harlan continued he answered questions from some other people. When he got ready to leave and go to his apartment Zed asked if he could take some of his time.

"Sure," Harlan said. "How's it going?"

"Not bad at all. You know, dealing with these people on the phone, striking deals, it's pretty annoying."

"I didn't know it was such a pain, sorry."

"Don't get me wrong, it's better than a regular gig, that's for sure."

"Ah, see that's the thing, it's all part of my plan of madness."

As they talked Zed wanted to tell him he didn't want to do any of it anymore. He wanted to get on with his own life, and he thought this whole thing of Harlan's would go away in due time.

49

When Harlan was done he told everyone he was returning to his apartment to see Tiffany and his son. As he walked to the apartment he talked to a few people along the way. He was excited he was going to see his family. The people he ran into had some questions for him.

He couldn't wait until their new house was built. He was tired of the little apartment. He unlocked the door to the darkness. He called out for Tiffany but got no response. He flipped on the light switch and closed the door. He called her name again. As he was making his way through the apartment he noticed the bedroom light coming through the bottom of the door. He pressed his ear up to the door. Light moaning came from the other side. He turned the knob to the door. Tiffany was there, and she was in bed with Laralyn. They were both naked, nothing on but smiles.

"What's going on, guys?" Harlan asked.

Tiffany got a stunned look on her face. "What you think is happening, yes, that's what it is."

Laralyn got out of bed and walked over to Harlan. "I can only imagine what's going through your mind right now. Relax. It's okay. You can join if you want. It'll be find with your girl

Harlan looked at both women, he said. "Could I talk to Tiff for a minute?"

Tiffany got out of bed, took Harlan out in the hall. "I know what you must be thinking."

"You do?" Harlan said. "I didn't know you

could read minds."

She cocked her head at him. "You know what I mean."

"When did this start?"

She said, "The other day. It's the third time."

"Three?"

"I like her."

"I can see that."

A shrug. "I'm not sure if it's gonna go any-where. Not sure at this point."

"Why, though?"

"I'm attracted to her. You were out with the guys one night. I was alone and she asked if I wanted to go out for drinks. We did. After we came here, one thing led to another, before we knew it we were in bed and I was licking her nipples."

"Sounds enjoyable, tasty after a long day."

She smiled. "You should join us. I see the way you look at her."

"I can't deny that, sure," Harlan said. "I'm al-ways up for new things."

"You'll enjoy yourself, trust me."

"I don't doubt it."

They went back into the bedroom. Laralyn told Harlan it would be okay. Both her and Tiffany undressed Harlan and kissed him all over. The next day Harlan woke with the two beauties sleeping beside him. He got out of bed and went to the restroom. After he showered, when he got back to the bed both women were awake.

Tiffany looked at Harlan. "Sleep okay, hon?"

"I did," Harlan said. "You?"

"Fantastic."

Laralyn said, "I'm so comfortable."
The three of them had sex again.

50

A few weeks later someone told Clint that the cops had been watching them. The person said that they have an undercover in the compound. It didn't take Clint long to locate Harlan so he could tell him. The thing was, they didn't really have anything else to go on. Harlan told him to wait and not to panic.

They should have been more alert.

When the local cops and FBI came to the compound it was a relief for most of Harlan's followers. They were finally free. They were now able to go out into the world and do whatever they loved. Harlan and the others, they really didn't put up much of a fight. At that point he didn't know what all they had on him. And he always told them to deny everything. He told them not to give them anything. It's their job to make a case against you. It took some time for the cops to sort things out. After they put people in cuffs and got the others out, they had to do a search. As they were gathering evidence against them Harlan assured Tiffany that it would be okay.

Mallory was the one who started freaking out, screaming, saying that they made her do everything, that they told her if she told they'd have her killed. At the same time Mallory was being led away by an officer, another officer had Gretchen in cuffs. Gretchen turned and spat in her face. The two started yelling at each other until the offices put them in separate cars.

It was a long ride for everyone to jail that day.

Most of them were thinking they could get out of it. After all, it was all Harlan's plan. It was all his work.

After everything was said and done Harlan and Denny were the only ones charged with any murders. The others were charged with smaller crimes.

51

They took Harlan into an room to question him—he was in there for a few hours. As they talked to him, going over everything again and again, he never broke. When they asked about the remains they found in the woods he told them it must've been someone else, that he knew nothing about anyone ever being buried out there. When they told him about all the people and bodies they found in the basement, again, he said someone else must have done it. When they told him the names of those who told on him Harlan just shook his head. "Those ungrateful motherfuckers! How are they gonna lie after everything I gave them?"

One of the officers, Brick, sat across from him. "Right now, in other rooms of this building, some of the others are being questioned, what do you think they might tell us?"

Harlan shrugged. "How am I to know that? If anything, I think they'd talk about how grateful they are that I found them, brought everyone together. See, what you have are boys and girls who have been cast out by society, pushed aside like garbage, thrown to the streets. It's a tough world out there, they could've been killed. Someone calls you a piece of trash all the time you start to believe it. They were looking for something. I showed them the way, the way to truth. They accepted. I wanted nothing but the best for them and still do. Some of those souls, they still need to learn, to grow, to experience everything life as to offer," Harlan knocked his fist on the table. "You guys had to come along and make it all go away. Just because you heard a few nasty rumors about me, guys had to come where I live and fuck everything up, twist things however you want to make yourselves look good. Well, buddy, great fucking job you did. I'm sure every agency will suck your dicks for years to come. And I'm sure if I were in your line of work it would be a good bust, everyone congratulating you. One problem, it's all a lie. You don't have any facts to back it up. While you're wasting time on me you could be out there catching real killers."

Brick laughed. "We have everything we need."

"That so?"

"Yes, sir."

"I'll tell ya this," Harlan told him, "I'm gonna beat this."

"Oh, you think?" the officer said.

"Without a doubt. You guys, you can't prove I did. The only thing I'm guilty of is reaching out to all of those lost souls, giving them a place they can be themselves, a place to worship God."

While Harlan talked two other officers came into the room.

After some more back-and-forth the officers got frustrated that he wasn't going to confess to anything. They had a pretty good idea Harlan was guilty of everything. They just had to prove it. Harlan told himself that they just couldn't go around accusing people of things with the hopes it will stick.

Harlan was able to get an expensive lawyer. After two weeks his trial started. They had everyone testify. The two main people they were going after were Denny and Harlan. Everyone said the two of them were really the only ones behind the murders.

At the end of it all both men got life in prison.

52

When they got to the prison the guards told the two men they weren't allowed to have any contact with each other. But the guards at the place couldn't watch everyone all the time. At the time, they didn't have the cameras and things they do today. When they were allowed to go outside the two would meet in the yard and talk.

"How you holding up?" Denny asked his friend.

"I'm still here," Harlan told him. "Yes, sir, I'm still here. Just have to keep thinking of the good things."

"You do. People say that in here, but it's true. Your worse day on the outside is better than your best day in here, that's for sure," Denny told him.

"That's one way to look at it."

"Shit, from where I'm standing' that's the only way to look at it. Just keep your head up, my friend."

"I like this place like I like a bullet. But it gives us some time to get our thoughts together, away from the bullshit on the outside."

Denny nodded at his friend. "So, buddy, what's the next step."

"From right here it's hard to say. I mean, I know what I wanna do, but I can't do it while in here."

"Yeah. Unless something happens we'll be in until the end."

"Might have to involve the whole family on this."

"Who?"

"Luke."

"Luke?" Denny asked.

"That's what I was thinking."

"What about that Luther guy, he always seemed to like

you? Thought you might be grooming him for something?"

"Fuck that shithead," Harlan said. "I couldn't trust him."

"Oh."

"I figure when Tiffany comes for a visit I could tell her about my plans for Luke. She can walk him through everything."

"Oh, man, that's a good idea. Think he'd be okay with that?"

"I assume he'll be fine with it. Why wouldn't he? It's the family business. It'll keep the name alive."

"That's a good plan, man."

"I should tell him as soon as I can."

"That would be best."

They laughed and traded stories of the past.

A guard called for lunch. The food wasn't that great but it was something. They lost their right to walk in a restaurant and order what they wanted. They lost all freedom.

The other prisoners knew who Denny and Harlan were. They were famous on the inside. The good thing for them was that they didn't have to fight with most people. As new guys would come in they would try their best with Harlan and Denny, trying to beat them down.

One of the new inmates got in an argument with Denny one day.

Denny laughed the whole thing off. If someone thought they could break him, let them try. And see what happens. The next day on the yard he told Harlan what happened.

Later that day, Denny was mopping the floor in the kitchen. The same guy from before came along with three big dudes. The three tackled Denny to the ground and beat him. One of the men took a homemade knife and stabbed Denny many times.

When Harlan learned of the fate of Denny he knew his time would be coming. He walked out in the yard and looked up into the sky.

www.ingramcontent.com/pod-product-compliance
Lightning Source LLC
Chambersburg PA
CBHW061115100726
47911CB00013B/547